Drop Dead, Gorgeous

Drop Dead, Gorgeous

Also by J. D. Mason

And on the Eighth Day She Rested

One Day I Saw a Black King

Don't Want No Sugar

This Fire Down in My Soul

You Gotta Sin to Get Saved

That Devil's No Friend of Mine

Take Your Pleasure Where You Find It

Somebody Pick Up My Pieces

Beautiful, Dirty, Rich

J. D. Mason

Drop Dead, Gorgeous

St. Martin's Press ≈ New York

DROP DEAD, GORGEOUS. Copyright © 2013 by J. D. Mason. All rights reserved. Printed in the United States of America. For information, address St. Martin's Press, 175 Fifth Avenue, New York, N.Y. 10010.

www.stmartins.com

ISBN 978-0-312-61728-8 (hardcover)
ISBN 978-1-250-02336-0 (e-book)

St. Martin's Press books may be purchased for educational, business, or promotional use. For information on bulk purchases, please contact Macmillan Corporate and Premium Sales Department at 1-800-221-7945 extension 5442 or write specialmarkets@macmillan.com.

First Edition: June 2013

10 9 8 7 6 5 4 3 2 1

Dedicated to those who just can't let

bygones be bygones

Drop Dead, Gorgeous

Drop Dead, Gorgeous

And So It Goes . . .

The Bible teaches us to turn the other cheek—forgiveness—and to love thy neighbor. It also teaches us another lesson—an eye for an eye. At the end of *Beautiful, Dirty, Rich,* the first book in this series, it looked like our girl Lonnie had come to the end of the road at the hands of lover boy, Jordan Gatewood. But as I was writing that scene, something inside me struggled against letting Lonnie Adebayo go.

A voice in my head screamed, "No! Not Lonnie! Let it be anybody else, but don't kill off Lonnie!"

I liked her, and the thought of losing her so soon, before I'd really gotten a chance to know her, left me feeling as if I was saying good-bye to someone who could've been my friend if only we'd had more time together.

Drop Dead, Gorgeous is the opportunity to do just that. It gives me a chance to know Lonnie and what makes her tick. So turn the page and let's see what she's working with.

Not the Place I'm Supposed to Be

She was raw meat; a muddy puddle of her former self, but Lonnie Adebayo was alive. Her eyelids were so heavy, and Lonnie wanted more than anything to close them and to rest, but if she did that . . . if she did that, she'd die. Or, she wouldn't, and he'd come back. Jordan would come back and . . .

"Her blood pressure is still high," someone said. "You're alright, Lonnie. You're safe now." Lonnie felt her head being stroked.

"No!" she heard herself say, as she cowered away from the person.

Her voice didn't sound like her voice. Her skin, her body—it all felt foreign to her. It wasn't a part of her. Her body wasn't her own. Not anymore.

Lonnie was surrounded by voices, and light, and sounds that came at her too quickly, too loudly. Clamoring noises, the sounds of machines, of people, all talking over one another. The light hurt her eyes. Dear God! Could someone please turn off the light? She tried to raise her arm to shield her eyes from it, but the pain shot up her arm and through her neck like knives. Lonnie cried out.

"Stop it," a woman said abruptly. "You need to stop!"

"Who . . . ?" Who was that woman? Perfume. It smelled . . . pretty. Lonnie tried to turn her head to where she thought the voice may have come from.

"Lie still, Lonnie," someone else said. Another woman. How did she know Lonnie's name?

Who told you my name? she wanted to ask, but when she tried, fits of coughing took her over.

"Drink," she was told. A plastic cup was pressed to her lips, which felt like they'd been injected with novocaine. The cold water soothed her swollen throat. "The police are on their way. You need to tell them who did this to you."

"Who called the police?" another woman asked.

"It's protocol in occurrences of rape. A counselor's on her way too, Lonnie. Her name is Nancy. She's very nice, and she'll help you through this." A woman with short blond hair pressed her warm hand to Lonnie's shoulder. "Try and get some rest."

The police. Yes. Yes, Lonnie needed to . . . to tell the police what he'd done. He needed to be arrested, and to have to stand trial for this. The police were coming and Lonnie would tell them everything, every nasty, filthy detail of what he did to her, and how she begged him to stop—how she told him over and over again that he was hurting her . . . killing her! The police would go after him. They'd find him, and it wouldn't matter who he was. He'd committed a crime. He'd beaten her nearly to death, and if it weren't for her . . . if it weren't for the woman with the perfume—

"The police can't know," the woman hovering over Lonnie said in a hushed tone. "You can't tell them."

"W-what . . . the . . . hell—" Lonnie struggled to say.

Of course the police needed to know. He needed to be punished. He needed to go to jail.

"You're alive, Lonnie," the woman whispered. The fragrance she wore wafted through her long hair, brushing against Lonnie's cheek. "Be glad you're alive and keep your mouth shut."

Lonnie forced her head back and forth. "No," she managed to say again. Lonnie's vision was so blurred that all she could see were the outlines of images. "I'm . . . tellin' . . . everythin'!"

"You do that and you'll be making the biggest mistake of your life," the other woman threatened. "You know how he is, Lonnie. You know what he'll do."

Was this bitch crazy? Lonnie had been brutalized. The police were on their way, and Lonnie wouldn't let them leave until they knew exactly what Jordan Gatewood had done to her. Until he was behind bars—until the whole world knew what that bastard had done to her—Lonnie would be looking over her shoulder. She'd be waiting for him to walk through the door of this hospital room, or any room where she could be, expecting him to find her and to finish what he'd started. He walked out of that house believing that Lonnie never would. And she'd be damned if she'd let him get away with what he'd done.

"Who do you think they'll believe?" that woman continued. "He's a Gatewood. He's *the* Gatewood, and ultimately, it'll be your word against his. Who do you think they'll believe? Why would a man like Jordan Gatewood put his hands on you? Why would he be bothered with a woman like you? What are they going to think, Lonnie?"

She wasn't serious. Lonnie couldn't believe what this woman was saying to her, especially now, especially when she was the one who walked into that house and found Lonnie lying there on the floor, naked and bleeding. Men had no right to put their hands on women. He had no right to put his goddamned hands on her!

"He'll be livid when he finds out what you've done. And he'll find you, Lonnie. They'll set bail, and Jordan has the money. You know he'll pay it, and he'll know that you turned him in, and he'll know you're alive, and he'll find you. He'll know you're alive. He won't stop coming after you."

"What—" A lump swelled in the back of Lonnie's throat. "Why . . . are you sayin' . . . this?" she asked bitterly. "Why?"

This woman had helped her. She'd practically carried Lonnie to her car, poured her into it, and gotten her to the hospital. And she'd stayed by Lonnie's side the whole time. She could've left her here, but she didn't. She had helped her, so why . . . why was she saying these things?

"Because I know him. You know him. And you know that if he knows you survived, he'll come after you. You know that he won't stop until he finds you, and you know that he will kill you. Maybe not with his own hands, but you can't beat him. You can't win, Lonnie. You know this. Be smart. Think! You know what I'm saying is true, Lonnie. You know what'll happen. You know."

Lonnie was afraid. She could not recall ever having this kind of fear before in her life, but it was here, blanketing her, and the realization took her breath away. Mental images of his fist slamming into the side of her face came rushing back to her. The searing agony of him violating her from behind, not with himself, but with something— He'd thrown her across the room, and Lonnie remembered the crashing sound of the table, splintering into pieces underneath her as she landed on top of it.

"*. . . he'll know you're alive, and he'll find you. He'll find you. He won't stop coming after you.*"

Jordan Gatewood wouldn't spend one moment of his life in jail. He'd call some high-powered attorney of his and have him waiting for him at the precinct before Jordan even climbed out of the back of the police car. And he'd know that it was Lonnie who had reported him. He'd know that he hadn't killed her, and he'd be free.

"You have your life," the woman said emphatically. "Your life, Lonnie. Take it and run before it's too late."

The woman had been kind enough to dial the number for Lonnie, and she held the phone to Lonnie's ear. When Phillip answered, Lonnie finally broke down sobbing, relieved to hear his voice, and desperate for him to come for her.

"It's me," she said weakly. "Phi-ip, it's Lonnie."

"Lonnie? What's wrong? What time is it?"

Hot streams of tears burned down the sides of her face.

"*He'll know you're alive. He won't stop coming after you.*"

"C-come get me?" she pleaded, praying that he would come for her and that he would hurry before Jordan somehow found out that Lonnie didn't lay dying or dead in that house and that she was here. "Come get—"

"Where are you, sweetheart?" he demanded in that British accent of his she loved so much. "I'm on my way, Lonnie, but you have to tell me where you are!"

The other woman pulled the phone away from Lonnie's ear.

"She's at Mount Sinai Hospital in Fort Worth. It's just off . . ."

Lonnie fixed her blurred gaze on the door of her room, half-expecting Jordan Gatewood to walk through it, praying feverishly to herself that he wouldn't.

Drop Dead, Gorgeous

Drop Dead, Gorgeous

He's Like My Freight Train

"*Do you know* who did this to you, Ms. Adebayo?"

Eventually she managed to answer the policeman standing at the foot of her bed. "No." She shook her head.

"Can you describe him?"

Lonnie could describe every inch of Jordan Gatewood, down to the birthmark on his thigh. But she swallowed. "No."

"He'll find you . . . and he'll come after you."

The next morning a different officer came to Lonnie's room, a woman. "Where were you when you were attacked? Had you ever seen this man before? What was he wearing? How tall was he?"

The woman shot off questions at Lonnie like bullets and Lonnie responded the same way. "No. I don't know? I don't remember."

Just when it seemed that the policewoman was beginning to lose her patience, the cavalry arrived. Phillip Durham, the man she'd spoken to the night before on the phone, burst into the room like the hero Lonnie had always suspected he was. He muttered something to the officer and to the nurse who'd followed him into the room, then pulled out his wallet and handed a business card to the officer. The female officer sheepishly handed him back his card, while the nurse turned a strange shade of red and left the room. The female officer followed.

"You called?" he asked, staring concernedly at Lonnie. "So here I am."

Phillip didn't bother with formalities. He didn't ask any questions. A few minutes after Phillip arrived, an orderly pushed a wheelchair into her room. Phillip lifted her off the bed, poured her into it, and wheeled her out of that hospital to a stretch limo parked out front. He put her inside and slid in next to her.

"What was that you showed that policewoman?" Lonnie asked.

"A business card," he responded casually, pulled it out of his wallet, and handed it to her. "A man I met at a party in Prague gave it to me."

She read the card:

MARTIN WILKINS
Associate Director
Central Intelligence Agency, European Division

They flew to Colorado in his private plane.

"We have a long drive ahead of us," he explained to her, as he poured her into the backseat of his SUV, covered her in chinchilla blankets, and buckled her seat belt for her. "You try and get some rest."

He wasn't handsome, but his mannerisms had always been his most attractive feature. Phillip was Mick Jagger–ugly, not as thin, but lean, with a swimmer's build and wide angular shoulders. He wore his silver hair cut close because he was balding, and most of the time, he dressed like he was some flower child from the sixties. But he was graceful, romantic, and careful with how he touched her. Phillip was thoughtful to a fault, accommodating, and filthy dirty rich, although you wouldn't know it from looking at him. He didn't wear his money like a badge because it was a part of who he was already, like skin.

The two of them had been lovers on more than one occasion, with the understanding that they would never do well together as a couple. He was always there for her, though; no matter what time of the day or night she called, he was the one she had always been able to count on. He was the one who never judged her, who understood exactly who she was and accepted her for it. Phillip loved her more than any man ever had or could, and Lonnie loved him.

Phillip had brought her to his château in Vail. Tonight he'd managed to coax her out of her room to actually sit down at the table with him for dinner, but Lonnie had no appetite. She was empty inside, void of that quality that had made her who she'd once been. That's what Jordan had stolen from her. Not pussy. Not even pride; but he'd taken her soul and raked it under his heel.

After dinner, Lonnie went into the living room and curled up on the sofa in front of the fireplace. Several minutes later, Phillip came and sat down next to her, handing her a glass of sherry.

"I thought only old white women drank sherry," she'd teased him once.

"If it's good enough for old white women, then it's certainly good enough for me," he quipped, in a staunch British accent that he turned on and off when he chose.

The two of them sat quietly next to each other, just watching the fire. The house was so quiet, she could hear him breathing. Lonnie listened to the sound of the fire crackling, to Phillip sipping and swallowing his sherry. Privately she hoped that Phillip would be as content as she was and not say a word.

"While you're sitting there, feeling sorry for yourself, I'd like to tell you a story."

Shit! she thought, exasperated.

"Oh, don't roll your eyes at me, young lady," he fussed. "It's been six months, Lonnie, and you've hardly said two words to me since I brought you here. At the very least, you could humor me and listen to what I have to say."

Lonnie used to love the sound of his voice. Phillip's voice was heavy, deep, rumbling almost. But now, it grated on her nerves.

"I'm listening," she said, sighing.

He paused for effect, and then began telling his tale, in dramatic, old-English fashion as only Phillip could.

"Once upon a time," he started, staring earnestly at her, "there was a beautiful princess."

Lonnie shot a hateful glance at him. If he thought he was being funny, he was dead wrong. There was nothing beautiful about her anymore. Jordan had slit open half of her face, and left her blind in one eye. Lonnie now walked with a limp that doctors said would probably never go away.

"Fuck you," she snapped.

But Phillip continued on, unabated. "This princess could have any man she wanted, but she chose the wrong one, and he hurt her, terribly."

Lonnie sat her glass down on the table and started to get up, but he grabbed hold of her wrist and held her next to him on that sofa.

"He left her wounded; inside he left her hollow and a shadow of whom she once was." Phillip pulled her closer to him, to his chest, and he draped his arm over the back of the sofa behind her. "She was afraid," he continued, "when she used to be fearless. She shrank inside herself, and refused to come out and let the world see who she was and how beautiful she still was."

Phillip was a romantic. And he was silly. And Lonnie felt like all she wanted to do was cry, because he was spot-on. She didn't know who she was anymore, and she was afraid to even set foot out of this house. For the last six months all she'd wanted to do was curl up and disappear, and that was all she had done.

"She was afraid of this man, the one who had been so cruel to her, because he was a king, and he ruled over a vast kingdom filled with infinite resources and all of his subjects worshipped him," he announced in grand style. "In her mind, there was nothing she could do to make him pay for the horrible things he'd done to her. He had committed a terrible crime, and the poor princess would have no choice but to live with the humiliation, the degradation."

By this time, Lonnie was crying. "Stop it, Phillip," she sobbed, helplessly. Why the hell was he saying these things to her? "Just . . . stop."

"But one day, the beautiful princess met a wizard," he said, pulling a copy of *Forbes* magazine from in back of the pillow behind her, and placing it on her lap.

Lonnie stared at the picture of Jordan, looking posed and poised on that cover. Bile rose in the back of her throat, and she looked at Phillip, shaking her head.

"What are you doing? Why are you doing this?"

She started to get up again, but he held her in place, staring into her eyes with those steely gray eyes of his. Phillip picked up the magazine and held it to her face, forcing her to look at it and to read the caption.

GATEWOOD TO MAKE A HOSTILE BID
FOR ANTON OIL AND GAS

"Suddenly the beautiful princess began to wake up and shake the fog she'd been living in," Phillip continued, staring passionately at Lonnie. "Yes, he was a king, but she was a princess. Yes, he was bad ass, but so was she!"

She looked at him again.

Phillip's expression was defiant. "The wizard said to her, snap out of it, lovely girl. And he waved his magic wand." Phillip fanned his fingers in front of her face. "And suddenly her eyes were opened."

"What are you talking about?" she murmured.

"'Make your wishes, princess,'" the wizard told her. As many as you like, and I will grant all of them to you. But first, you must answer one question."

Lonnie was transfixed on the wizard Phillip. "What?"

"How do you topple a king?"

Phillip was quirky. He was odd, and eccentric. Some people thought he was crazy, and maybe he was. Lonnie had always found him amusing and wise, and a little bit scary. But the two of them had connected years ago on some cosmic level that had always drawn them back together to meet in the middle.

Lonnie stared deep into those hypnotic eyes of his. This wasn't a game, and Phillip wasn't simply telling her a story. Suddenly, the answer came to her. "You find his weakness," she whispered.

Relief washed over Phillip's expression. "And what is the king's weakness?"

She looked down at the magazine in her lap, and her eyes drifted to the word "Gatewood."

"His name." It dawned on her.

"His name, Gatewood, holds the power to all that he is, princess. And all that he is not," he said smugly. "Jordan Gatewood is a king. Joel Tunson is no one."

She knew his secret. Lonnie knew that Jordan's father wasn't the late, great Julian Gatewood like everyone believed. His real father was a man named Joel Tunson, a nobody. "I have a friend who works for *Forbes*," she said, feeling life creep back into her all of a sudden. "I can send him a copy of Jordan's real birth certificate. I have a copy of it in a safety deposit box in—"

Phillip shook his head disapprovingly. "No, no, no, princess," he groaned. Phillip's full lips cocked to one side in a crooked smile. "That's too damned easy." His expression hardened. "The king nearly killed you. He tried to ruin you. You don't simply tell his secret to some reporter. You showcase it, put it up on a neon sign for the whole world to see. You strip him of every ounce of power and dignity he has." Phillip's eyes narrowed. "You make that mother fucker suffer."

"So says the wizard?" she asked, seeing the magic in this man and feeling it spark inside her.

He smiled. "So says the wizard."

Dear Jordan,
You missed.
xoxo, Lonnie

Up Jumped the Devil

She stared out of the window from the living room in the house and watched his car pull into the driveway. Jordan Gatewood climbed out of his black and shiny Panamera Porsche sedan, came toward the house, but stopped long enough to study the only other man outside that house, casually leaning against his restored Chevy Caprice. Lonnie was no fool. She was guilty of doing foolish things, but she knew better than to show up here, alone. That man was her outside assurance that she would be safe in this house. Her inside assurance was locked and loaded inside her purse. The yummy and beautiful Jordan Gatewood continued his journey to the front door. For a moment, a lump filled with fear the size of her fist threatened to choke her running and screaming from this place out the back door, but Lonnie swallowed that shit. It had taken two long years, but in that time, she'd mastered the art of putting things in perspective. Jordan Gatewood was a monster, but maybe not so big— not so bad.

"Mind telling me how you managed to get into my house?" he asked, as he came inside and shut the door behind him. Jordan started to turn the knob to the deadbolt, but stopped when Lonnie cleared her throat.

This moment had been a long time coming. Lonnie had spent the last two years avoiding this confrontation in her nightmares, but she'd savored it in her fantasies. Jordan was every bit the handsome, delicious man she'd remembered—on her best days. But hidden behind those dark and heavily browed eyes of his was the boogie man.

"The Realtor let me in," she eventually responded. "How much are you asking for this place?" She surprised herself and smiled at her own attempt at sarcasm, a pretty good attempt too.

Her worst memories had been of this room. Jordan had stripped her down to nothing in this room, taking full advantage of her naked body, mind, and soul. He had raped her in so many terrible, terrible ways that night. Jordan had not only assaulted her body, but he'd assaulted her pride, her ego, her true-soulful-self. He'd stripped her of the woman she'd always known herself to be, fearless and ready to face any and everything. He had made her helpless for the first time in her life.

Lonnie had faced bigger monsters. She'd stood nose to nose with wars and dictators, drawn back her shoulders and defied them without hesitation or trepidation. She'd been one of the few photographers in Zaire during the first Congo War when Mobutu was being thrown out on his ass. Lonnie had locked gazes with rebels, getting up-close-and-personal photographs of their rage, victories, and deaths. Her editor sent her to the heart of what was once Yugoslavia, when eighteen thousand Serbs lay siege to the city of Sarajevo, assaulting the city with machine guns, tanks, and bombs. She was there, close enough to touch everything going on around her, and capturing it all with her camera.

And this motha fucka right here had left her running and screaming for her life? She'd pondered it for the last two years, and for the last two years, she'd found that shit unacceptable.

Lonnie took a defensive step back when she noticed him walking toward her. "Don't even think about it, Jordan," she threatened.

He stopped. "I wasn't thinking about it," he said, sounding almost—almost—apologetic. "I would apologize, but I know that it wouldn't matter."

Lonnie raised her brows in awe. "No, it wouldn't, but I have to admit, it surprises the hell out of me."

Jordan shook his handsome head in dismay. "What are you doing here, Lonnie? Why here? Why this house?"

"This house," she murmured, looking around the room at the pristine and expensive furnishings he'd bought to replace the shit he'd used her body to smash the other stuff with. This place looked brand-spanking-new. The smell of her blood, sweat, and tears had been washed away, and the body of the woman he'd left behind here to die blended into the shadows. "This was the scene of the crime, Jordan," she explained, looking into his eyes.

He didn't like hearing that. Lonnie took note of the slight cringe in his face when she said it, but it was true, and he needed to remember that. He needed to understand that some things could not neatly be disposed of and replaced with his version of the truth. All the money in the world couldn't make what happened in this house go away. Lonnie wouldn't let it.

"I never meant for it to go that far," he finally said. "I lost it, Lonnie, I lost it in a way I never thought possible, and I will never forgive myself for what I did to you."

Her face lit up. "What you did to me! Yes, Jordan. Yes, that's what I needed to hear. I needed to hear you say that you did something terrible to me. I needed to hear you admit it, because I swear, at first, I thought I had imagined the whole thing. For the past two years, I've been hoping and praying to wake up, warm and safe in my own bed, wiping sweat from my brow, exhausted but relieved that it had all been nothing more than a bad dream."

That brief bout of empathy he may have expressed moments ago faded quickly, replaced by the real Jordan. The one who bucked the system of fate, and rejected any form of responsibility that didn't match his three-thousand-dollar suit.

"It's been two years, you say?" he asked defensively. Jordan tucked his hands into the pockets of his slacks.

Lonnie held up two fingers and mouthed the word: *"Two."*

His ice-cold gaze washed over her as he took a step again, toward her. He stopped when he noticed how her ass was holding on to that purse. *Good boy,* she thought approvingly.

"What the hell do you want?"

There he was, looking just like the good-old lovable pit bull he really was. Lonnie knew that he was in there somewhere, feigning regret, trying to lure her into his circle so that he could grab her by the neck with those steel jaws of his and squeeze until she fell limp in his teeth.

"To do to you what you did to me," she murmured coolly.

A glint of something sinister flashed in his eyes. "Is that why you got your boy outside? Is he going to hold me down, Lonnie? Is he going to make me beg him to stop?"

Jordan took another step in her direction, but this time, Lonnie didn't flinch. She didn't take a step back. She didn't blink, and that nervous ball bouncing around in the pit of her stomach stopped bouncing, and she took a step toward him.

"You've got me confused with someone else, Jordan. Oh, you got the drop on me, caught me off guard, but you have no idea who I really am," she explained menacingly. "You have no idea what I'm capable of."

"Oh, I think I know. I know that it was you fueling the Desi Green machine," he said confidently. "When I saw the two of you together, Lonnie, I knew exactly who you were. Desi's a great victim. She's a master at playing that role, getting people to feel sorry for her, and even to believe her pitiful little lies about me and my family. But she's no rocket scientist. You, on the other hand, were masterful in the way you unraveled that mess that ultimately made her America's sweetheart. It was you who exposed that pedophile judge and the fact that he'd murdered that kid. How can a man like that, who passed judgment on someone like the sweet and pretty Desdimona Green, ever be validated? Of course she didn't do it. Of course she was set up, and someone else pulled the trigger that night, killing the late, great Julian Gatewood."

Lonnie waited patiently for Jordan to round out his diatribe. He was spot-on, of course, about all of it. Desi Green was her friend, closer to Lonnie than any sister could be, and yet, Desi Green was a pathetic blob of downtrodden uselessness that would've curled up and died had it not been for Lonnie.

"The world watched in horror as the truth came out about the upstanding law enforcement official who'd arrested Desi—even taken the gun from her hand that night as he stepped over my father's body, and escorted her to that police car in handcuffs—fall from grace when the story broke of his involvement in that human-trafficking ring, shaking the hell up out of this whole goddamned state. He was no saint, but maybe, just maybe, Desi Green was. Poor, poor little thing." He smiled all of a sudden. "That was you too."

Lonnie thought for a moment, waiting, just in case he had something else to add. But Jordan held back.

"You've summed me up pretty damn good."

"Damn good," he said convincingly.

Lonnie felt an unexpected sense of relief. She had underestimated him. He knew what she was capable of, and as she looked at him now, it dawned on her that he was more afraid than he was willing to let on. Jordan stood there, looking as calm and cool as a spring day, but hidden inside that façade, he had to know that he was in for one hell of a ride.

"Time to put on your big-boy pants and gird up your loins, baby," she said, walking past him. Lonnie held open the door, took a good, long deep breath, held it, and slowly let it go. "I don't play fair, Jordan. I'm not nice like you." She turned to him and smiled. "I choose not to live with any regrets. I'll see you in the ring."

"You survived, Lonnie. That's got to count for something."

The line had been drawn in the sand. Would he cross it? Of course he would. She'd dared him to and it wasn't in his nature to walk away. "You should've killed me."

She left him standing there, looking a wee bit squeamish.

Son of a Man

Frank Ross had been minding his business in Paris, Texas, when this broad walked through the door of his office and told him that she wanted to hire him for protection. Sitting across from her crazy ass now, in this broken-down hole-in-the-wall outside of Fort Collins, Colorado, it dawned on him that he was the one who needed protection, and he needed it from her.

He should've known something wasn't right when she offered to pay him more money than his services were worth. And a damn siren should've sounded after the two of them left that house, outside of Dallas, headed straight for the airport, and he found his ass sitting in a private jet on its way to Colorado.

"You can close your mouth now, Frank," she said, after she'd finally finished telling him that bullshit story about that cat she'd just met up with at that house. He hadn't even known that his mouth was hanging open. "You look like you don't believe me," she said, looking cool as a fan.

"If I'd told you some shit like that, would you believe me?" he asked indifferently.

"It's the truth," she said, smiling.

She tried covering the side of her face with her hair, he could tell that something was wrong with her. But the rest of her—damn! Thick up in all the right places, and she knew it too. She was fine and knew it, and those were exactly the kind of women he'd learned to avoid.

She'd laid a magazine on the table with that dude's picture on the cover. "Gatewood," he said, studying the picture. He looked up at her. "And you really expect me to believe that he's kin to me?"

"He's your brother, Frank. Your half brother."

Nah, he didn't believe her. "We have the same—"

"Father," she repeated with him. "Yes. What part of that don't you understand?"

Now she was just being belittling. "Look at this cat." He motioned toward the magazine. "We don't even look like we're from the same planet, let alone the same daddy. How do you expect me to buy into this?"

"Joel Tunson is your father."

"Joel Tunson is my father, yes. But I barely know the man. I may have seen him a half dozen times in my life. He was a child-support check to my mother. That's all I know about him."

"Then you know more than Jordan knows. His mother was married to Joel for a hot second. Either she was pregnant when he married her, or she got pregnant on her wedding night," she said sarcastically, "but they weren't married long before a man named Julian Gatewood sped through town in a white Cadillac, spotted the beautiful Olivia Tunson, and stole her away from her husband, along with her infant son. They changed his birth certificate and his name to Gatewood, leaving poor

Joel Tunson standing in the dust and wondering what the hell just happened."

"That's fucked up."

"Way fucked up. But what they didn't count on was Joel having a copy of the original birth certificate tucked away under his mattress for posterity's sake."

"How come he didn't try and get his woman and baby back?"

"Money, caveman," she said sarcastically. "Gatewood was loaded, and Joel couldn't touch him. Not to mention, Olivia had made her choice. She wanted Julian and all his money and her kid. She didn't want Joel."

"So, this kid grows up a Gatewood."

"Essentially. But he's not a Gatewood. And that's the punch line, Frank." She leaned toward him. "He was never adopted. He was never legally made a Gatewood, and yet he inherited his father's position at one of the largest oil companies in the world, becoming president and CEO and filthy rich. If the board of directors knew that he wasn't who they think he is, they'd kick him out the door on his ass so fast, he wouldn't know what hit him."

Lonnie was making one hell of a case for the argument he was already preparing in his head. She might've thought Frank was dumb as a rock, but he was smarter than he looked, and he knew where she was going with this. He knew why she'd come all the way to Paris, Texas, to hire a bodyguard when she could've found a hundred of them in Dallas. He knew why she'd asked him to stand outside that house earlier that day, instead of coming inside. She wanted the two men to take a good, hard look at each other. She wanted them to remember each other's faces. And she wanted Frank to sound the alarm.

"The last thing that man would want is for the truth about who he really is to come out," he finally said.

The woman's pretty smile showed up again. "That's the last thing." She shrugged. "At least, one of them."

The wheels started turning in his head. Frank was an ex-cop. He'd spent nearly ten years on the force, and in that time he'd learned to read between the lines of what a person was saying and what they were really saying, and he could see red flags waving all around this woman's head.

"I'd be willing to bet he'd do just about anything to keep that secret, if it's true," he added quickly.

"It is true, and yes, he would do anything to keep it secret."

The man had money and plenty of it from the looks of that magazine cover. He looked like money, and he looked like he'd put a bullet or have someone else put a bullet in another man's head if he tried to mess with his money.

Frank cleared his throat. "So, where you going with this?" he asked, but Frank already knew.

"I'd be willing to bet that Jordan has kept tabs on Joel Tunson and his other two sons, Woody and Malcolm. He's careful and thorough like that. And he'd keep a close eye on them, making sure that none of them got too close to him, or said too much."

"They know?"

She shrugged again. "Joel knows, of course, but I'm not sure about his sons. A deposit is made every month to Joel's account for ten thousand dollars. Comes on the first, like clockwork, and he doesn't spend a dime of it."

"How do you know that?" he asked suspiciously.

She didn't answer. "As thorough as Jordan is, I don't think he knows about you, Frank."

Frank hadn't been raised a Tunson either. Joel had had an affair with his mother, Shirley, and she'd ended up pregnant with Frank. Joel sent a hundred and fifty dollars every month, and once in a while, he'd show up for Frank's birthday or football game, but other than that, he'd never spent much time with the boy. The words stuck in his head. Joel Tunson had been getting paid ten thousand a month for years, and the best he could do for Frank and his momma was a lousy hundred and fifty a month? That was some serious bullshit! But if Gatewood, with all his cash hadn't been able to find Frank, then that left him curious.

"So, how'd you find me?" he asked.

"I looked," she said simply. "I'm a reporter by trade, and we know how to look for things that other people overlook. For years, Joel Tunson drove a truck for a living, traveling one route going east to west, ending up in El Paso, dropping off his load, then turning around and coming home. There's a halfway point, in a small town called Cotton."

Frank was born in Cotton.

"When I found the monthly ten-thousand-dollar deposit in his account, I saw another pattern, a debit for one-fifty every month going to a credit union in Cotton to a Shirley Ross."

Was she serious?

"That still didn't tell you that I was his son," he argued.

"No, it didn't. But you did." She looked at her watch. "Not five minutes ago."

Frank leaned back in disbelief. "You didn't know?"

She shook her head. "I was spitting in the wind, Frank. And I got lucky."

What the hell kind of people was he dealing with here? All of a sudden, Frank felt like he was definitely in the wrong place, hanging out with the wrong kinds of people, and every instinct in his body warned him to get up and fly back to Texas.

"I don't know what you expect me to do with what you've just told me, lady."

"You know exactly what I expect you to do."

"Do I look crazy to you?" he said, trying to hold his voice down. "Before a man like that let me get up in his face about any damn thing, he'd have somebody chop off my head, especially if the word *Tunson* comes out of my mouth!"

"If we play this right, Frank, you could end up with more money than you can make in a lifetime," she argued.

"Or I could end up floating facedown in the Red River," he snapped, standing up to leave.

"Frank, just listen—" She grabbed him by the arm, but he jerked away.

"If you can't get over what he did to you, then you might want to learn to live with it. People do it every day. But I'm not the solution to your problem, lady." He dropped a ten dollar bill on the table to pay for the coffee. Frank was going home.

Texas was a different kind of place. It ran by different kinds of laws that flowed just underneath the surface of the real ones. If a man like Jordan Gatewood ever got wind of Frank, or thought that Frank was a threat to that empire of his, he'd scrape Frank off the bottom of his shoe, and she was crazy if she thought that Frank was dumb enough to sign on to some shit like that!

I'm a World of Power

"You put your hands on her?"

Edgar Beckman was a relic. He was pushing eighty and had watched Jordan and his sister June grow up. He was the keeper of all the Gatewood secrets.

"I put my hands on her," Jordan solemnly admitted, staring out the window of his Dallas office.

In the two years since that night had happened, so much had changed in Jordan's life. It had been as if that night he'd spent with Lonnie in that house was the exclamation point at the end of an era. Jordan was forced to put away the fantasy he'd had about riding off into the sunset with the woman of his dreams. The tapestry of lies that he had come to believe were true had started unraveling in front of the whole world. The woman he'd loved had set him up while the one he hated had risen from the ashes like a phoenix. Desi Green had moved on, whoring herself and that book of hers to anyone who'd listen to her lies. But despite the press and the pressure, Jordan and his family survived.

Police had come sniffing around his mother's home like dogs, wanting to get a statement from an old woman who could hardly remember what year it was. Jordan had had Olivia placed under a doctor's care and tucked her away safely in a nursing home where the law couldn't touch her. If what Desi wrote in that book of hers was true, and his mother had been the one to pull the trigger that night, killing her husband, Julian, then it was a truth that would go to the grave with her. Jordan had even gone so far as to reconcile his marriage to Claire and had recommitted himself to making it work this time.

Edgar had been a fixture in Jordan's world since before Jordan was even born. He'd been Jordan's father, Julian's, best friend and personal attorney. The two men had grown up together, but when Edgar went off to college, he had left a black man, and came back white. Julian had been light enough to pass too, but he'd never even entertained the notion.

Edgar had been the one to help Julian get the permits and licenses he needed to start up Gatewood Industries. Edgar had convinced investors that putting their money behind that black man's oil business was an investment that absolutely could not and would not fail, and if it did, he'd personally pay them back their money, with interest. Edgar had authored Julian's will. He knew everything there was to know about Ida Green and her child. He'd had that house bought for Ida and paid for it, in her name, using Julian's money.

"And she wants money," Edgar muttered, bringing Jordan's thoughts back to the immediate matter at hand.

Jordan turned to face the old man. If all that Lonnie Adebayo wanted was money, this would be an easy problem to solve. "She wants my head on a platter."

The old man huffed, "And how does she plan on getting it?"

"Lonnie's resourceful, Edgar," he reluctantly admitted. "She was the engine behind the Desi Green freight train. Lonnie was the one who exposed the sheriff, the judge."

Seeing her again had brought all those things and more flooding back to his memory. Jordan had given Desi too much credit when it came to exposing the corruption behind her trial. The woman just wasn't that brilliant. But Lonnie— That night he saw the two of them together, it all made so much sense.

"If there's a needle in a haystack, Lonnie can find it."

Edgar looked worried. "You've got a lot of needles, son."

Lonnie shouldn't have come back here. A knot tightened in his stomach as he thought about where all of this was leading.

"I haven't been able to find her, Edgar. She's in the city, but I can't pin her down."

Edgar nodded thoughtfully. "Well, if she's in the city, then we'll find her."

Find her and then . . . what? She had made it clear that she would go to any lengths to make him pay for what he'd done to her. Lonnie was smart, she was cunning, and she was determined. But as resourceful as she was, she had nothing on Edgar Beckman. The old man was loyal to a fault, and he was as loyal to Jordan as he had been to Jordan's father, Julian.

"Let me know when you do," he said to Edgar, half smiling, "before you do anything."

"Of course," Edgar assured him, standing to leave. The two men embraced.

"Uncle Edgar!" Jordan's sister, June, came bursting into his office without bothering to knock. "I heard you were here." She cast a sly glance at Jordan, and went over to Edgar and embraced him.

The old man laughed. "My little June-bug," he said as he hugged her back. "I heard you were back. How are those children and that husband of yours doing?"

June grimaced. "The kids are adjusting, and I left the husband behind in Georgia."

"For good?" he asked.

She nodded. "For damn good. I decided it was time to come home, and help my big brother run this place." June smiled at him, looped her arm in Jordan's and gushed, "Not that he needs it, but I appreciate him giving me a job."

June hadn't asked for a job. She'd come into Gatewood Industries and demanded an office.

"What's he got you doing?" Edgar gave Jordan a bewildered look.

"She's working with the acquisition team on the Anton buyout."

Edgar looked at her.

June shrugged. "Just call me the number cruncher," she said laughingly, glancing at Jordan.

June had a master's in finance, and even Jordan had to admit that he was impressed, but what he wasn't impressed with was the impeccable knack that June had for stepping on toes. Namely, his.

"Thank you for coming, Edgar," Jordan said, placing his hand on the old man's shoulder and ushering him toward the door.

Edgar looked at June. "Bring the children by when you get some time, June. I'd love to see them."

"Of course." She kissed his cheek. "I'll give you a call. Maybe we can get together next weekend."

"Excuse me, June?" June's assistant was standing just outside Jordan's door. "That call you were expecting is on the line."

"Oh," June said excitedly. "I need to take this. I'll call you, Edgar," she said, hurrying away. "Jordan, don't forget that we have a conference call in an hour with Michael."

Michael was the corporate attorney.

Jordan and Edgar watched as June rushed off, whispering with her assistant.

"It's good to see her," Edgar said warmly. "It's good to have her home."

Jordan didn't respond.

Edgar's driver held the door open for him as he laboriously climbed into the back of his car. That sonofabitch was just like his father, thinking with his dick instead of his head. Edgar was getting too damn old for this. He'd been putting out Gatewood fires for longer than he could remember. The boy wasn't Julian's by blood, but he'd certainly inherited his penchant for letting pussy get him into trouble.

"I know you love her, Julian, but you've got a wife. You've got children, and you've got a corporation to run. What the hell are people going to think when they find out that you left Olivia for that woman?"

"What difference does it make, as long as I'm happy? Ida makes me happy."

"But Olivia made you who you are in society," Edgar argued. "Gatewood Industries has just gone public, Julian. You do this now, and stocks are going to plummet."

"My personal life's got nothing to do with my business!"

"It's got everything to do with it! You are Gatewood Industries. Look at

how long it's taken these people to finally give you the respect you're due, Julian."

He was a black man, stepping on white folks' toes, and they begrudged him for it. But times were starting to change, and they were beginning to see that Julian Gatewood was a brilliant oil man who could make them money. That's what they wanted. They wanted his black ass to make them rich, and if he shook things up, and made them any more nervous than they already were, by replacing his beautiful, light-skinned, unthreatening woman with that black, nappy-headed Ida Green, all those supportive white folks would run away screaming, taking their money with them.

"I'm not telling you to let Ida go, Julian," he said sincerely. *"But don't rock the boat man. Not now."*

Edgar was an old man who had been running interference for that family since before Jordan was born. He'd kept the secret that Jordan wasn't Julian's biological son, and doctored that birth certificate listing Julian as the father just in case—just in case.

Someone had found out the truth, though, and had somehow gotten their hands on a copy of the real thing.

Jordan had come to his house late one afternoon and shoved both documents at him. "Is this your handiwork, Edgar? Did Julian put you up to this?"

Edgar lied. "For all intents and purposes, Jordan, you are his son. He wanted to protect the truth because you were meant to sit at the head of his company. Your father asked me to do this to protect your inheritance."

Julian had no idea that Edgar had changed that document. But Olivia knew.

Edgar was a stockholder in Gatewood Industries. He had made millions off of that company, and Jordan had been the driving force behind those millions. That boy had taken GII to heights Julian could've never imagined. Edgar had a vested interest in this boy's success. He did what he had to do. He would always do what he had to do as long as there was a breath in his body.

"Hello," Edgar said over the phone. "I need you to find someone for me. Lonnie Adebayo. I have no idea where to look," he said irritably. "That's your job. Start at the beginning, and work your way to Dallas. Let me know when you find her." He hung up.

Jordan wanted to be informed when Edgar found Lonnie. Jordan had created this mess and called Edgar to fix it, and fix it he would. This Adebayo woman was a pimple on an ass. Edgar would get rid of her and then he'd tell Jordan to get control of that wayward dick of his once and for all before it cost him more than an inconvenience.

THE CHIC CRITIQUE

Featuring, Fashion News from Around the World

The Spring Issue

TRUE "KONVICTIONS"

Desdimona Juliette Green was only eighteen when she was convicted of murdering oil mogul Julian Gatewood. She would spend the next twenty-five years of her life serving time in a women's federal prison for that crime in Texas.

"I was a baby when I went in, and a different kind of fortysomething-year-old woman when I came out. My mother had passed away, and I had no one. I had to try to start over, but how? And from what?"

At the debut of her new shoe and accessory fashion line last month, Desdimona "Desi" Green stood a world apart from that hopeless woman we've read about in her memoir, *Beautiful, Dirty, Rich: The Desi Green Story*. After her release from prison, no one was more surprised than Desi to learn that she'd inherited more than twenty million dollars from her deceased mother's estate, money reportedly left to the woman by the same man Desi went to prison for killing: Julian Gatewood.

Desi could've rested on her laurels, taken the money and run with it, but instead, she decided to share her story with the world, and use the money she inherited to start her own fashion line, Konvictions.

"Konvictions has nothing to do with me being convicted of a crime. It's about determination to overcome what seemed impossible to over-come. It's about being true to yourself and being real with who you are and what you know, and not being afraid to show the world your

Konvictions," Desi stated in a recent interview with the editor at *Shoe-Shine, Inc.*

Recently Miss Green debuted Konvictions to an audience of two hundred of the industry's fashion elite at a private event at the Montage Hotel in Beverly Hills.

"I was nervous," she admits, "because I knew that all of these people came here expecting to see the dog-and-pony show that was Desi Green. I mean, come on. Ex-murderer coming out with a high-end fashion shoe line? They expected to see combat boots, heavy metal, and spikes [she laughs], but I'm not a heavy metal kind of girl."

The elegance of the show took many by surprise, and the exhibition of women's shoes, boots, belts, scarves, sunglasses, and jewelry was surprisingly impressive.

"I've had tremendous help from some of the most talented young designers in the world, all of them, like me, up-and-coming, and hungry. We want people to see these shoes and say, 'I gotta have those!' We want women to walk up to other women asking, 'Girl! Where did you get those shoes!' We want to stand out, and the women who love this line will be those kinds of women. They don't want to blend in. They want people to take notice of them when they walk into a room, and they want to impress, but without screaming 'Look at me! Look at me!' It's more like, 'I know you're looking at me, and I know you're digging what you see.'"

Members of the audience had a great deal to say about the new Konvictions shoe and accessory line.

Kim Reid, editor in chief of *Fashion Moguls* magazine, said, "Oh, it was fabulous! Unexpected and fresh! I admit that I didn't know what to think when I first heard about this, but I am a believer, and I'm looking forward to seeing what else she has coming at Fashion Week in New York next spring."

Carleen Brice, president and CEO of the Fancy Pants Uptown retailer chain, had this to say. "The whole line is so organic and so naturally exciting that it's impossible not to be intrigued. The fashion-forward woman will love this line, and we're looking forward to carrying it in our stores."

Desi Green has become the poster child for reinvention. She has overcome years of struggle and hardship in the first part of her life, and has started over from scratch, living her dreams in the years going forward.

"Not every woman getting out of prison is going to inherit the kind of money I did, so yeah, I can admit that that helped me tremendously to put my past behind me, to be able to move on and realize a few dreams. I do feel obligated to give back, though, so I've started a foundation, the True Konvictions Women's Foundation, to help women who have been down on their luck, but who want to make positive changes in their lives. The foundation offers scholarships, job-hunting assistance, housing assistance for women who've served time in prison. Your life isn't over just because it may have stalled. You have the power to turn it around and to take control of your future. It's not impossible. I'm living proof of that."

Diamond Life

Lonnie sat alone in the dark corner of a coffee shop in downtown Dallas and closed the magazine when she finished reading the article. *Little Desi Green is all grown up now,* she thought, feeling surprisingly smug. It was hard for Lonnie not to take credit for the woman Desi had become now. When she first met Desi, the woman had just gotten out of prison and was a mouse of a broad who was scared of her own shadow, despite the fact that she'd inherited millions from the Gatewood estate.

"I should feel different," Desi said to Lonnie in a Blink, Texas, hole-in-the-wall dump after she'd finally won the right to her inheritance from Jordan, who'd made it his personal vendetta to see to it that Desi never saw a dime of her inheritance. But surprisingly, the judge ruled in Desi's favor. She hadn't inherited the money from the Gatewoods. She'd inherited it from her mother's estate, and if they'd had issue with the money, they should've taken it up with Desi's mother, Ida, before she

passed away. The only thing was, no one knew that Julian Gatewood, Ida's lover, had left her any money.

Lonnie swallowed half of her bottle of beer before finally agreeing with Desi. "You're fuckin' loaded, Desi. So, yeah. You should feel pretty different."

"So, how come I don't?"

That was the twenty-million-dollar question, and Lonnie just remembered looking at the woman like she was a freak. Looking at the photograph of her now in that article and having seen clips of past interviews of Desi Green, Desi had changed. She was no longer that mousy, shy, reluctant little martyr she'd once been. Desi had become a goddamned brand now. She'd taken her reluctant fame and embraced it. Desi was riding that wave of her past and building an empire on the foundation of it. Lonnie hardly recognized the woman.

"Can I get you anything else?" the waiter came over and asked.

"No, thank you," Lonnie responded.

She'd called Desi once since . . . A few months after Phillip had taken her to Colorado.

"Where are you, Lonnie! What happened? Are you alright?"

"I'm right as rain, Desi," Lonnie lied.

"What happened? What did he do to you? I saw Jordan right after you disappeared, and I know he did something, Lonnie. Where are you? Tell me where you are and I'll come get you."

The thought of sharing space and breathing the same air as Desi nauseated Lonnie. It wasn't her fault, but . . . maybe it was—kind of. Lonnie had butted into Desi's business, riding in on a white horse, thinking that she was doing that woman a favor by helping her to get the money that rightfully belonged to her. Lonnie had championed Desi from the beginning, exposing the conspiracy behind the machine that put that woman in prison for twenty-five years. She'd shoved the shit down Desi's throat until she had no choice but to swallow it and regurgitate it on every page inside that book of hers. Lonnie had loved Desi like a sister, and put her own ass on the line for the woman.

"I had to get away, Desi," Lonnie finally told her.

"But . . . Lonnie." Desi's voice cracked. "C'mon, girl. Just tell me what he did to you? Tell me what happened."

Why? So that Desi could fix it? The notion was laughable. Desi hadn't been able to fix her own damn self. How the hell was she supposed to fix Lonnie? If Lonnie was a fool, then Desi was a bigger fool, and if Lonnie was weak, then Desi's ass was absolutely helpless.

"I'll be in touch," she said before abruptly hanging up.

The woman featured in that article was a star now, a real live celebrity, and she wore her new status like a brand-new dress. As Lonnie drove back to her Dallas loft thinking about her friend, she happened to glance in the rearview mirror. She'd seen that car before, in the parking lot of the café she'd just left, and earlier, at the gas station.

Lonnie made a mental note of the license plate number, and repeated it over and over again in her head until she had it memorized. Instinct was a bitch, or was it paranoia? Either way, she'd learned to listen to them both, because both of them were usually dead-on.

Panic threatened to take over when she made an abrupt turn at a stop sign down a side street, and the car followed.

Lonnie took several deep breaths, and gripped the steering wheel with both hands. She willed herself to try and stay calm, and to focus. She was being followed, and yeah, her ass was scared shitless. How long had this fool been following her? Did he know where she lived? Even if he knew the building, there was no way he'd know which loft she lived in. The thought gave her some solace, but not much.

Jordan was trying to be slick. Who else would put a tail on her but him? She swallowed and took another sudden turn, right into the parking lot of a police station. Lonnie pulled into one of the parking lanes facing the street, and watched the gray sedan slowly drive past her.

Lonnie pulled out her cell phone. "Yeah, I need a taxi," she said, giving the dispatch the cross streets.

A knock on her window made Lonnie damn near jump out of her skin. She reluctantly rolled down the window.

"Is everything alright, Miss?" the policeman asked, concerned.

Lonnie must've looked crazy, but the lie came almost immediately. "I think my ex-boyfriend is following me." She swallowed, glanced quickly out at the street, and spotted him parked half a block down. "He's uh—" She looked helplessly at the officer. "He's got a bit of a temper."

"Is that him?" he asked, nodding in the direction of the car that was following her.

She nodded. "He can't know where I live, officer," she said, playing up that damsel-in-distress role to the max. "I'm afraid that if he finds out—"

"Calm down. Calm down. I'll go talk to him."

The car pulled away from the curb and drove away before the police officer could get to him.

"Would you feel safer if I followed you home?" he asked kindly when he returned.

She nodded again, and smiled. "Yes, sir. Oh, thank you. Yes."

Lonnie waited for the officer to climb into his car before pulling back out onto the road. This was real now. Jordan had just showed her a card in his hand. And Lonnie needed to pull up her big-girl panties, and get ready to show him hers.

Back inside her loft, Lonnie bolted the door shut, took some deep breaths, and poured herself a drink.

"You're okay," she chanted over and over again until she was finally convinced. This was her game, not his. Lonnie had this. She pulled her new cell phone from her purse and dialed the number to Jordan's office. Of course, she got his voicemail.

"You've got me confused with an idiot, Jordan!" she said angrily. The thought that she'd gotten complacent and let her guard down, even for a moment, infuriated her. "I'm not a fuckin' amateur, you sonofabitch! This is my script! I wrote it, and I know how this is going to end!" She abruptly ended the call.

Jordan was devious and capable of anything. Lonnie had to pay attention. Because she knew the consequences of underestimating him better than anyone.

We're a Hell of a Nation

Marauders made the best pan-roasted sea bass in the city. Jordan had spent his whole morning in meetings, so by lunch time, he was famished.

"It's been a while, Mr. Gatewood," the petite, brunette hostess said, leading the way to his table. "We have your favorite table waiting. Can I bring you your usual lager?"

"Please," he said cordially, as he took his seat next to the window.

She set the menu down in front of him. "Carlos will be your waiter today, and I'll send him right over."

"Thank you."

Half an hour after arriving, and well into his meal, Jordan suddenly lost his appetite.

"Mmmmm, that smells good."

Lonnie sat down at his table, across from him. Long, dark waves of hair cascaded past her shoulders. A simple but brilliant diamond hung from a thin chain around her neck and the red wrap dress fell open at her thigh as she crossed her shapely legs.

Jordan put down his fork, leaned back, and wondered how the hell she knew he'd be here.

Lonnie seemed to read his mind. "'The bass is always the freshest on Tuesdays at Marauders,' you told me once." A wave of hair strategically hid the left half of her face. "You never miss the sea bass unless you absolutely can't help it." Lonnie slightly leaned over the table, exposing that pretty neckline of hers. "You showed your ass," she said casually. "I figured I'd stop by and give you a quick view of mine."

Edgar had told him about the tail he'd put on Lonnie and about how she'd shaken him by pulling into that police station. The message she'd left on Jordan's office phone was her idea of a warning. She was no amateur. But neither was he.

"She saw him because she was looking for him, Edgar," he'd told the old man, agitated. "It was a mundane move. A bit of a cliché. I expected better from you."

Out of the corner of his eye, Jordan spotted the waiter start toward his table. He put up his hand to stop him. Lonnie noticed, and poked out her bottom lip.

"Damn. Can't a sister even get a glass of water?"

"I thought this visit was all about ass-showing, Lonnie. You can drink water someplace else."

She casually leaned back in her seat. "You really should be nicer to me, Jordan."

"When was the last time you saw nice in me?"

The question quickly wiped that cocky expression off of her face. Loving Lonnie had gotten him played by her and Desi Green. Being weak for Lonnie had left him looking like a fool. Jordan was over being nice and foolish.

"I try not to think about it," she muttered, vulnerably. "But you had your moments."

"*We* had our moments, Lonnie," Jordan said, surprising even himself. Jordan pulled his napkin from his lap and tossed it on top of what was left of his bass. "I wanted you," he said bluntly. "I needed—you."

"Having somebody followed is tired and old-fashioned, Jordan. If you want to know where I live, why not just ask?"

He leaned forward. "So, where do you live?"

"If I didn't know better I'd think that you wanted me to hurry up and get this over with."

"Yes," he said, with certainty. "I want this to be over, Lonnie."

"But not too soon, Jordan," Lonnie said coyly. "I want to see you squirm."

"I don't squirm."

"You will."

He smiled. "I'll never put my hands on you again, but I'll be damned if I let you fuck with me and get away with it."

"That's your problem, Jordan. You think too small. Of course I'll fuck with you, and I'll get away with it." Lonnie stood up to leave, relishing the dismal expression on his face. "You lack vision. You always have, and that's to my advantage." Lonnie picked up his glass and took a sip of his beer. "Mmm. Always could count on you for the good shit." Lonnie winked and walked away.

Turn It Loose

Frank should've known better than to bring up the encounter he had with Lonnie Adebayo to Colette. There was no such thing as casual chit-chat with a cop, even an off-duty one lying naked and next to you in bed, hot and sweaty after thirty minutes of oral foreplay. When he worked on the force, she was his partner. At the time, both of them were married to other people, and both of them were cheating on their respective spouses with each other. Frank's wife divorced him four years ago, and Colette and her man were in the process of going through.

She was a big, white girl with green eyes and jet-black hair that she wore cut short and spikey. Colette was five-ten, had melons for boobs, and at least a dozen tattoos all over her body. The first time he laid eyes on her, he thought she was a lesbian, but Colette was far from it. She loved dick every which way but loose, and had him knotted up like a pretzel, drooling, and sucking his thumb. He'd been her love slave ever since.

"Jordan Gatewood is *your* brother?" she said in a tone that pretty much said she didn't believe it.

He shrugged. "If what that woman said was true, then technically, he's my half brother."

"And you believed her?" she asked, smirking.

No. He mostly didn't. "She said we had the same father."

"His father had the last name of Gatewood, as in Julian, as in dead millionaire. Is your father a dead millionaire?"

Frank cut his eyes at her. "What did I tell you about sarcasm? Didn't I tell you I hate sarcasm? I know I told you that."

"I'm sorry, but this shit is hilarious. So, who is this woman? What's her game? Blackmail?"

"Basically," he said matter-of-factly.

"No, for real."

He looked at her. "Yes."

"She wants to blackmail him?"

"I told you yes."

"And what did you say?"

"I left."

Colette raised herself up on her elbows. "So, she was serious?"

Frank sighed, staring down at his dissipating erection. "She seemed to be."

He could feel her studying him, the way cops tend to do to people when they're looking for signs that someone might be keeping something from them. "You believe her."

"How many times do I have to tell you not to try and profile me?"

"It's second nature, Frank. I can't help it any more than you can. You believe her? You believe that Gatewood is your brother?"

"Half."

"Whatever. Do you?"

Shit, Lonnie had been pretty convinced and convincing. Maybe he hadn't believed her in the beginning, but ever since then, he'd been pulling up pictures of Gatewood online, and there was a resemblance, if not to Frank, then definitely to Malcolm, Joel Tunson's oldest son.

"I don't know," he finally said.

"What do you mean you don't know? You don't know if it's true?"

"It was how she said it. She knew things."

"Like what?"

"Like, she knew about my father sending money to my mother for child support for me every month. He still sends it, like clockwork, a hundred and fifty bucks, every month on the fifteenth to the credit union."

"So, have you ever met your real father?"

"Oh yeah. He'd come through every once in a while. I'd spend a day or two with him here and there. He'd bring pictures of my brothers and show them to me."

"That's fucked up."

Frank thought about it. She was right. It was fucked up. It was especially fucked up finding out that the motha fucka was being paid sick money and was only coughing up one fifty to Frank's mother.

"Was Jordan Gatewood in any of those pictures?"

"Hell, I don't know. He didn't mention a Jordan. He talked about Woody and Malcolm."

"So why is she so convinced that there's a connection between you and Gatewood? I don't get it."

Frank didn't get it either. And that's the part that didn't make sense no matter how many different ways he spun it. How would a man like Joel Tunson, factory worker, end up with a woman like Jordan's mother, socialite Olivia Gatewood? He'd seen pictures of that woman in her heyday and she was definitely out of his league.

"I mean," Colette continued, "she'd have to have some kind of proof. Right?"

He nodded thoughtfully. "She would."

"So, what is that proof, Frank?"

Frank's gaze drifted over to meet Colette's. "Where you going with this?"

"Aren't you curious? Don't you want to know if it's true or not?"

Sure he was curious, but— "Lonnie Adebayo could very well be crazy."

Colette nodded. "She could be. But you said she tracked you down and plucked you out of the crowd. She could've found a bodyguard anywhere. Dallas is full of them. Why you?"

Colette's imagination always did work in overdrive, even when they were partners. She had a tendency to spin these crazy-ass theories, hoping that shit was more fantastic than it really was. Colette was the reason he'd left the force, and the reason she was looking for her own way out without raising suspicion.

"Stop it, Colette," he warned.

She knew what he meant, and he could see in her eyes that he'd struck a chord. "You need to look at the possibilities, Frank. All of them."

"No, I don't. And neither do you. I'll cut you short the same way I did her. Leave it alone."

"But what if it's true?"

"And what if it isn't?"

Most of the time, Colette was good at hiding it, but it was never far enough away from the surface, that desperation, that fear that the two of them would be caught. Frank had told her to just be cool and bide her time.

"You didn't bide yours," she'd snapped when they had last talked about it. *"You fuckin' left, Frank! You left me here, hanging, by my damn self, so don't you sit here and try and tell me to bide a goddamned thing because I'm the one who has to check in at that precinct every day and pretend like I don't know what happened! I'm the one who has to play this role wondering if they know what we did, and worrying that every damn time someone knocks on my door that it might be the fuckin' police!"*

"Gatewood's worth millions," she continued with a spark of enthusiasm in her eyes.

"Do you hear yourself, Colette? I said, it's bullshit. I don't know that woman from Eve, and I sure as hell am not going to take her word for something like this."

"Then ask your father?" she suddenly said.

Frank shook his head, crawled out of bed, found his underwear on the floor, and started to get dressed. "I knew I should've kept my mouth shut," he grumbled.

"What harm could it do to ask your father about Jordan, Frank?" She sat up behind him. "At least you'd know."

"Why the hell would I want to know some shit like that? What difference does it make?"

Colette looked at him like she couldn't believe he'd just asked that question. "If it's true, it could make all the difference."

He knew what she was thinking. Frank and Colette had been partners, they'd been friends for more than a decade, and there were times when he truly believed they shared one brain. Frank knelt on the bed, gently cupped her chin with his hand, and gazed deeply into those big, green eyes of hers.

"Our problems are big enough already, baby. Even if this happened to be true, Jordan Gatewood is not the kind of man either of us is equipped to fuck with." He stood up and started slipping into his pants. "If things were reversed, and I was in his shoes, I'd make sure that any motha fucka coming at me with some shit like this never took another breath. Do you understand what I'm saying?"

Powerful men like Gatewood, men with so much to lose, would go to any lengths to protect what they had. Frank didn't need to be smart to know this. He just needed to be empathetic.

Tears of frustration clouded Colette's eyes. "I don't know how much longer I can do this, Frank," she said weakly. "I need to resign, just like you did."

"You do that now, and they'll get suspicious. I already told you."

"How do you know they're not already getting suspicious?" she shot back bitterly. "For all I know, they're just building a case right now as we speak."

"I don't believe that," he said calmly.

"Because you're not there every day like I am," she snapped. "You took off! You left me there to take the heat by my damn self!"

"So what the fuck are you thinking, Colette? Threaten to tell the world that Gatewood isn't who he says he is if he doesn't pay up?" Frank hadn't realized that he was yelling until he saw the look on her face.

Colette nodded.

"And add blackmail charges to murder," he said coolly.

Colette shrugged. "There'll only be charges if we get caught, Frank. We could take the money and run—Canada, Mexico. Wherever you want, baby. I'll follow you to the ends of the Earth. You know that."

Frank should've known better than to mention Lonnie's proposition to Colette. As ridiculous as it all sounded, he should've known that Colette was desperate enough to make it make sense in her mind.

"Just talk to your father, Frank. Ask him if Jordan is his son. If he says no, then—"

But what if the old man said yes? That's what scared him the most. Then how tempted would Frank be to really take this thing to the next level?

"I'll call you when I get to Paris," he said, kissing her on the head before he left.

He's Like My Blue Sky

Norman's was Jordan's favorite restaurant. He and Claire had a standing reservation at a table next to a window overlooking the city, the pianist played flawlessly, as usual, and the filet mignon practically melted in your mouth. But tonight, Jordan seemed more preoccupied than usual. He'd been unusually quiet, which always made Claire nervous. She was sensitive to his moods. Claire used a great deal of energy reading her husband, and anticipating his needs, but she loved him, and she lived for him.

It had been his idea to go out to dinner tonight, but Jordan had hardly touched his food. It had been a while since she'd seen this side of him. Things between the two of them had gotten better these last few years. Jordan was more attentive, even more caring and considerate. Most of the time, Claire could almost believe that he was in love with her.

"June called," she said, breaking the silence between the two of them. "We're flying to Taos in a few weeks for a spa weekend."

He looked at her. It was the kind of look she'd come to love. There was a time when Jordan hardly acknowledged that Claire was in the same room with him. Now he took notice of her, and for Claire, that spoke volumes.

"That sounds nice, baby," he said, almost smiling. "The two of you should have a good time."

Jordan didn't like a clingy woman. Claire worked hard not to be that woman. He seemed to miss her when he was gone, and he was genuinely glad to see her when he came home. He'd changed so much in the last few years. Claire had nearly lost him. She'd nearly lost herself over him, but slowly, their relationship was on the mend, and she couldn't have been happier.

She reached across the table and rested her hand on top of his. Instead of pulling it away the way he used to, Jordan laced his fingers between hers. Her heart fluttered.

"Is everything alright, Jordan?" she asked carefully. "Is there something bothering you?"

Her handsome husband gazed into her eyes, and it was all Claire could do not to swoon. There was no man as fine as Jordan Gatewood, and no other man in this would could affect her the way he did. There's nothing she wouldn't do if he asked. There's no place she wouldn't follow him to. Claire had come so close to losing him, but God must've been on her side, because when the dust finally settled, he was still hers.

"I'm just tired, sweetheart," he eventually said, raising her hand to his lips, and kissing it.

"Do you want to go?" she asked, holding back her excitement.

Jordan nodded, and flagged down the waiter.

Claire had the most beautiful mouth. Jordan lay back on the bed, holding back her hair with one hand, watching in awe, the magic she worked with that pretty mouth on his dick. He'd have been a fool to let her go, and he'd come so close to doing just that. He'd gotten his head too wrapped up in Lonnie to see straight, and he'd almost made the biggest mistake of his life, and left his wife for that woman. Claire looked up at him with beautiful amber eyes, hooded in lashes that were so long they didn't look real.

"Are you happy?" she asked sweetly, smiling up at him.

His rigid penis pulsed in her hand. "You make me happy, baby."

Men envied him for having a woman like Claire. He'd seen the way they looked at her when she walked into a room. She was breathtaking, accommodating, and loyal. There was no doubt in his mind that this woman loved him, and that he could trust her with just about anything, and all it had taken for him to see that was the last night he'd spent with Lonnie.

He'd left Claire in the hospital to get to Lonnie. Claire had slit her wrists, and come parading to the park, bloody and hysterical because she'd found out about the two of them. Fortunately, the ambulance came and Jordan whisked her away before anyone could figure out who he was, or that she was his wife. Doctors wanted to put her on one of those seventy-two-hour holds, but Jordan made sure that didn't happen. He didn't need the negative press, and Claire needed to accept that he didn't want her anymore.

After Lonnie, Jordan went to his downtown penthouse, showered, and slept all day and all night. When he finally did make it back to the house, Claire was there, waiting. She sat slumped on the sofa, her wrists still bandaged, her hair pulled back, and she had packed all of her things.

"I was going to write you a note," she said, not bothering to look up at him. "But I didn't know what to say."

It was in that moment that what he'd done actually became real. For two days, he'd slept to keep from thinking about what he'd done to Lonnie, and what had happened in that house. Jordan had gone numb, almost to the point of believing that the whole thing had been one bad dream that couldn't possibly have had anything to do with him.

"I'm tired, Jordan," she said, defeated. "You don't want me. You never have, and I'm tired of trying to make you change your mind."

He didn't want her. Jordan had had this beautiful, sweet woman all these years, and he had never really wanted her. Was it true? Watching her stand up, he noticed how thin she looked, how frail, and fragile. And noticing those things in her stirred the realization in him that Claire was all he had. She had been there with him, standing by his side, being his cheerleader, pumping him up when everybody else around him fully expected him to fail. She had been true to him, and real. He'd been all caught up in Lonnie but for all of the wrong reasons. A man like him didn't need the bullshit game-playing that came with a woman like Lonnie. He needed a rock. He needed someone stable, like Claire. He had a corporation to run and to grow, and in his world the last thing he had ever needed was a woman more interested in the game than in him.

She picked up her suitcase, and started to walk past him. A voice in his head screamed, *Don't you dare let her walk out on you!*

Jordan grabbed hold of her arm. "Claire," he whispered her name, and tears stung his eyes. Letting her go would be a mistake.

She tried to jerk away from him. "Jordan, don't." She began to sob. "I can't do this anymore. I'm sorry, but I can't."

She wanted him to let her go, but Jordan made his mind up, right then and there, that he would never let her leave him. He slipped his arm around her waist. "Claire," he said again, pulling her closer. He took her bag from her hand and let it fall to the floor. Jordan inhaled the floral scent of her hair, his nose pressed into the curve of her neck, and pulled her against his chest, as she cried.

"I'm sorry, baby," he said, passionately, desperately holding on to her, as if his very life depended on her.

Claire was his life raft. She was his anchor. He'd been selfish and blind before, but now it was clear to him that night just how much he had needed this woman.

Claire's head bobbed up and down on his shaft, and Jordan felt the eruption start to build. She knew what it took to make him cum. She knew what he liked better than any woman, and he knew her. When she finished, he would take care of her, his wife, his woman. Jordan would bury his nose between the soft folds of her sweetness, and lose himself in her until she cried out, calling his name as she came all over his face.

"That's it, baby," he gasped. "I'm cumming, Claire! Damn! Baby!"

I Can Take Your Fears Away

"*It's two* in the morning, Phillip," Lonnie said sleepily, answering the phone. "What are you up to?"

"I'm lying in bed, thinking of you, my love. Oh, hold for a moment, please."

Lonnie held the phone to her ear, and heard him talking to someone. "It looks delicious, sweetheart. Oh, could you go back to the kitchen and fetch me the jar of peach preserves in the cupboard? I do so love peach preserves with my scones. Thank you, darling. Lonnie?"

"What do you call this one?" she asked, referring to the woman he was obviously with. "The one *fetching* you some preserves?"

"A beautiful, petite, big-bosomed, fair-skinned redhead named Anna. You would like her."

"Where are you, Phillip?"

"Athens. The weather's beautiful. You should've come with me."

"But I have work to do," she said solemnly.

He paused. "Yes. I suppose you do. How's it coming along?"

"He looked like he'd seen a ghost when he first laid eyes on me, and then he just looked pissed."

"Pissed is dangerous, love, especially for a man like him."

"I know. I'm being careful."

"You have to be, Lonnie. Gatewood's more dangerous now than he ever was before. He's a man who's spent the last two years believing that he'd literally gotten away with murder. You don't give him that kind of a gift and then snatch it away from him. There's a witness to his crime, and that witness is you."

Phillip was right, of course, and he was doing his part, even from as far away as Athens, to try and keep her safe. He'd bought the downtown Dallas loft, in a secure building; she was staying in it under his name. The cars she drove were registered to various aliases, and a different one was parked in the designated spot every few days.

"What about the brother? Did that pan out?"

She sighed dismally. "It did. He is Jordan's half brother but he doesn't want to get involved. Turns out his brain is bigger than the needs of his empty wallet."

"Did he say no right away?"

"He said hell no, immediately, then tucked tail and ran."

"Smart man."

"For real."

"But don't write him off just yet, sweetheart. He probably just needs time to digest what you've told him. He'll go home, peruse the Internet for any and everything he can find on Gatewood, and just when he's downed his last Budweiser and last packet of ramen noodles, he might just dial your number."

She laughed. "I'll cross my fingers and toes."

Was she crazy? Was Lonnie out of her mind for coming back to this place, and purposely putting herself in the same arena with Jordan Gatewood? So far, she'd only shown up with threats, but Lonnie had such a long way to go to get Jordan where she wanted him. In the meantime, she had to try and stay off his radar, out of sight, and alive. He wouldn't make the same mistake the next time. He probably wouldn't use his own hands to try and take her out either. She wasn't safe as long as she was in the same state with the man. Lonnie might as well have been walking around with a bull's-eye on her back.

"What are you thinking?" Phillip eventually asked her.

"I'm thinking, what if I don't get this right, Phillip? What if I made a mistake coming back here and getting in his face like I did? And I'm thinking that maybe I should just pack up my things, and drive my ass to the airport and fly to Athens to meet your new girlfriend."

"I'm thinking that if you do that, if you leave now, you'll regret it for the rest of your life. I'm thinking that if my new girlfriend gets a good look at you, she'll dump me for you. And I'm thinking that there will be casualties, Lonnie. This is one ugly game you've got yourself into, and it can only get uglier."

"Casualties I can handle," she said quietly. "What's the saying? It's a dog-eat-dog world? I just don't think I could live with myself if Jordan walks away from this unscathed."

"You're not alone, love. I'm in your corner, and all you have to do is ask. You know I'll do whatever it takes to help you get through this."

Lonnie smiled. "I know, baby. You have always been so good to me."

"I promised you that I'd keep you safe, and to the best of my ability that's what I'm going to do. Knowing you, Lonnie, and what you're capable of, I believe in you. I believe that you can do this, and I believe that you should. He had no right to hurt you the way he did. And you have every right to make him pay the price."

"A normal woman would go to the police."

"And Jordan Gatewood owns the police. It would be your word, two years after the fact, against his. Who do you think would win?"

Jordan, by a landslide.

"I can't let him get away with what he did to me," she said, more to herself than to Phillip.

"Of course not. Just remember that men like Jordan don't play by rules, unless he makes them up. So, you throw your rule book out the window too, love."

"Consider it gone."

"Oh, and one more thing," he added. "The brother?"

"Frank Ross."

"Maybe he's not the Gomer Pyle he wants to make you think he is. I'm sending a newspaper clipping to your phone. It may be nothing, or it could be everything. It's up to you to figure it out. I'm just the messenger."

A few minutes after ending the call, Phillip's file came through attached to a text message.

Coincidence? I wonder. . . .

Two Off-Duty Police Officers Found Dead

Tuesday morning, a fisherman stumbled upon the bodies of two men lying facedown in the Rio Grande River just north of Ernie, Texas, a small community ten miles outside of Cotton. The two men were later identified as Edward Brewer and Jake Boston, both members of the Texas State Highway Patrol.

So, Frank Ross was born in Cotton, and he may have even been a cop there, but . . . What was Phillip implying? What was going on in that brilliant brain of his, and what was he hoping she'd connect? Frank Ross, a cop killer? The big, good-looking lug could've been a world heavyweight wrestler, but a killer? Before she dismissed the notion too soon, Lonnie took a few minutes to let it sink in. In her line of work, she'd seen all sorts of things, met all sorts of people, and in all these years, she'd learned one thing: that people were capable of just about anything, even those you least expected to be capable of anything.

The article was a year old. Frank had moved to Paris a few months after that story was published and started his own security business, Ross Security. Reading further along into the article, the local police forces suspected drug dealers, but the case was still open. It was a stretch, putting Frank behind a gun that killed those men. But then, finding him had been a stretch, and finding out that he was Joel Tunson's illegitimate son had been a taffy pull. Lonnie turned off the light and closed her eyes to try to sleep, but it was too late. Phillip had flipped the on switch in her brain. Damn him!

We Are the Genius of Love

Damn! She tasted like apples. He explored her mouth with his tongue, marveling at how the taste never seemed to disappoint him. As much as he regretted breaking the seal of their kiss, there were other parts of her that begged to be tasted too. Jordan found her nipples swelling instantly as the tip of his tongue grazed over first one, and then the other. She arched her back, opened her mouth and released a satisfying moan.

The scent from between her legs smelled as sweet as she tasted and made his mouth water. Jordan gently drove two fingers in between the folds of her warm pussy, and slowly stirred them inside her before pulling them out, and putting them in his mouth. His dick was so damn hard it ached, but he resisted the urge to push into her now. Jordan needed to make this last.

She was a gorgeous, dark beauty, who wore her hair cut as short as his, and she represented absolutely nothing that reminded him of the world he'd come from.

Lonnie spread her legs wide to accommodate him. Jordan greedily lapped *his tongue against her clitoris, and then drove it in between the folds as far as it would reach. Damn! If all of her didn't tasted like apples.*

"Jordan!" she gasped, holding his head in place. "You're going to make me cum," she said, breathless.

He stopped, looked up at her and smiled. "Not yet."

Jordan wanted to be inside her when she came. He raised himself up and hovered over her and expertly guided his rigid penis inside her. Jordan lowered his mouth to hers again, and slowly began driving himself into her, and then just as slowly, eased himself out to the tip.

"Did I ever tell you that you taste like apples?" Jordan said, after making love to her.

Lonnie laughed. "You've mentioned it."

"How the hell does that happen?"

She shrugged. "You gotta eat a lot of apples."

Jordan was on a plane headed for Houston. He stared out of the window, shaking loose the memory that had taken root in his head. The last thing he needed to be thinking about now were memories of making love to Lonnie.

It had been that good, though. The two of them together had been so good that he lost his head over her, and got so caught up that he hadn't been paying attention to what was really going on.

"Can I get you another drink, sir?" the flight attendant asked him.

He handed her his glass. "No, thank you."

Lonnie rolled over on top of him, straddling him. Jordan privately willed his dick to rise to the occasion of round two, but he was spent.

She grazed his mouth with soft, sweet kisses, occasionally dipping her tongue in between his lips, tapping the tip of it against his.

"You've got me sprung, Gatewood," she whispered. "There. I said it."

"What does that mean?"

She laughed. "Sprung? It means that I am your love slave. All you have to do is ask, and I'll come running because you sex so damn good."

She was teasing him. Lonnie started to kiss him again, but Jordan held her back.

"What if I want more than that, Lonnie?"

"What else is there, Jordan?"

"There's you. There's all of you."

"You've got me, baby," she said demurely. "And you've got your wife. What more could a man ask for?"

But he didn't have her. Not really. Lonnie was a bird who could fly away from him on a whim, and Jordan wasn't comfortable with that.

"I want you."

"Of course you do." She smiled. "You want what you can't buy or own. But you can borrow it."

"Until you say otherwise?"

"It's a good deal, baby." Lonnie seductively licked his bottom lip. "Take it or leave it."

"Good afternoon, Mr. Gatewood," Jordan's driver said, greeting him outside of baggage claim, taking Jordan's bag and holding open the back door for him.

Jordan climbed in and smiled at the nervous young man sitting across from him.

"Mr. Gatewood," the younger man said politely.

"How you doing, Bruce?"

He nodded. "I'm good, sir. Surprised." He smiled shakily.

"Surprised?" Jordan asked coolly.

"Yeah, that uh . . . you'd ask me to meet you out here."

"You ever been to Houston?"

"No, sir." He swallowed.

Jordan looked surprised. "You're from Texas, aren't you? And you mean to tell me you've never been to Houston?"

Bruce Johnson couldn't have been any more than thirty, thirty-five maybe. Jordan hadn't seen or spoken to him in two years. Jordan glanced out of the window, staring out at the highway as the driver maneuvered his way into traffic.

Bruce smiled nervously. "I always meant to, but no. I've never made it down here."

Jordan studied him. Bruce was more than nervous. He was scared. And he had every right to be. "It's been a while, Bruce."

"It has, Mr. Gatewood. It has." He nodded, unable to make and hold eye contact for very long. Men with nothing to hide, or at least nothing to be ashamed of, had no problem looking another man in the eyes. Jordan didn't trust a man who couldn't look him in his eyes.

This man had let him down. The disappointment filling Jordan's chest almost took his breath away. A man like him, in his position, relied heavily on people he could trust. He counted on men like Bruce Johnson to deliver on whatever task he assigned to them, and if they couldn't, he expected them to be truthful with him.

Bruce Johnson had started to sweat under the weighted gaze of Jordan.

"Do you remember the last conversation we had, Bruce?"

Bruce's expression went blank. "Not really," he lied miserably.

Jordan had no respect for liars, either. "Unfortunately for you, I do remember it."

Bruce cupped his hands together between his knees.

"You told me that you'd taken care of her, Bruce," Jordan said gravely.

"You promised me that I had nothing to worry about, and that you'd cleaned up the mess I'd left behind."

Fear flooded that man's eyes like tears. "I—uh . . ." His eyes darted back and forth. Bruce pursed his lips together. "The house was empty when I got there, Mr. Gatewood." He started talking fast, too fast. "I mean, I got there as soon as I could, and there wasn't anybody there, so I cleaned up the mess. I burned the purse and clothes, washed the floor. I thought that was all I needed to do. I figured that's what you wanted . . ."

The rage came out of nowhere, and before Jordan realized what he was doing, he drove his foot into the gut of Bruce Johnson. When the man doubled over, Jordan grabbed him by the collar of his shirt, and pulled him out of his seat and onto his knees on the floor of the car.

"You fuckin' lied to me!" Jordan growled. "When I asked you if you'd taken care of *her*, not clothes, not purses, not floors, but *her*, you looked me in the eye, and you told me something! What the hell did you tell me?"

Bruce struggled to breathe. His mouth flapped open and closed before he finally made an audible sound.

"I-I told you . . . that I did," he gasped.

"That you did what?"

"That . . . I took care of her."

Jordan shoved him back into the seat across from him, adjusted his suit and tie, and casually leaned back, noticing that the driver was starting to slow down inside the parking garage of Jordan's hotel.

"If you'd just told me the truth, Bruce." Jordan shook his head in disappointment. "I'm not unreasonable, man. The truth I can live with, but lies make me sick to my fuckin' stomach."

The driver parked, and moments later, opened the back door for Jordan to get out.

"Lock it," Jordan told him, as he exited the car. "Call me and let me know when it's done."

"Wha—Hey, man! Mr. Gatewood! I'm sorry, Mr. Gatewood!"

As the driver pulled away from the curb, Jordan headed inside, ignoring the cries coming from the back of that car.

We Stand for Nothing

Forty-two-year-old Frank Ross hadn't seen his father in nearly twenty years. Joel Tunson had never been a regular fixture in his life, but there were no hard feelings from Frank. The situation was what it was. He was a grown man. He knew how things worked in real life. Frank and Shirley had met at a club, had a few drinks, shared a few laughs, and then got busy. She ended up getting pregnant, and the two of them kept on living their lives despite the bump growing in her stomach and the boy who'd been born as a result of their short-lived acquaintance. Joel came around from time to time when Frank was growing up, bringing him a toy truck or a baseball. He always took Joel out for ice cream, then dropped him back off at his momma's house, patted him on the head, and promised to spend more time with him in the future.

Colette had talked him into making this drive to see his father. "Don't you want to know the truth, Frank?" she asked, naked and straddling him. "I'm not saying you have to do anything about it, but wouldn't it be something if you really were related to a man like that?"

She was desperate and looking for an answer to the situation the two of them had gotten themselves into. *The situation.* That's what he called it. She didn't bother to call it anything, Colette just wanted out of it. She saw Gatewood as an opportunity, her own personal piggy bank, and a light at the end of a long, dark tunnel that seemed to go on forever. Frank was in that tunnel too, but he'd just learned to keep his eyes closed and pray that it would eventually come to an end, hopefully with him outside of prison walls, and not behind them.

He had gotten a card from Joel when he graduated high school, a card and a hundred-dollar bill. This address was on the outside of the envelope, and Frank had it memorized. The small house sat back off the street on a lot big enough to hold twenty houses that size. Frank pulled his car onto a patch of dirt, behind the old Buick already parked there. Frank spotted a large vegetable garden over to the side of the house, and an old doghouse toward the back. Overalls hung on the line. Never in a hundred years did he think he'd ever come to this place. And Frank sat in his car, realizing that he had no business being here now. This was wrong. All of it. He had no place in this old man's life, and Joel Tunson had no place in his. And neither one of them warranted anything remotely related to Jordan Gatewood.

"Get in the car, Frank," Colette demanded. She'd asked him to meet her in the parking lot of a convenience store just outside of Cotton.

"What's going on, Colette?" he asked irritably.

"Just get in, dammit!"

She was more agitated than usual. Colette had always been high strung, but something definitely had her upset. He climbed in on the passenger side, and looked at her sideways. "Mind telling me what the fuck is going on?"

Their shift ended hours ago, and Frank had settled into his place with a six-pack and the schedule to all the playoff games for the weekend.

"I got a call from Ed Brewer." She glanced at Frank. "You know him?"

Frank nodded. Ed Brewer had come on the force not long after Frank had joined. "I know him."

"He knows, Frank," she said, staring wide-eyed and frantic at the road ahead of her. "How the fuck does he know?"

Frank couldn't believe what he was hearing. "He can't know, Colette," he argued.

"He does, Frank. He called me, and he said shit that only you and me would know. He knows about Reggie." She shot a nervous look at him. "He knows about the money, and the drugs."

Frank's heart started to pound. If this shit was true— "He called Reggie by name?"

She nodded. "Reggie Rodriguez," she said, panicked. "Reggie's been giving you and Frank a cut." That's what he said. "Reggie's been cutting the two of you in on the action," she repeated. Colette raked her hand through her hair. "If I didn't tell him, and you didn't tell him, then it had to have been Reg," she concluded. "Right? I mean, he's the only one."

"But how would he even know to talk to Reggie?"

Colette had his head spinning with more questions than answers. Reggie was a meth dealer living in Cotton, but his small-town, country ass distributed the shit all over west Texas, Arizona, and New Mexico. Frank and Colette weren't sure how much money he made, because Reggie kept a low profile, living in his mother's basement, and driving an old beat-up Mustang, but for a percentage, they turned a blind eye when they saw him coming. Not much.

Colette had made enough to get her mother's roof fixed, and pay off her car, and Frank had been able to catch up on some child-support payments, and give the kids some pretty nice Christmases.

"Where're we going?" he asked, as she exited the highway.

"He told us to meet him here," she said, sounding preoccupied. Colette drove to a secluded spot off the Rio Grande River, and pulled up next to a black pickup truck. Ed was in that truck, but he wasn't alone. Jake Boston, a dude who'd transferred in from El Paso, was with him. Both men climbed out of the truck and walked over to the edge of the river, waiting for Colette and Frank to follow.

There was no sense in beating around the bush. This was exactly what it appeared to be, a good old-fashioned Texas shakedown. Colette trailed behind Frank, keeping her arms folded protectively across her chest.

"What's going on?" Frank asked, staring back and forth between the two men. Ed Brewer was around Frank's age, a white guy with brown hair and eyes. He and Frank stood about the same height. Jake was a brotha, short and stocky, built like a running back.

"You know what's going on," Jake spoke up.

Ed turned and glared at him for speaking out of turn. Then he turned back to Frank. "Your boy Reggie's got a big mouth when he's threatened with jail," Ed calmly explained. "We pulled him over off Highway 10 the other night for speeding. One thing led to another," he explained in that slow Texas drawl that Frank seemed to hear in everyone's else's voice but his own, "and we searched the vehicle." He paused for effect.

Colette groaned, and muttered. "Shit."

"That's right," Ed said, looking briefly at her. "When we threatened to take him in, he offered us a deal." He turned to Jake. "The same deal he'd given you and Colette here."

"What deal?" he asked, thinking that the best way to play this was to play it dumb.

Jake laughed.

Ed didn't. "An idiot like Reggie is lucky to be alive, and he's even luckier to be walking around a free man," he said coolly.

"Then why didn't you just arrest him, Ed, for speeding, transporting meth, and trying to bribe two upstanding officers like yourselves?" Frank caught on to the game Ed and his sidekick Jake here were trying to run on them. They had the word of a drug trafficker making accusations against two of Cotton's finest. So, what the hell did he want?

Ed's eyes narrowed. "We want what he's really giving the two of you."

Frank raised his eyebrows.

"He offered us pennies on the dollar, Frank."

Frank turned and glanced at Colette. Yeah. That's about all he was giving the two of them. Pennies. But it was enough to help out their bank accounts a bit, without drawing too much attention to either one of them.

"What's he really giving y'all?" Ed probed.

Frank decided to play it smart. "I never said that he was giving us anything," he said coolly.

Ed started to get angry, and his buddy behind him was getting noticeably agitated.

"You trying to play us for fools?" Ed said menacingly, taking a step too close to Frank.

Frank took one toward Ed. "If I didn't know any better, I'd say Reggie already did that."

"Tell the truth. How much did the two of you take in from that little wetback last month?"

Frank shook his head. "I can't believe you dragged my ass all the way out *here for this," he said, getting angry. Ed and Jake had nothing but the word of Reggie. They were pissing in the wind, literally, trying to get Colette and Frank to confess to something that, for all they knew, was bullshit. And he could see it in both of their faces that they had nothing concrete.*

He turned to Colette. "Let's go," he said, motioning her back to the car.

"Where the fuck are you going?" Jake called out. "Where the fuck are they going?"

"This conversation never happened, Frank!" Ed said, sounding reluctant all of a sudden.

He'd come here with an underlying threat, accusing the two of them of being dirty, but he had no real proof. And when Frank called his bluff, all of a sudden, that dog stopped barking.

"What if they tell— Naw, man! What if they—"

The agitation in Jake's tone sent a chill up Frank's spine, and Frank looked up in time to see that fool pull out a gun and point it at him and Colette. But what he didn't see was that Colette already had her weapon drawn and aimed at Jake. She pulled the trigger before he did. Ed pulled a gun from behind him, but he was too slow. Instinct had kicked in. Instinct from being on the force for close to ten years, and always having to watch his back.

A knock on the driver's side window startled Frank back from the past.

The old man peered through the glass. "You gettin' out?"

Frank climbed out of the car and stared into the eyes of his old man. He opened his mouth to talk, but all of a sudden, he had no idea what to say.

Joel peered curiously at him. "Frank? Frank, is that you?" And then he laughed, held open his arms, and embraced Frank for the first time in nearly twenty years.

When We Seek and Hide

The woman had saved Lonnie's life, but they weren't friends. They weren't even close to being friends.

"Hello, Claire," Lonnie said, as Claire Gatewood sat down at the table across from her.

Lonnie thought that she was more prepared for this meeting, but the flood of emotions coming back to her just now were almost too overwhelming. Claire was as beautiful as Lonnie remembered, before Jordan assaulted Lonnie. She'd never understood why he'd chosen Lonnie over Claire, except that maybe he was attracted to Lonnie's edge. Claire was Barbie perfect, almost too good to be true perfection. Lonnie was the polar opposite. She broke the rules and he fell in love with that part of her. She didn't fit the mold, and he adored her for it. Lonnie had been the rebel to Claire's debutante.

"Thank you for coming," Lonnie said to the woman, who was noticeably pensive and guarded.

Of course Claire didn't want to be here. Lonnie had heard the repugnance in her voice when they spoke over the phone.

Claire wouldn't even look at her. "Did I have a choice?" she asked defensively.

Lonnie didn't bother to answer that question. It was redundant. She inhaled deeply, taking in the scent of Claire's perfume. It hadn't changed.

"Wha-what happened to— Wh-who did this?"

Lonnie was so grateful to hear her voice. It was the voice that called her out of the darkness, that pulled her back from death.

"Who did this? Who— Can you walk? Can you get up? Can you walk?"

The woman was her angel, her savior. Yes! Yes, Lonnie would get up—if she had to. She would walk if it meant that she wouldn't die here in this place.

"How did you get my number?" Claire asked abruptly, snatching Lonnie back to the present. This time, Claire did look at her, she glared angrily at her.

Lonnie noticed the large yellow diamond on her ring finger. Jordan must've given it to her. Lonnie studied the woman, searching her face, her demeanor, for any signs that her husband knew that it was her who helped Lonnie to leave the house that night.

"I wanted to thank you, Claire," Lonnie said calmly.

Claire Gatewood was a nervous and unstable volcano, threatening to erupt at any moment. If looks could kill—

"I never asked for your thanks," Claire snapped abruptly. The dropdead gorgeous Claire Gatewood's chest heaved, and for a moment, Lonnie truly believed the woman would burst. "I should've left you there." She dropped her gaze to the silverware on the table.

The waiter showed up in that moment. "Hello. Can I get you—"

"No," Claire snapped, but then quickly composed herself. "Thank you." After he left, she turned her attention to Lonnie again. "Why did you ask me to come here, Lonnie? I didn't want to see you again." She clenched her teeth together. "I had hoped I'd never have to see each other again. I don't give a damn about you, and you know that."

"But you couldn't let me die, either."

Whatever her motives, Claire hadn't left her there, lying on the floor in her own blood. She'd made it clear that she hated Lonnie, but she hadn't let her die. In this moment, just like in that one, that's all that mattered.

"Does he know?" Lonnie asked softly. Of course she knew the answer to that question already, but she needed for Claire to say it out loud. She needed for Claire Gatewood to acknowledge verbally that she knew who had beaten Lonnie, into the bloody pulp Claire had stumbled upon that night, and that he had no idea that his wife had been the reason behind Lonnie's resurrection from the dead.

Claire looked as if she were going to break down crying.

Lonnie almost felt sorry for her. But what did Phillip tell her? In this war, there would be casualties, and Lonnie was sitting across the table from one of those casualties.

"He thinks you're dead," Claire admitted shakily. "Don't be a fool, Lonnie. Let him believe that."

Claire had been the one who had convinced Lonnie not to tell the police what had happened to her that night in the hospital.

"He'll know it was you and he'll come after you."

Lonnie shook her head in disbelief. "You know what kind of man he is. You know what he's capable of," she said, disgusted, "and you are still with him?"

Claire bravely held Lonnie's gaze. "He'd never do to me what he did to you."

Lonnie couldn't believe what she was hearing.

"You pushed him, Lonnie. You had to have pushed some button in Jordan that made him snap, and do that to— I know my husband. I'm safe with my husband because he cares about me."

Lonnie couldn't believe the shit coming out of this woman's mouth. "But he didn't always care about you, did he, Claire?"

She hadn't asked Claire to come here to hurt her, only to get a feel for where her head was. She'd wanted to understand the relationship Claire had with her husband, and to see if she was still the wounded bird Lonnie so vividly remembered.

"Tell me," Lonnie said, leaning over the table. "Did he care about you when he was fucking me?"

The sting of those words showed in Claire's eyes.

"Did he care about you when he whisked me down to Cabo for a weekend, laid me out on the patio, and licked my pussy raw? Did he care about you when you found us in the park that day, with the blood dripping down your wrists because he had driven you to try and kill yourself?"

"You fuckin' slut," Claire snapped bitterly.

"He was leaving you for me," Lonnie stated bluntly. "That's how much your man cared for you."

"I should've left you to die!"

"But you didn't, and if all you've ever wanted was to live happily ever after with your man, then you're right. You should've left me there."

The woman looked shocked to hear it, but Lonnie had driven that revelation home. She hadn't intended to come at her like this, not this soon, and not this hard, but Claire had forced her hand. She'd pushed the issue, and now, it was clear to Claire that by saving Lonnie, she had made the biggest mistake of her life.

"You're married to a monster, Claire. You know it as well as I do. I do thank you for saving my life, and I caution you to be careful."

Tears flooded Claire's beautiful amber eyes. "Let him think you're dead, Lonnie," she demanded. "He doesn't know . . . what I did, and he'll never know. You leave Dallas, and don't ever come back."

Lonnie reached for her purse. She put ten dollars on the table, and stood up to leave. But she stopped and stood over Claire before walking out. "I'll always be grateful for what you did for me. But you pay attention, Claire. I'm not your enemy. Your husband is."

I Got a Jones

It was late, but Lonnie didn't care. She dialed his number again and again until he finally relented and answered the phone.

"What is it?" he asked, sounding like he'd been asleep.

"What happened, Jordan?" Lonnie blurted out, raking her hand over her hair. She sat with her knees drawn to her chest, in the bay window of her loft, looking down at the city streets.

Lonnie had tried to sleep, but seeing Claire again had raised too many memories, and too many questions that all of a sudden she needed answers to.

"Hang up and I'll call right back," she threatened. "I'll show up at your goddamned door!"

"What the hell do you want?"

"I want to know why the hell you felt you had the right to put your goddamn hands on me, Jordan! How the hell did some shit like that pop up in your mind?" she demanded, crying.

Lonnie was a different kind of distraught. She was losing it, finally. She'd gone crazy. Of course she'd known that Jordan and Claire were still together, long before she'd sat down with that woman. But after seeing Claire again, knowing the bullshit mess that the woman must've seen when she found Lonnie that night in that house— How could she let a man like that put his hands on her? How could she love him so blindly, so ridiculously, even after all the shit he'd put her through? How could she have ever forgiven him?

"I'm telling you—no, I'm warning you not to keep pushing this, Lonnie," he snapped.

"You couldn't stand her, Jordan," Lonnie yelled at him. "You were through with Claire! You told me yourself that you didn't want her!"

"Where is— Where's this coming from, Lonnie?" he said, suddenly in a hushed tone. "What the hell are you talking about?"

Lonnie was drunk, but she wasn't that damn drunk. She couldn't let him know that she'd spoken to Claire, and Lonnie trusted that Claire wouldn't tell him about their meeting either. She regretted buying that bottle of Ciroc on the way home from seeing the woman. Alcohol had a way of making the dirty shit rise to the surface.

"You're still with Claire," she said, almost as if she couldn't believe it. Lonnie grimaced. He had blatantly disrespected that woman, and that fool still nipped playfully at his ankles like a puppy desperate for attention. "How the hell does that happen?"

"You sound jealous," he said smugly.

She laughed. "Oh, now that's funny! Is this Richard Pryor I'm talking to or Jordan Gatewood! Funny as hell."

"Then why the hell are you calling me with this bullshit?" he snapped back.

Because that bitch saved my life, asshole! she wanted to scream into the phone. Jordan couldn't know that she was alive because of Claire. Not yet. Lonnie stood up and walked back and forth to compose herself. *Think! Be smart! Think, Lonnie.* She needed to get him off balance. Jordan was in control. He was always in control even when he was making you believe that you were the one holding the reins. She couldn't underestimate him. She couldn't let her guard down. And more than anything, Lonnie had to get him off balance.

"You asked me a question the last time I saw you," she said, metering her speech. "When was the last time I saw nice in you." Lonnie closed her eyes and focused on the path she needed to be on, the one she needed to stay on. Keep him distracted. Keep him guessing. Keep him unprepared. "It was in the park, Jordan," she stated with clarity. Lonnie stopped and stared out of the window. "The day was perfect. The sun was shining, a cool breeze blew, and there wasn't a cloud in the sky. It was beautiful." Lonnie was suddenly caught up in that moment—in that day again, recalling the sounds of kids and music playing, birds singing, and of the two of them laughing. It was the fantasy of a high school girl, romantic and sweet.

"You dared me to catch the football," she said, remembering him throwing it at her. It was so unexpected, so playful, and childlike. The great mogul Jordan Gatewood, running around a city park, in jeans and sneakers, throwing a football to his girlfriend. Lonnie laughed. "Oh, God! I caught it," she said, raising her hand to her forehead and closing her eyes. "I couldn't believe I caught that damn ball, Jordan. Do you remember?" Lonnie began to spin around slowly in a circle with her eyes closed. "We were like teenagers," she murmured, almost forgetting that he was silent on the other end of that phone. "Like kids without a care in the world. I fuckin' loved that!" she blurted out. Lonnie stopped, and a wave of heat washed over her as the revelation hit her like bricks. "I loved you . . ." her voice trailed off.

The sound of her own declaration suddenly snapped her out of whatever trance she'd been in. This was not the way to punish him! He was the one supposed to be off balance, not her! Lonnie caught up with her train of thought, wandering recklessly off track, and pulled it back on course. Hurt him! Remind him of the man he really is! Jordan's no teenage boy trying to impress a girl. He's a fuckin' terror!

"And then we saw Claire," she said, forcefully. Lonnie stopped spinning and remembered the image of that woman, walking over to the two of them. "Her eyes wild and glazed over, and the oversized white blood-stained shirt she wore, one of yours . . ." Lonnie's voice trailed off. "Claire stumbled, and blood dripped down off of her fingertips. She knew about the two of us, Jordan. And she tried to kill herself because of—"

Jordan had done that to that woman. He'd driven her to do that to herself. She waited for him to say something, but he never did. All of a sudden, the line went dead.

Can You Dig That Mess?

Olivia Gatewood was like a priceless art piece tucked away in the attic and forgotten about. After Desi Green's book was published, naming Olivia as the one who actually pulled the trigger on the gun that killed her husband, Julian, all those years ago, investigators began sniffing too close to the Gatewood compound. Jordan did what he had to to protect his mother and she'd resented him for it ever since.

Oakwood Assisted Living was one of the premier and most exclusive senior communities in the country. It cost more to live there than most people made in their lifetimes, but she hated it. Jordan had had his mother, who suffered from dementia, placed under the direct care of one of the most prominent physicians in Texas. Detectives couldn't talk to her without her doctor's approval, and as far as he was concerned, Olivia Gatewood was physically and mentally not well enough for questioning.

It was the third Sunday. Edgar always visited her on the third

Sunday. Some visits were better than others. Today, she knew who he was. Olivia was in her full presence of mind, and when she was, she was as sharp as a tack. Edgar watched admiringly as Olivia's long, slender fingers expertly manipulated those knitting needles and lavender-colored yarn. Well into her seventies, she was still a breathtaking-looking woman. Edgar had always marveled at how lovely she was, and he'd always been dumbfounded by Julian's indifference to this woman. She was elegant, intelligent, and she loved Julian Gatewood, literally to death.

"I warned June not to marry that fool," she said disappointedly, shaking her head, and curling her lips at the corners. "He was beneath her, and I told her as much, but her silly behind had to try and prove something," she said, glancing at Edgar. "If I told her to go left, then she went right. If I'd told her to go ahead and marry the man, she'd have dumped him like a hot potato."

Edgar nodded. "June never did like following the rules."

"She never liked following *my* rules," she corrected him. "Even when they're right."

June had divorced her husband and moved back to Dallas as soon as she had, and she'd moved into a position inside the family business.

"I guess she's got something to prove now." When she was in her right mind, Olivia was acutely aware of everything and everyone. "She's got another thing coming if she thinks that brother of hers will sit by idly and let her take over the business. Jordan loves his sister, but he loves his position at Gatewood Industries more."

"He'll accommodate her to a point," Edgar concluded. "As long as she doesn't overstep her boundaries . . ."

"Boundaries he'll no doubt set for her. My children played nicely together when they were young, Edgar. I don't believe that's the case anymore, especially since they're both after the same thing: Anton Oil."

He was surprised that she knew about the acquisition of Anton.

She seemed to know what he was thinking. "I may be crazy, Edgar, but I can still read. Anton Oil's gulf oil spill was an unfortunate accident, but they were struggling long before that happened. That oil spill was the last straw on the back of a company that could hardly support it. Jordan's been eyeing that company for years. My daughter needs a feather in her cap. She needs to prove herself, especially to him and the board. If she can land this acquisition, without the lawsuits and federal charges, she'll come out shining like a brand-new penny, and he won't be able to dismiss her so easily. That's all she wants, her brother's approval. That's all she ever wanted."

Edgar couldn't help but be impressed by her prowess. She was the matriarch of this family, and wore the title like a crown.

"Once again, I've been talking your ears off, Edgar," she said with a smile. "How've you been? How's that lovely young wife of yours, Bridgette? Is that her name?"

He was surprised she remembered. "That is her name," he said graciously.

"What is she? Wife number three? Number four?"

There was a flippancy to her tone that he didn't approve of. Edgar challenged Olivia's gaze with his own, but of course, the woman wasn't about to back down.

"She's my third wife, Olivia," he said begrudgingly.

She smiled. "As long as she makes you happy."

"She does."

"Well," she said with a sigh, setting aside her knitting. "I've had about enough with the small talk. What about you?"

"Indeed."

"Did you send Joel Tunson his money?"

He nodded. "I send it every month, Olivia, although I don't believe he ever spends a dime of it."

"It doesn't matter. Keep sending it. What about Desi Green?"

"What about her?"

"Where is she? Hanging out with Oprah, I suppose?"

"Oprah was last month. This month, I believe it's Anna Wintour at *Vogue*," he joked.

Olivia looked perplexed by his attempt at a joke.

"She's launched a new business. Shoes, I believe. And purses."

Olivia laughed. "All of a sudden she thinks she's Coco Chanel?"

"Basically. She's lost interest in the Gatewoods and seems to have moved on with her life, Olivia. If you ask me, Desi Green's a nonissue, and you no longer need to waste your money or your time worrying about her."

"Your advice is appreciated, but unsolicited, Edgar," she said coldly. "As long as my husband's blood flows through her veins and I am still here on this Earth, I will always worry about Desi Green."

That was the bane of this woman's existence and it had been since that child was born. Edgar had tried talking sense into Julian. He'd warned him to leave that woman alone. Ida Green was not worth losing his beautiful wife over or the scandal he would suffer and the damage it would do to the business he'd worked so hard to build.

Edgar didn't tell Olivia the truth to betray his friend. He told her so that she could make her husband see just what was at stake if he continued that foolishness.

"H-how do you know, Edgar?" she'd asked him, sinking onto her knees and finally down on the sofa, shocked by the news. "How do you know he's the father?"

Ida Green was several months into her pregnancy. Edgar had known

Julian well enough, and he'd known Ida well enough to know that she had been loyal to Julian. She loved him, and like Olivia, she lived for him.

"I just know, Olivia," he said dismally. "I wouldn't be telling you this if it weren't true."

"You shouldn't be telling me this period!" she suddenly snapped. "I don't believe you! That whore is not carrying my husband's child, Edgar, and shame on you! Shame on you for coming to me with this nonsense!"

The seed had been planted that afternoon in Olivia Gatewood, and they never spoke of it again, but at some point in her life, she'd accepted the truth that Desi Green was a Gatewood, and she'd never let the reality stray too far from her thoughts. It was the driving force behind the reason Olivia put that gun in Desi's hands instead of Ida's the night Julian was shot. She'd never said it, but Edgar had reached the conclusion on his own.

"Speaking of Desi, how is my son?" she asked coolly.

The relationship between the two of them had become strained at best since he'd had her placed here. Olivia resented him for trying to save her life, and he loved her enough to let her resent him.

Edgar had never kept secrets from Olivia. He'd always cared for her, probably in ways that were inappropriate for a man to care for his best friend's woman. But despite his loyalty to Julian, Edgar always believed that Olivia deserved better than to ever be lied to. The Gatewood name, the family's position, always seemed to mean so much more to her than it did to her husband. She relished it, and it was Olivia Gatewood who had added the grandeur to the name.

"I'm afraid he's gotten himself into a mess," he casually explained.

A thoughtful expression crossed her face, one that was hard to read. "How so?"

"With a woman."

Olivia shrugged. "That was going to be my next guess," she said in that delicious Southern accent of hers.

"Does the name Lonnie Adebayo ring a bell?" he asked curiously.

She thought about it and shook her head. "No. I'm afraid it doesn't. Is he fuckin' her?"

He smiled. No one said the word *fucking* quite like the beautiful Olivia. "He was, until he lost his damn mind and tried to beat the woman to death."

The amusement vanished from her face. "She's lying."

"He admitted it."

She looked shocked to hear Edgar say those words. "Jordan's never put his hands on a woman, not even Claire."

"He put his hands on this one, Olivia," he said coolly. "And he made the mistake of not finishing what he started," he continued.

Olivia stared wide-eyed at him.

"The worst thing he could've done was to leave that woman alive," he explained without batting an eye. "Now he wants me to help him clean up behind him."

"Don't tell me that," she muttered.

As angry as she was at her son, Olivia still believed that boy walked on water. She believed he was still her little prince, and that he could do no wrong. Edgar owed it to her to set her straight. He'd tried to get her to see the light where Julian was concerned, and she refused, until it was too late. The woman was getting too old to still believe in fairytales.

"The sonofabitch may not be Julian's by blood, Olivia, but he's certainly his by circumstance," he said coldly.

Olivia raised her chin in defiance, but said nothing.

"The bitch is a beast, a reporter or photographer, or, hell, both—who's covered some of the most incredible events around the world, and she is a pit bull," he said, curling his hand into a fist. "She is relentless, and once she gets her teeth into something or someone, she doesn't let go."

In recent weeks he'd read every article Lonnie Adebayo had ever written, viewed every photograph she'd ever taken, and her work showed him more than any other human being on the planet could've ever told him about the woman.

"He should've made sure she was dead," he said, in a hushed, angry tone. "Because if she can bring him down, she will! And she'll do it at the expense of your last name, Olivia!"

She stared unemotionally at him. "There you go again, overstating things."

Olivia Gatewood had a knack for taking the things he told her, and tucking them away safe inside herself for processing later on. Edgar had learned long ago not to force more on her than she could handle at any one time. He picked up his hat and put it on his head.

Edgar composed himself. He knew better than anybody that he had a problem with being melodramatic at times. "But don't you worry your pretty little head about this Lonnie woman, Olivia," he stated calmly as he stood up. "No one cleans up messes left behind by the Gatewoods better than I do. And I assure you, I'll wipe up this dirty little stain the same way I have all the others." He smiled at her one last time.

Olivia's gaze drifted off. "Thank you, Edgar. You're a good friend," she said casually.

He paused before leaving. "Yes," he said, nodding reassuringly. "I certainly am."

The Makings of You

"*You could've* just met me at the motel room where I'm staying," Frank said irritably, sitting next to Lonnie Adebayo in a crowded mall.

"Believe me, Mr. Ross. I've learned my lesson about not meeting an angry black man anywhere alone."

"I'm not angry."

"But you're anxious, and that's almost as bad."

"I'm concerned," he corrected her. Lonnie wanted to see him crack and he wasn't about to give her that satisfaction. "You call me up with some cryptic shit about Cotton, Texas, and why I left there, sounding like you got something to say about it." He looked at her. "You know something I don't know?"

He waited, giving her the stage to stand up and say whatever it was she thought he should know. This one was manipulative, and cool as hell. Now that he knew what her game was, he'd made up his mind not to volunteer any damn thing. If she thought she had something on him, then let her tell him what it was.

"Edward Brewer. Jake Boston," she said coolly. "Those names ring a bell?"

He nodded. "Sure they do. They were police officers in Cotton back when I was on the force," he stated matter-of-factly. "They were found dead about a year ago."

Lonnie stared at him, watching and waiting for Frank to give her some sign that this topic of conversation was making him uneasy.

"Any idea who killed them, Frank? Or why?"

"Not a clue," he responded. "Last I heard, their murders were still unsolved."

Frank didn't blink. He didn't sweat or swallow. She watched him, looking for those signs, indications that he knew more than what he was saying, but he wore that poker face like he'd been born with it.

"Why'd you agree to see me, Frank?"

"Why'd you ask me to see you, Lonnie?"

She smiled. "Why're you so guarded?"

"Why don't you tell me what you want?"

"Did you kill those men?" she asked, straight up.

Admittedly, hearing her ask if he killed them put a lump in his stomach. And it took every ounce of will power in his body not to flinch.

"Why would you ask me that?" he asked, trying like hell not to sound defensive.

"Because if you did, I'm sure you had a good reason for it. Ed Brewer had a gambling problem, and needed money. Lots of it. Jake Boston was just plain mean and greedy. He had a history of abusing his girl-friend, and getting in random fights whenever the hell he felt like it."

He knew what she was doing. Lonnie was trying to reel him in. "I didn't kill anybody, Lonnie."

"But just for argument's sake, let's say you did," she said, looking hard into his eyes. "How far can you run, Frank? How much money do you have? And what about Colette?"

He was shocked to hear Colette's name come out of Lonnie's mouth.

"She's a mess. She's a meth head, Frank. Or haven't you noticed?"

Keep your mouth shut, man! Don't fall for this shit. She was dangling raw meat in front of him, tempting him to say what she wanted to hear. He just shook his head.

"How long do you think it'll be before she falls apart?"

Colette was fragile. She was getting more and more brittle every time he talked to her. Frank made the mistake of blinking not once but twice, quickly. He saw a spark in Lonnie's eyes. "Colette's a good cop," he started to explain. "At least she was when we were partners. If she is on drugs, that's news to me."

Even he cringed at the sound of the lie coming out of his mouth.

"Texas is big, but it's not big enough, Frank. And Paris, Texas, isn't far enough away. You know how these things work. You've been a cop, and time always shines light on the truth, sometimes sooner, rather than later."

"I didn't kill anybody, Lonnie," he repeated with certainty.

"The Cotton police force recently questioned a man named Reginald Rodriguez, a suspected drug dealer."

Frank's heart stopped beating.

"They found his address in Ed's cell phone, and a series of phone calls to Reggie's number."

Why was she saying these things? Did she know, or was she just pissing in the wind, guessing and hoping he would come clean and tell her everything, like before? Frank swallowed when she wasn't looking.

"I think Reggie's afraid," she continued. "I think he's afraid that whoever had the balls to kill two cops might just come after him too."

"What do you want, Lonnie?"

"I want you to be safe, Frank. I want you to be able to get as far away from whatever bullshit you left behind in Cotton, Texas, as you possibly can, and live to be a crunchy, old man."

"You want me to press down on your boy, Gatewood?"

"Jordan's got his eyes set on buying out this company, Anton Oil. If he does that, he'll be worth double what he is now. Wouldn't it be nice to get your hands on some of that money?"

"You don't give a damn about me, so let's just keep it one hundred, Lonnie. This ain't about nothing but you getting back at the brotha for doing you wrong."

She smirked. "Yeah. He did me wrong, alright."

"So, you know who he is. Why don't you come out with it to the press and leave me out of it?"

"Because all I got are words. You're living proof, Frank."

"You got papers on him?"

The look on her face told her that she probably did.

"Then you've got your proof. Use it."

"Me putting papers out there would only irritate him. You'd make him nervous."

"Nervous?" He shook his head. "I doubt seriously that that brotha has patience for anything that'll make him nervous."

"He's used to having things his way."

"And I'm supposed to shake him up? Go up to him and say, 'Hey bro! Look, you don't know me, but uh . . . we got the same daddy, and well, how 'bout you hook me up with a few hundred thousand, and uh . . . I'll disappear like a ghost and you'll never even know I was here. But if you're not interested, then I'll make a phone call to the Channel Three news and let them know that you ain't who you say you are.' Is that about how you see it going?" he asked sarcastically.

She laughed. "Yeah. That's it."

"And you don't see how ridiculous that is? My word against his? So, maybe I do have papers, but how hard would it be for him to counter what I have with what he has and make me look like some gold-digging fool from the sticks? You don't see anything wrong with this picture?"

"Oh, I've seen it. And I know how it'll play out. You'll go to him for money, and he'll laugh in your face."

He looked at her like she was crazy. "So you know I won't get anything out of this?"

"I don't know any such thing, Frank," she said seriously. "He may pay you to go away, just like he's paying Joel. But if he doesn't . . ."

"If he doesn't, and I go public, then I'll end up looking like a fool."

"Or you could end up with more money than you ever dreamed of."

This didn't make sense. What did she really want? And then it dawned on him.

"You need a distraction," he said, finally figuring it out. "If he's busy with me, then he's not going to be paying attention to something else." The look on her face told him that he was right. "What is it?" This time, he was the one looking for her to give away her secrets. "That oil company," he eventually said. "That's it. Isn't it? I start a scandal now, and old boy's too busy trying to clean up one mess while you start another one."

Lonnie looked out into the crowd walking past the two of them. "When was the last time you spoke to your father, Frank?"

He didn't answer.

She looked at him. "Did he tell you that Jordan was your brother?"

He thought back to his visit with Joel, the first one in nearly twenty years.

"You came all the way out here to ask me that?" the old man asked, looking disappointed, and looking something else too. "Who told you about him? Who you been talking to?"

"Is it true?" Frank didn't want to hear that it was. He'd hoped his father would laugh at him and ask him what kind of joke this was he was trying to play on him.

Joel squinted at him. "What you askin' for?"

"Because I'm your son too. Like it or not, I am."

Joel rolled his eyes and groaned. "I never said you wasn't," he growled.

Frank had a long-ass argument that he could've come back with about how he barely ever saw Joel, and how it was easier for his ass to send a check than it was to pick up the phone and call. But now wasn't the time.

"Is that man my brother?"

The old man's face turned to stone. "He ain't your brother any more than he's my son," he said gravely. "And it's best you leave that alone, boy. He ain't the kinda man you wanna know."

"How do you know?" Frank asked bluntly.

The muscle in Joel's jaw ticced as he clenched his teeth.

"Because he is your son," Frank concluded.

The man shifted his focus toward the window, trying to hide the pain in his eyes. "Not anymore." His voice was ragged. "Not in a long, long time."

"What if he does pay up, Frank? What if he thinks it's easier to pay you then deal with the scandal, publicly? Like you said, a public scandal would be a distraction, one he doesn't need right now. Or, if you like, you can put your faith in Colette and Reggie, and take your chances with them. It's up to you."

Lonnie pulled her purse onto her shoulder, stood up, and walked away, and left Frank with one hell of a dilemma.

Right On for the Darkness

"What the fuck do you mean they held the meeting?" Jordan marched through the long corridors of Gatewood Industries headquarters, leaving his office and heading toward June's. He was talking to the chief financial officer on his cell phone. "I canceled the goddamned meeting before I left for Houston!"

"June rescheduled it, Jordan," the man said apologetically. "I reminded her that you had canceled the meeting, but her assistant had sent out the meeting notice before she'd ended the call."

Jordan cut the man off and stormed into June's office at the end of the hall. She was perched on the edge of her desk, talking to that sidekick administrative assistant of hers. June had handpicked the woman for the job.

"Jordan," she said, startled, hopping off of her desk. "I thought you weren't due back until tomorrow."

Jordan glared at Vickie or Nickie or whatever the fuck her name was. "Leave," he said simply.

She paused, looking at June for permission.

"We'll finish up later, Lisa."

He waited for Lisa to leave, closing the door behind her.

"How was your flight?" she asked casually, taking refuge behind her desk.

"Who told you to convene the acquisition team meeting, June?"

With everything else going on in his world right now, the last thing Jordan needed was to babysit his little sister. June had been a mild annoyance since she'd moved back to Dallas and insisted on coming to work for the company. He'd entertained it, only because she was his sister.

"I didn't see a reason not to, Jordan," she said, calmly crossing one leg over another.

She looked like Julian. June was lighter-skinned, with green eyes. People always marveled over how much more she looked like their father and how he looked so much like Olivia, their mother.

"It was a simple enough agenda," she continued. "And I figured that we could handle it while you were gone. One less thing for you to have to worry about." She smiled.

Now she was just trying to push some buttons. Jordan found himself uncharacteristically amused.

"I've been running this business a long time, June," he said with a smirk. "You'd be surprised by all the things I'm capable of worrying about."

"You're worried that I'm stepping on your toes?" June smiled. "Don't, big brother. I'm here to help, and if I can take some of the heat off of you, then why shouldn't I?"

June stood up, walked over to him, and pressed her hand against his chest.

"Baby sister has a great big MBA with an emphasis in finance. She's mere inches from getting her PhD, big brother." June smiled up at him. "I know what I'm doing."

He looked down at her, and forced away the image of his twelve-year-old sister. "So do I, June-bug," he eventually said.

He'd allow her some room to push, but only to a point. Jordan would entertain her muscle-flexing as long as it didn't get in his way. But the moment she pushed too hard, or those muscles of hers got too big, Jordan would have to do some flexing of his own.

"I'll have Lisa send you the meeting minutes right away," she said assuredly. "And you'll see. The meeting went great, and you'll be signing the deal on Anton before you know it."

As promised, Jordan had the meeting minutes in his inbox by the time he made it back to his office, and the notes did look promising. As he read through them, Jordan's cell phone vibrated. He had a new e-mail from Edgar with an attachment.

Call me, his message said.

Jordan clicked the PLAY button for the video, and then picked up the phone and dialed Edgar's number.

"I got your e-mail," he said when Edgar answered.

The couple were sitting on a bench inside the mall talking.

"You recognize your former lady love, Lonnie Adebayo," Edgar said sarcastically. "But do you know who the man is?"

Jordan paused the feed and studied the man's face. "No."

"Frank Ross," Edgar explained. "She hired him for protection."

Suddenly, Jordan thought back to the day when Lonnie first contacted him a few weeks ago. There had been a man leaning next to a car outside the house.

"Okay," he said cautiously.

"He's an ex–police officer from a town called Cotton, just east of El Paso, and now owns a security firm in Paris, Texas, about a hundred miles northeast of here."

"I asked you to find me Lonnie, Edgar. Not some ex-cop turned bodyguard," he said irritably.

"The woman is staying in the Fuller Building downtown. Condos— but the property isn't in her name."

"Whose name is it in?"

"That I don't know," he said with a sigh. "But I didn't send you that feed because she's in it. I sent it because of the gentleman she's sitting with."

"What about him?"

"Are you telling me that you don't see the resemblance, son?" Edgar said gravely.

Jordan was already frustrated from his earlier encounter with June, and now Edgar wanted him to play guessing games?

"Edgar, I really don't have time . . ."

"He's Joel Tunson's son, Jordan. A son from an affair he had with a woman in Cotton. Frank is your half brother, and I suspect she knows that and that she and good old Frank are planning to *out* you, so to speak," he said.

"Out me," he repeated, introspectively.

All those threats and this was as good as she could do? Jordan leaned back and sort of chuckled to himself. Lonnie's evil scheme was to dangle some wayward Tunson over his head, and expect for Jordan to tuck his tail, cringe in fear, and what? Beg and plead for the man not to tell his story to the media? Or pull out his checkbook, sign it, and hand it over, letting this cat fill in the blanks with as many zeros as his little heart desired?

"This has got to be a joke," he said, unimpressed, as he stared at the video and focused his attention more on that Frank Ross than he did on Lonnie.

He'd squashed the Tunson threat a long time ago. Jordan had confided in Edgar, who didn't seem surprised at all about Jordan's confession that Julian wasn't his biological father.

"If Desi Green wants to produce a photocopy of your so-called birth certificate"—he shrugged, casting his lure into the lake—"let her. She's got copies but we've got an original to dispute it."

"But what about Joel Tunson?" Jordan asked, concerned, while Edgar continued to fish.

"What about him? If Joel Tunson hasn't come forward by now, he's not going to, and even if he did, it's his word against yours." He smiled. "My money's on yours."

"She has a knack for flair, this Lonnie Adebayo of yours," Edgar said. "Beautiful woman too, still."

Edgar was careful not to say it, but his remark implied that she was still a beautiful woman, even after what Jordan had done to her.

"She's got a knack for the sensational," Edgar continued. "She could've avoided all of this, had one of her reporter friends publish the birth certificate indicating Joel Tunson as your father."

"But her intention is to make me suffer, to drag this thing out in dramatic fashion and make me sweat, wondering what she could possibly have on me. If this is as good as it gets, then I must admit, I'm disappointed."

"I can imagine what she's promised Frank Ross: money, maybe fame," Edgar said dismally. "It's a shame to drag him into this."

"He looks like a big boy from here, Edgar," Jordan quipped. "If he thinks he can hang with the big dogs, let him try."

Keep Some Proud on My Face

"*Seventy-two hours,* my ass." It was Jordan's voice Claire heard arguing with the doctor outside of her room. "*Do you have any idea who she is? Who I am?*"

"Your wife tried to kill herself, Mr. Gatewood. Do you understand what I'm telling you? She tried to take her own life! A seventy-two-hour hold is protocol in cases like this."

"My wife accidently cut herself gardening," he grunted. "Get me the administrator!"

"Sir, that's not—"

"Get me the damn administrator or you let me take my wife home!"

Claire just wanted to sleep. She was so tired of trying so hard, for so long, to get him to love her. She was tired of the women . . . of this woman— How come he needed another woman so much? He had Claire. She would do anything for him. She would die for him. He knew this. She'd proven it.

"Alright! Alright! Just leave her overnight for observation. Please! We need to keep her at least for the night, and then—she can go home tomorrow."

Claire waited for him to come back into her room, pull a chair up close to her bed, and to stay the night with her. She'd only done this to show him how much she loved him. Claire had done this to herself to prove to him that she would do anything for him—anything! She fell asleep thinking about him. When she woke up the next morning, Claire was alone.

They had sold the house. Claire sat next to Jordan in his office at home, across from Geneva Harris, signing the document formally accepting the buyer's offer.

Years ago she had begged her husband to buy the cottage. Three months ago, she'd suggested that they sell the place, since neither of them had set foot in it since . . . Jordan didn't protest when she asked him about selling it. His indifference about the issue was classic Jordan, and a few weeks later, the house was on the market.

She watched as her husband signed his name. Was he as relieved as she was to be rid of this place? This should have been the end of it, finally. That dark episode in both of their lives should've ended with his signature, but seeing Lonnie the other day resurrected a part of Claire's life that she'd regret for as long as she lived.

The image flashed in her mind of the night she walked into that house and saw Lonnie lying there, naked and beaten on the floor in the living room. Claire had left the hospital and had gone to the cottage instead of going home because she wasn't ready to see her husband. She remembered driving down the road toward the house, crying and accepting the fact he never loved her, and it was just a matter of time before her marriage was over.

"Mrs. Gatewood?" Geneva held the pen out to Claire.

Claire took it and signed next to Jordan's signature.

"This was a fabulous offer," Geneva went on to explain. "Twenty-five percent above asking is unheard of these days in this market, but the buyer was determined, to say the least." She smiled.

"Well, his determination is our gain," Jordan said, glancing at Claire. "You say he's European?"

"Yes. I believe he's from Wales. Mr. Durham. Phillip Durham."

Jordan had been quiet during dinner. Claire showered, and stood in front of her bathroom mirror, staring at her reflection, rubbing moisturizer into her face.

"He was leaving you for me. . . . If all you've ever wanted was to live happily ever after with your man . . . you should've left me there."

In that moment when she saw that woman lying there on that floor, Claire knew. She knew that it was Lonnie lying there and she knew, instinctively, that Jordan had done that to her. Claire had seen, first-hand, how cruel Jordan could be. He'd never hit Claire, but he'd said things . . . done things, uncaring things that left her wondering if he really understood the damage he could cause in another person.

Claire's heart began to race, and she started to turn and leave. If Jordan knew that she'd been here, if he knew that she'd seen what he'd done to this woman—he could just as easily have killed Claire, too.

"Help."

It was a weak and fragile cry for help, but it was strong enough to stop Claire in her tracks.

"P-please."

Claire wouldn't have left a dog to die. Jordan wouldn't just leave her there, dead, in his house. He was coming back. Claire knew it as sure as she knew she'd take her next breath. Jordan wasn't finished with that woman.

"H-h-help . . . me," Lonnie whimpered.

Every instinct warned Claire to leave and to get as far away from that house—from Jordan—as possible. This woman, Lonnie, had mocked Claire. She'd practically ruined Claire's life, taking from her the only thing that ever mattered—her husband. But even with all of that, something inside of Claire wouldn't let her leave Lonnie in that house. Claire should've left her there.

Jordan had beaten that woman to within an inch of her life, but Claire loved him. She loved him to toxic levels, and hated herself for it. But she'd trained herself to see what she loved in Jordan, and to block out those parts of him that scared her.

"What's that?" he asked, standing in the doorway to her bathroom as Claire washed down her pill. She had been taking antidepressants even before her attempted suicide.

The muscles in her back and neck immediately tensed whenever he caught her by surprise. Jordan wore only the bottoms of his pajamas and she had thought that he was in bed already.

She nervously started to put the pill bottle back in her medicine cabinet, but Jordan came over and took it from her hand before she could.

He looked at the label. "Prozac?" he asked, concerned.

Jordan never came into her bathroom, and she'd never told him that she was taking anything.

"How long have you been taking these?"

She shrugged, and took the bottle from him. "Awhile," she said, nervously.

She tried to walk past him, but Jordan blocked her way. "Claire, do you really think you need these?"

Claire needed them to cope, to try and heal, to think rationally, to believe that her marriage wasn't the farce she knew deep down that it had always been.

The expression on her face must've spoken volumes. Jordan tenderly pulled her close to his chest, and wrapped big strong arms around her. Claire melted against him.

"I'm sorry," he said sincerely. "Sorry that I've left you feeling so vulnerable." Jordan kissed her head, and Claire marveled at the fact that he would actually apologize to her and admit something like that to her.

She pulled back and looked up at him.

"You're my wife, Claire," he said, staring into her eyes. "And my wife should not have reason to be unhappy."

Jordan had no idea what depression really was. It was deeper than just being unhappy. It was not knowing how to give herself permission to be anything else. Unexpected sincerity filled his eyes and his voice, and Claire couldn't help but to feel touched by his sentiments.

"It's alright, Jordan," she said sweetly. "The pills help. I'm okay, really."

He seemed to examine her, searching for clues that she really was fine. His expression softened.

"I want you to stop taking them," he said gently.

The thought terrified her, but so did disappointing him. Conflict inside her began to swell, and he noticed.

"If we're going to have a baby, Claire," he continued calmly, "then I don't think you can take antidepressants."

A baby? Since when had Jordan wanted to have a baby with her? He had a daughter, grown and living in California, that he barely saw or mentioned, but he'd made it clear a long time ago that he wasn't interested in having more children.

Claire, on the other hand, had dreamed of having his children since before he proposed.

"Jordan, I—"

"It's what you want. Isn't it?"

Claire was overwhelmed. "Yes. Yes, but you never wanted it."

He sighed. "My wife wants a family," he said assuredly. "And I want her to be happy. That's what I want."

Jordan kissed her, then took her by the hand and led her into the bedroom. He wanted a child. Jordan wanted her to have his child. If this was a dream, Claire never wanted to wake from it, and the nightmare of Lonnie or of the transgressions of her husband would not ruin it.

How Did I Get So Far Gone?

"Reggie's dead."

Those two words, coming from Colette over the phone, abruptly snapped Frank out of the fog he was in. He pushed himself up in bed, and focused on the numbers on the clock by the nightstand until they came into focus. It was just after one in the morning.

"What did you just say to me?" he asked gruffly.

He hadn't spoken to Colette in days, and she calls him up out of the blue to tell him this?

"He's dead, Frank," she repeated.

Frank rubbed sleep from his eyes. "What the fuck happened, Colette?"

The grinding in his stomach warned him that he didn't want to know the answer to that question. But Frank absolutely needed to know the answer to that question.

"Shot," she said simply.

"How? Who the fuck shot him?"

He knew who? Jesus! He knew!

Colette didn't answer him.

"Where are you?"

"He was nervous, Frank." She spoke as if she were under some kind of spell. "How the fuck can you be a meth dealer and be that damn nervous?" she muttered, more to herself than to him.

"Colette." He nearly shouted her name. "Where the hell are you?"

"In my car," she said quietly. "I'm driving, Frank. Just driving. They kept pulling him in for questioning, and I knew . . . He's going to break, they said. This one here's got something and it won't be long before he gives it up," she told him, repeating what she'd overheard investigators say around the precinct. "He was a fuckin' pussy!"

All of a sudden the room got hot. "You fucked up, Colette." Frank said it before he could stop himself. Right now that woman was a loose cannon. Those damn drugs she claimed she wasn't doing had fried her judgment. "If you thought you were in a shitty spot before, baby, you sure as hell are in one now."

"We," she said simply. "We, Frank, because I'm not going down for any of this shit by myself."

"I didn't put the bullet in Reggie," he snapped.

"No, you just shot a cop!"

"*We* shot cops and you pulled the trigger first, baby girl," he argued.

Colette had turned into a lunatic. She'd shot Reggie Rodriguez. Maybe the cops had no concrete evidence leading the murders of those cops back to Frank and Colette, but he could hear sloppy in her voice. Colette had left evidence, and it was only a matter of time before it led to her, and she led them to him.

"I'm leaving town," she said.

Frank lost it. "You fuckin' leave and they'll know it was you, Co-lette," he grunted. "You leave and you might as well paint a bull's-eye on your back and mine too for that matter!"

"It's too late, Frank! I can't do this anymore! I can't stay here and take the heat while you bask in the afterglow of the murder you got away with. I won't do it!"

"What the hell do you expect me to do?" he snapped.

"We need to leave. We need to go far and we need to go fast. Money, Frank. We need money and lots of it!"

He knew what she was saying, and unfortunately, he knew that in this case, she was right. If the cops got their hands on Colette, it was over—for both of them.

"We don't have time for you to keep bullshitting, Frank," she said gravely.

"We'd have had plenty of time if you hadn't shot Reggie."

"Reggie was going to talk. Hell, maybe he already did, and maybe they already know," she said dismally. "I bought us some time. Not much, but some. Now you need to do what you have to do. I, uh . . . I can't say how much longer I'll be in town. I can't say how long it'll be before they find out what happened to Reggie, but I can say without a doubt that if they pull me in, I'm pulling you in with me, baby. I mean it." She hung up before he could say another word.

All of a sudden, the heat was turned up and Frank didn't have the luxury of time or rational thinking on his side anymore. He had five hundred in his savings account, and a credit card with about two hundred dollars left on it. Put it together and maybe he had enough to get him to Florida.

Frank had never put much thought into running. In the back of his mind, he'd always thought that this whole thing would magically blow over, and eventually, the deaths of those two men would be filed away in the back of a storage room somewhere. But the dead men were cops, and he knew that the police wouldn't stop until they found who did it.

"Lonnie," he said wearily, over the phone.

The sun was just starting to come up, and Frank had been up since getting off the phone with Colette.

"It's early, Frank," she said irritably. "This better be good."

Frank had been playing out every possible and plausible scenario in his head before finally calling her. A man like Gatewood wasn't going to make this easy. Frank would need to let him know what was up. He'd need to let him know who he was, and what he wanted, and then, duck and cover and stay out of sight.

The Gatewoods of the world didn't get their hands dirty on men like Frank. He'd either report Frank to the police for extortion or he'd dismiss him and dare Frank to say a word to the press. And then it would be the word of a Gatewood against the word of a nobody like Frank. In either of those cases, Frank could become interesting all of a sudden, even as far away as Cotton, and that would get the cops back home to looking at him again with fresh eyes. Some bright motha fucka would begin to put the pieces of the puzzle together, and *bam!* He'd be in handcuffs.

There was one more path Jordan Gatewood could take. He could just nip this shit in the bud right away, and Frank could end up being a smudge on the wall, or cemented to the bottom of a lake someplace. None of those alternatives set right with him, but what choice did he have? Frank needed money, and he needed it fast. He had to take a chance that somehow, fate wouldn't hold his sins against him, and that he'd catch Gatewood on a good day.

"How do I get in touch with Gatewood?" he asked apprehensively.

Lonnie took a breath. "I'll text you his personal cell phone number."

He nodded, forgetting that she couldn't see him. "How come I get the feeling that I'm going to regret this?"

"Because you probably will."

"Then why do it?"

"In the last two years, he's deposited two hundred and forty thousand dollars in Joel Tunson's bank account, and he won't stop buying that old man's silence until he's dead. How far could you go on a quarter of a million or more, Frank?"

He thought about it before answering. "Pretty damn far."

"It's a risk, yes. Maybe it'll pay off, maybe it won't. But what do you have to lose? And what could you possibly gain?"

He had everything to lose. Just thinking about it made Frank sick to his stomach.

"Send me that number. Let's get this ball rolling," he said, before hanging up.

We're All Cannibal

"So let me get this straight," Lonnie said, standing in the open doorway of her loft wearing panties and a tank top and eating an apple. Phillip Durham had showed up out of the blue like he was a rabbit who'd just popped out of a hat. "You flew all the way from Greece and some hot babe just to take me to lunch?"

He smiled. "I know of no other woman in the world more deserving than you, love."

She couldn't argue with that. Lonnie stepped aside and motioned for him to come in. "Thought you had a key," she said to him.

"Of course I do," he responded. "But it would've been rude to use it."

Phillip kissed her forehead, came inside, and shut the door behind him. "I like what you've done with the place," he said, looking around.

"I didn't do anything," she said, taking another bite of apple. "I just moved in."

He turned to her and smiled. "That must be it. It looks lived in and smells like girl."

"When did you get back to the States?"

He took hold of her hand and led her toward the armoire in the bedroom. "Do you have a pretty dress?" he asked, flipping through hangers.

"Of course I have a pretty dress, lots of them. Why?"

He pulled out an orange number with a wide belt, and a plum-colored pair of suede pumps. "Huh?" He laid out the ensemble on the bed, looking for her approval.

"Um . . . creative."

"Get dressed, love. I am famished."

Lonnie plopped down on the bed. "I ate already," she said casually. "Tell me about Athens." She patted a place beside her.

He took hold of her hands and pulled her to her feet. "I'll tell you about Athens over lunch."

"But I said I'm not hungry."

"I am. So you can watch me eat and I'll tell you all of my adventures."

So, Phillip was hungry, and insistent. Lonnie shrugged, pulled her top off over her head, and started to get dressed.

The hostess led Lonnie and Phillip through the crowded restaurant to a table facing the lake.

"No," he said, stopping her. "Would it be possible for us to sit over there?" Phillip pointed to another table across the room.

"Sure." The hostess smiled and seated them.

Phillip ordered a bowl of lobster bisque soup and salad. Lonnie just ordered the salad. For twenty minutes, he told her every detail about his trip to Greece and the four times he fell in and out of love while he was there. Then suddenly he changed the subject. "So, tell me how your little vendetta is coming along?"

"My little vendetta?" she asked, slightly offended, and slightly amused by his pompous, belittling tone.

Of course, Phillip caught on. "Oh, come on, darling. I'm English. You know we are naturally condescending. It's in our DNA."

Lonnie quickly recovered. After all, this was Phillip, her savior, best friend, and occasional object of her affection. "I think Frank Ross has finally gotten with the program," she explained, toying with her napkin. "He's ready to get in touch with Jordan. Asked me how to do it a few days ago."

Phillip's blue eyes twinkled. "Wonderful." He smiled. "What is your prediction? Do you think he'll fare well?"

Lonnie thought before responding. "No," she said remotely. "I don't think he'll fare well in any of this. But I need him."

"That's all that matters," Phillip said unemotionally.

Lonnie nodded. "We're all actors in this play. We've all got our roles."

There was something sad and dismal about it all.

There will be casualties, Phillip had warned her. Frank was going to have to be one of them, eventually. So would others.

"I spoke to Jordan's wife," Lonnie volunteered, thinking back to her meeting with Claire.

"The woman who saved your life."

Phillip had just missed Claire when Lonnie was in the hospital, but she'd told him who she was.

"He still has no idea?" Phillip probed.

She shook her head. "Not yet."

"You plan on telling him?"

Lonnie stared at him. "I plan on getting her to tell him."

"How?"

She shrugged. "Claire's weak," she said matter-of-factly. "She's a puppet with strings. You just gotta know how to pull them."

"And I take it you do?"

Lonnie was thoughtful. Of all of them, Claire was the easiest to read, the most vulnerable, and the one with the most cracks in her armor.

"Once upon a time," Phillip started, "there was a beautiful princess." He stared deep into her eyes.

The last time he'd started that once-upon-a-time shit, she'd told him to shut up, but now she knew better. Lonnie sat quietly, patiently, and listened.

"The evil king said he loved the princess, but he hurt her terribly, nearly took her life, and never gave it a second thought."

She hung on every word, putting images behind those words, making Phillip's story three dimensional and layered.

"She thought she was too weak to fight him, but she was wrong."

"Because she was just as strong as he was." She finished that part of the story for him.

Phillip smiled approvingly. "How do you topple a king, princess?"

"You find his weakness," she muttered.

"And what is this king's weakness?"

"His name," she said, with confidence.

"His name. You've found the king's weakness. The next step in toppling this king is . . . ?"

He waited for her to find the answer on her own. Lonnie thought about it. She thought about the conversation the two of them had been having, and it dawned on her that Phillip hadn't just been asking her those questions for casual conversation. The answer was in there. She might have even said it herself. Frank came to mind, and then Claire. Claire had pulled Lonnie out of that house, and Claire would die if her husband ever found out what she had done. Claire lived for Jordan, and she would die for him too. She'd already proven that. She was his biggest cheerleader, and for whatever reason, from what Lonnie had seen in the society pages, Jordan proudly braced her at his side. He needed her.

"You turn his most loyal subjects against him." The answer came to her as she made eye contact with Phillip.

"Look over my right shoulder," he told her. "The couple seated next to the window."

Lonnie focused where he told her. "The old man and his daughter?"

"See the rock on her finger?" Phillip asked. "Do you really think she's his daughter?"

Just then she saw the man lace his fingers into the woman's. He brought her hand to his lips, and kissed it. "Guess not."

"His name is Edgar Beckman," Phillip continued, as he dipped a corner of bread in his soup. "The young woman is his third wife."

Lonnie shrugged. "Okay."

So, the old dude had a young wife. It happened.

"He was the executor of Julian Gatewood's estate after he died."

Now he had her attention.

"Edgar's name showed up on a great number of publicly filed documents related to the Gatewoods through the years. Apparently, he was Julian Gatewood's personal attorney for many, many years."

Lonnie wasn't getting it. Julian was dead. "So?"

"Men like him are loyal to a fault."

She wasn't convinced. "Then why is she his third wife?"

"The other two got old," Phillip said, without missing a beat. "And he's as loyal to the Gatewoods now as he ever was."

"How do you know?"

"He visits Olivia Gatewood once a month at the retirement community," he said casually.

"She was married to Julian. Nothing special about that."

"Did I mention that he was the executor of—"

"Julian's will," she said impatiently. "I know. I know. But what does that have to do with—"

"The day after Julian Gatewood died, his will was filed with the state of Texas with the probate courts."

"Naturally."

"The day after that"—Phillip pulled documents from the pocket inside his sports coat—"another will was filed in the probate court, superseding the original one."

She picked up the document, unfolded it, and looked at it. "It looks like a will," she said, after examining it. "Julian's will. How'd you get this?"

"It's the original will, Lonnie," he said coolly. "Take a closer look." Lonnie studied Phillip's expression, which had never, in all the years she'd known him, betrayed the mystery of the man. He was a great friend, but she suspected that he was also the last person on earth she'd want for an enemy.

"Don't look at me like that," he said impatiently.

"Like what?" she asked.

"Like you're trying to see inside me."

"What would I find?"

He shrugged. "Blood and guts, Lonnie, and the person who is forever on your side. Today I am the Caped Crusader," he boasted. "And as long as I have my super powers, justice will be served."

"*I, Julian Gatewood, being of sound mind and . . .*" Lonnie read on in silence, then suddenly stopped, and looked up at Phillip.

"I fuckin' knew it," she snapped. "I knew it!"

Lonnie happened to glance in the direction of the old man, Edgar, and he stared back at her, like he couldn't believe what he was seeing. Phillip slipped on his sunglasses, and casually glanced over his shoulder at Edgar and then turned back to Lonnie.

"He knows who I am," she said, stunned. "Phillip, he knows who I . . ." Lonnie looked back at Phillip. "He knows who I am."

"He knows who you are, sweetheart. And now, you know who he is. He is the Gatewood guardian. He is the one who filed the second will, and he is the one who has kept this secret all of these years."

She read on.

I leave behind my wife, Olivia, my stepson Jordan, and my two daughters, June and Desdimona . . .

A Man of Odd Circumstance

"Hello. My name is Frank Ross. Joel Tunson is my father. I think we need to talk."

Jordan was in his car, stuck in traffic on Interstate 635 when he got the call. Jordan had expected it. He was actually relieved that it had finally come. Now, he could get this shit over with. "So talk," he said coolly.

The man on the line hesitated, as if he had to think about what he was going to say next. Jordan felt himself start to get irritable. "Mr. Ross, if you're going to back a motha fucka up against the wall, at least have your shit ready," Jordan groaned.

"In person," Frank shot back. "Not over the phone."

Jordan waited, then listened patiently while Frank Ross told him where he wanted to meet.

After hanging up, Jordan pressed his button on the steering wheel and called his assistant to cancel the two meetings he had scheduled that afternoon.

Jordan nearly stepped on a little girl who bolted out in front of him, running across the grass to get to the slide. Frank sat on the opposite side of the playground in the park on a bench, looking as ominous as a predator, in dark jeans, a black T-shirt, and a ball cap pulled down low on his head. Of all the places the two of them could've met, the brotha had really thought outside the box with this one. He moved over when Jordan arrived. Jordan sat down next to him.

"Frank Ross," Jordan eventually said, trying to let this moment soak in. He couldn't believe he was here now, with this fool. And he couldn't believe the conversation that was about to go down. "What could you possibly have to say to me, Frank Ross?" Jordan looked at him for the first time.

If there were any type of resemblance, Jordan refused to acknowledge it. But he was getting impatient with the reluctant attitude of this dude.

"Joel Tunson's your father too?" Frank asked, trying to sound hard.

If a man wants to sound hard, Jordan thought, he doesn't ask another man a goddamned thing; he states it, emphatically. "I don't know any Joel Tunson," he answered simply.

"Just because you don't know him doesn't mean he's not your father, man." Frank finally dug up some courage from somewhere and dared to look back at Jordan. "He knows you though," Frank continued, and gradually, Jordan could sense this man was starting to grow some balls. "So, I've been thinking about it, and it looks to me like you might have yourself one hell of a dilemma."

Jordan stared at the children playing and swinging on the playground. "What kind of dilemma could I possibly have with a man I know nothing about?"

Frank Ross chuckled. "Oh, I see. You wanna play word games. What? You think I need to sit here and convince you that you ain't a Gatewood by blood? That I need to try and get you to believe the truth when you already know it?" He shook his head. "Man, I'm not even going to waste my time with that shit."

"But you're wasting my time, right now."

"Then make me disappear," Frank stated simply.

The implications were so deep in those four little words that Jordan almost admired him for saying them. But he was still so far out of his league that it wasn't funny. "Is this how you've made your way through life, Frank?" Jordan asked calmly. "By taking things that don't belong to you."

"And you're different—how? You've taken another man's name, his business, and even his legacy, and strut around wearing all of it like some goddamned peacock feathers. What the hell do you have that you didn't take from somebody else?"

Now he was just starting to piss Jordan off. "I have no idea who this Joel person is that you insist on throwing up in my face. Julian Gatewood is the only father I have ever known. His name is the name I've grown up with and into. He left his legacy behind for me in his will, motha fucka, so don't try and compare the two of us, because other than both of us being black men born and raised in Texas, we ain't got shit in common."

"Then you won't mind me going to the press and telling them that the great Jordan Gatewood isn't who the world thinks he is?"

"You run and tell the press any damn thing you want, Frank. You are a gnat on an elephant's ass, son. And you might as well be invisible," Jordan said, glaring at him. "I've gone up against governments, Frank Ross, corporations, and men who would just as soon run over your ass with their golf carts if they didn't think your black ass would dirty their wheels," Jordan said, casually adjusting the cuffs of his shirt and standing up to leave. "If I can give you anything, it's a word of advice." He turned to look at him. "You run. Run as fast and as far away from this mess that Lonnie's pulled you into, and you keep on running and forget that you ever laid eyes on that bitch and me. Because you don't have what it takes to play this game." Frank met his gaze, and he looked as insulted as Jordan had intended. "She's using you to get back at me."

"You think I don't know that?" Frank retorted.

"So you're just doing your part to try and help a sista out. Is that it?"

Frank shrugged. "If it works out that way then fine, and if I can get something out of it too, even better."

Jordan laughed. "I must admit, I haven't been this amused in a long time."

"Probably not since the night you beat and raped a woman," Frank blurted out.

"I'm almost impressed, Frank," Jordan said unemotionally. "That was definitely below the belt."

"Thank you."

"If you truly care about Lonnie, tell her that eventually my patience will run out, and remind her that getting even with me is not worth her time or effort. I can't turn back the hands of time, and I can't take back what I did to her. Believe me. I understand where she's coming from, but she doesn't give a damn about you. If she did, she wouldn't have given you my number, and she wouldn't have encouraged you to leave that closet of an office you have out there in Paris-fuckin'-Texas to come here and to fuck with me."

"If these kids weren't here right now, man, I'd put my big-ass foot up your fancy, princess ass," Frank threatened. "That three-thousand-dollar suit ain't armor, Jordan. And that stuck-up attitude you got is all for show, and maybe it works for some people, but that shit don't faze me. Yeah, I had issues with getting involved in this mess, because I'm not that kind of brotha. I work for what I get. Always have. I ain't never held out my hand to another man and said, give me your fuckin' money."

"But now all of a sudden, you've decided to try something new?" Jordan asked sarcastically. "See, Frank, the thing is this. A man in my position understands and accepts that the world is filled with people who resent what he has, and will do whatever they can to try and fuck with his success. I've given you some sound advice, and if you're a smart man, you'll take it and you'll stay the hell away from me." Jordan stood up and adjusted his suit jacket. "But if you decide that you want to challenge me, you go ahead and have your little press conference. Because for every document you can dig up, I've got half a dozen attorneys sitting back waiting to discredit your shit. I've got people waiting to discredit you. You can try and bring up my demons if you want to, son, but we all have them. I'm sure you've got your share. And believe me, if you do, I will find them and hang your black ass from the highest tree and show the whole world what they look like." He slipped on his sunglasses and slid his hands into his pants pockets. "You came to play," Jordan said with a shrug. "So, let's get it on." He began to leave, stopped, and looked over his shoulder. "And tell that bitch to call me."

He walked away from that fool, leaving him with something to chew on. The Frank Rosses of the world were incidentals. Most of the time, Jordan barely knew they existed. But this one had gotten up in his face. He'd called Jordan to the center of the ring, and thrown the first punch. Either Lonnie had given him one hell of a pep talk or a big bite of that delicious ass of hers, because he was definitely not thinking with the head on his shoulders.

Just a Hustler in Spite of Myself

Edgar was old enough to be her grandfather, and Bridgette, his wife, was a cokehead, slave to his money and his will. He sipped on brandy, and sat at the foot of their bed, with his shirt unbuttoned, and the soft puddle of what used to be his cock lying limp in his lap as he watched another man fuck his young wife.

"You watching, Daddy?" she purred, bracing herself on all fours while the other man drove a dick as long as Edgar's arm into the pink, soft, sweet folds of what he knew was the best pussy in the whole state of Texas.

Her eyes rolled in the back of her head, Bridgette raked her moist tongue across her pretty pink lips, and she moaned.

"I'm watching, sugar," he said enviously. "Make it good."

He loved them young, not jail-bait young, but Edgar had a thing for firm, ripe tits, a plump, springy ass, tight enough that you could bounce a quarter off of it. But as much as he loved these things, the best he could do was to taste them, to kiss them. He couldn't get hard anymore. And on those rare times that he did, Edgar's meager erection would fall apart as soon as the thought of putting it inside a woman threatened to become real.

He didn't even know this man's name. He was a valet. A damn valet, and she decided that she wanted him. So, Edgar let her bring him home, but only if he could watch. The tall, slender man was even younger than she was, with an athletic build, smooth, dark skin, and enviable skills. As he pushed into her from behind, he leaned over her, cupped the two teardrop-shaped orbs hanging from her chest, and rolled pink nipples between his thumb and index finger until they sprung to life and grew right in front of Edgar's eyes, like magic.

Bridgette's tousled blond hair cascaded over her face, but she still managed to peek through the strands and gaze deep into Edgar's eyes with hypnotic brown eyes. The other man reached up and slipped a long finger in between her beautiful lips, which she eagerly wrapped around it, and made love to it with her tongue.

"Yesssss," she hissed, as he drove into her, with long, slow, even strokes.

Edgar sipped on his brandy, and savored the kissing sounds that their bodies made together. Her moans were like music to his ears, and before long, Bridgette forgot all about her husband watching her. Her lover's moans mixed with hers, and there were times when Edgar was so caught up in the moment that he heard the sound of his own voice erupting from deep in the back of his throat, escaping into the air and mixing with theirs.

This was the price he paid for loving young women. Age wasn't kind and didn't give a damn how much money he had. But she gave a damn. Edgar let her spend his money like there was no end to it, and in return, she would be another man's porn star, another man's whore and slut. But Edgar—he could watch. Neither of the young people noticed when he exited the room. Edgar quietly left them to their pleasures, and took his brandy with him downstairs to the living room. An hour later, he heard the front door open and close. Bridgette had no doubt been fucked into a stupor and was fast asleep and reeking of the smell of that sonofabitch who'd just left.

Lonnie Adebayo knew who he was. Every fiber in his body screamed that to him the moment their eyes met in that restaurant earlier that day. It wasn't just a casual glance across the room. The expression on her face, the way she held that look of hers to his, had said it all. But how did she know him? And what was it that she thought she knew about him? Of course, he'd felt silly for getting so shaken by this. After all, who was Edgar Beckman except an impotent old man and retired lawyer? He was no one, and Miss Adebayo had better figure that out, rather than waste any of her precious talents for fact-finding on him.

The ringing of his phone annoyed him. Whoever was calling was calling so late that it was disrespectful. He glanced at the number, and rolled his eyes. "Yes, Jordan."

Edgar didn't bother trying to hide the irritability in his voice, but Jordan glossed over it. "Frank Ross asked me to meet him today."

Edgar rubbed sleep burning his eyes. "And did you?" he asked, unconcerned.

"I did."

"And?"

"And it's just like I thought. He's a nobody, trying to get something to make him somebody."

"So, there you have it," Edger said with a sigh.

"I warned him to walk away."

"Do you think that he will?"

"I don't think he's bright enough to."

"And you're calling me this late because . . . ?"

"Oh, I'm sorry, Edgar. Were you busy fucking the brains out of that young wife of yours?" he asked sarcastically.

"Little pricks grow into big pricks, I see," Edgar said coldly.

"Frank Ross mentioned something about going to the press."

"Let him go," he said hoarsely. It was late, and Edgar was tired, and nursing a decent buzz and wounded ego.

"The last thing I need right now is any kind of controversy in the middle of this Anton takeover. Maybe he won't make a ripple in the media, but then again, what if he does?"

"You said yourself that he's a nobody, Jordan. Mr. Nobody comes out of nowhere and claims to have the same sperm donor as you, who happens to be someone else besides Gatewood, so what? They'll think he's a crackpot."

"But it'll still be news, crackpot or not."

"So, what are you asking, son?" he asked irritably.

Jordan was getting a little too used to asking for favors from Edgar. He was a big boy now, old enough to handle his own shit. Jordan was taking liberties where favors had once been the norm, and Edgar was beginning to tire from it.

"I need you to find me something that'll shut him up."

"Why do you need me for that? Can't you find something on him yourself?"

Jordan was silent on the other end of the phone for several beats before finally responding. "You make it sound like I'm overstepping my bounds, taking advantage of a friendship."

"Yes. I'd say so."

"But isn't that what this friendship is built on, Edgar? You scratch my back, and . . ."

There it was. Edgar had made mistakes with Jordan. He'd gotten too close, shared too much, let his guard down, thinking that that boy would always be beholden to a sense of loyalty and respect to Edgar by virtue of the friendship he'd had with his father, and because Edgar had been there for all of them, after Julian's death.

"I can't believe you're going there," he said hesitantly.

"I can't believe you're making me go there."

Edgar paused, rubbed his eyes again, and finished the brandy in his glass in one gulp. "What do you want, Jordan?"

"Nothing hard, Edgar. Frank Ross looked like a man with a lot on his mind. He claimed that he didn't come to me because of Lonnie, which means that something else drove him to me. I need to know what that is."

"And what if it's nothing more than pure and simple greed?" Edgar asked, rubbing his burning eyes.

"I've seen greedy. This man was desperate."

Jordan had resources. He could've hired a private detective to find dirt on this Ross fellow. Jordan was flexing, reminding Edgar who had the bigger muscles, and tonight, maybe because of the booze, or maybe it was watching his wife get her rocks off with Mandingo—he hated Jordan for it.

"I'll see what I can find," Edgar said wearily. Jordan hung up first, without so much as a thank you.

His bedroom smelled like sex. Edgar didn't have to actually smell it to know it. He dragged his heavy, tired, dangerously-close-to-eighty-year-old body up the stairs, and went down the hall opposite of where Bridgette slept. He was too old for all of this, his life. Edgar was too old for a thirty-year-old wife, and for getting mixed up with the likes of Miss Adebayo, who was proving to be much more of a factor than he ever thought she could be. And he was far too old to be Jordan Gatewood's errand boy.

Don't Wanna Be Your Girlfriend

"*It was a freak accident, really,*" *Phillip explained in that British, pompous demeanor of his. Leaning back on the sofa at the loft after lunch, he crossed his sockless ankle over his knee, and explained to Lonnie how he'd managed to find a will that no one even knew existed. "A friend of mine is just naturally curious," he continued.*

Lonnie, wearing sweats and an oversized T-shirt, sat next to him with her legs crossed.

"The topic of Julian and Desi and all that nonsense came up in the course of casual conversation. She found it fascinating, the whole bit about her going to prison for murdering him, and that his son, who now ran the company, wasn't really his son." He waved his hand dismissively. "Confounded by the gossip," he said, frowning. "I don't know, but a few weeks later, he gave me a call."

Lonnie sat up. "He? I thought you said it was a woman?"

Phillip raised a brow. "Did I? Of course I didn't."

Lonnie wasn't a fool. She'd made her living on details. Phillip had distinctly said "she" when he first mentioned his friend, which indicated to her that he was making up this story of how he came by this will on the spot. "Go on."

"Anyway, she called a few weeks later, with some fascinating news about a discovery he'd made pertaining to Sir Julian's will. There were two probate records of the document recorded on two different dates. Curious," he said, intensely, reminding her of Sherlock Holmes or somebody. "So, she dug a little deeper, one thing led to another, and here you have it." He motioned to the will lying on her coffee table.

"Can I keep it?"

He smiled and patted her cheek. "Dear Lonnie," he said, smiling. "Of course. Why do you think I flew all the way out here?"

Lonnie bit down on her bottom lip before asking the million-dollar question. "How do you know it's real?"

Phillip looked at the document on the table, and shrugged. "How do you know it's not?"

Lonnie had taken the elevator down to the lobby on her way out, and she saw Jordan leaning against his car parked out front on the other side of the secured door. How the hell did he know where she lived? She stopped. The thought raced across her mind to run back upstairs and hide in her apartment, but she quickly dismissed it. It was broad daylight. The concierge was posted a safe distance inside the door, and thanks to Phillip, Lonnie had more ammunition against Jordan Gatewood than she knew what to do with.

She walked out and stopped a few feet in front of him.

"I'd ask you to take a ride with me, but I know I'd just be wasting my breath," he said.

"I guess I should've known that you'd find me eventually," she said.

He paused and considered her for a few moments before finally answering her. "This whole thing is getting ridiculous, Lonnie. You've got to know that," he said earnestly. "Frank Ross is a joke. He's a damn puppy dog afraid of his own damn shadow, and you've got no business dragging him into our mess."

Lonnie rolled her eyes. "First of all, I didn't drag him into anything. I asked him if he wanted to come along for the ride, and left it up to him."

"And that's your big plan?" Jordan asked, amused. "You came back here, to face me, waving Ross's black ass in front of my face like I'm supposed to snarl and foam at the mouth and trip like some rabid dog?" He laughed. "He doesn't scare me and neither does this weak scheme of yours, Lonnie. I mean, honestly, I expected more."

More. Lonnie had a ticking time bomb in her purse. She had the truth that had been kept hidden all these years. Lonnie felt a smile start to creep across her lips. Jordan obviously didn't like the looks of it.

"I'll tell you what I told him. Walk away, honey." Jordan's tone dripped with sincerity. His eyes bled the stuff. "I don't have time for this. Frank doesn't have the stomach for it, and you—" He shook his head, and looked away.

"Now that's a threat of enormous proportions if I ever heard one," Lonnie spoke up and said.

"I didn't come here to threaten you. Baby, I have no intentions of ever hurting you again. I went too far, Lonnie, I know, but when I saw that you were alive—Getting back at me isn't worth putting your life on hold for. You have always been and are still a gorgeous woman, and there's something more important waiting for you out there than this bullshit you and I are entangled in."

Lonnie took a fearless step toward him. "No, you did not just say that." She pushed her hair back from the scarred side of her face, and tucked it behind her ear. "Don't you dare turn away," she warned, catching him averting his gaze. "Eighty-five percent of my vision is gone in this eye," she angrily explained. "Six teeth in my mouth aren't mine, Jordan. I have a metal rod in my hip, and chances are I couldn't have a baby even if I wanted one. So don't you dare stand there looking like you've just walked off from a cover shoot with *GQ* magazine and tell me that I need to forget what happened and get on with the joyous life that's waiting for me! Not when I still wake up in the middle of the night, just in time to see your big-ass foot coming out of nowhere and landing on my face. Any chance I had of finding true love was left on the floor of that house that night! There is no happy ending here for me, and I'll be damned if I'm going to let you squeak by and get to ride off into the sunset like a hero after the shit you did to me!" Lonnie was crying. God! When did she start crying?

Jordan moved so fast she didn't have time to react. He wrapped one strong arm around her waist, and pulled her in to his chest, grabbed hold of her chin, pulled her face to his, and pressed his lips hard against hers.

"Feel that! Remember that!" he said passionately, holding on tightly to her despite her struggles. "That's what we lost, Lonnie! That's what we both lost! I wanted you then, and if I knew you'd take me now, I'd—"

Lonnie pushed away from him in disgust, spat, and wiped her mouth with the back of her hand.

Jordan turned, quickly climbed into his car, and peeled off from the curb with squealing tires.

"Are you alright, Miss?" the concierge asked, concerned, rushing from inside the building.

Lonnie was shaken, but she nodded. "Yes, I'm fine," she said, breathless and trembling.

"Are you sure? I can call the police."

She shook her head. No, the police wouldn't know what to do with this. She didn't know what to do with it. This was some low-down-dirty-funky shit right here. "It's alright," she said, still stunned by the fact that he'd not only put his hands on her, but his mouth. "I'm fine. Thank you," she said, starting to walk away.

The smell of him made her sick to her stomach. Lonnie's head was spinning from physical contact with Jordan. She made it to the parking garage, stumbled against her car, and drank in buckets of air to calm the wave of nausea washing over her. Without thinking, she raked her tongue across her lips, and she tasted Jordan. Lonnie closed her eyes, and released a sound akin to a whimper, and a moan. He tasted the same. Jesus! He tasted just like she'd remembered, and Lonnie cursed herself for the rush of emotion coursing through her.

Gimme Some. Some. Some.

Frank didn't need this shit now. He was back in Paris, but the last person he expected to see show up in the middle of the night at his door was Colette, eyes wide, bloodshot, and looking like they were going to pop out of her head. Her short, black cropped hair was wild on her head.

"I need to sleep, Frank," she said frantically. Colette paced back and forth in his small living room like a caged animal. "I can't sleep, baby. I don't know—my nerves. My nerves are shot, and that place is just getting to me. It's like I always think they're watching me or talking about me behind my back, like they know, Frank." Tears flooded her eyes. "Oh, God! Please don't let them know!" Colette covered her eyes with her hands. "Please! Please! Please!"

He went to her, and pulled her over to the sofa to sit next to him. "What the fuck are you doing, baby?"

She was high, and if she wasn't high, that wasn't good either. Colette was falling apart, literally before his eyes, and Frank was feeling the pressure of her pulling him apart too. They'd never been like this before. Frank and Colette were cops, and even a non cop had more cool than either one of them had.

"You shouldn't have come," he blurted out. "You shouldn't be here."

She looked at him like he was crazy. "You can't tell me that. I'm here because I need you right now, Frank. You've got me sitting back in Cotton on a fire pit, all by myself, waiting for them to find out what we did and drop the shit load of bad news all over my ass."

He was tired. Frank was already stressed, and her being here was making him start to come apart. Frank was starting to accept the truth about Colette. He'd always known it, but he'd always felt responsible, even protective of her in some strange way. But looking at her now, he knew that if it weren't for her, he wouldn't be in this mess. If she hadn't agreed to meet those men at the river—if she hadn't shot first—he would still have his life. It wasn't much, but it was his, and he'd be where he should've been, back home in Cotton, driving his squad car, protecting and serving, and—

"Don't look at me like that," she warned, shaking her head. "Don't you dare fuckin' look at me like this is my fault!"

"I didn't shoot Reggie, Colette," he blurted out. He shouldn't have said it. Frank realized it as soon as he saw the look in her eyes, but it was too late. And it was the truth. "You fucked up, baby. All you had to do was wait it out. You needed to sit tight and let it pass. It would've passed, Colette."

Out of nowhere, Colette's hand landed flush against the side of his face. Frank grabbed hold of her arm, and the other hand almost landed on the other side of his face, but he grabbed her by the wrist and stopped it.

"You're coming loose, Colette, and you're bringing us down," he snarled.

"And you left me!" she spat. "You left me behind to take the heat for murder, Frank! You think that shit was just going to pass? But you weren't there, so you have no idea what I've been going through! You don't have to walk through the doors of that precinct every day, wondering what they're whispering about. Reading things into the way they look at you that couldn't possibly be right. But you don't know if it's true or not. Maybe they know what we did. Maybe they're just waiting for us . . . me to slip up and make a mistake, or waiting for the lieutenant to call me into his office because they know it was my gun who killed a man. You ran away like a bitch! Tucked your tail and took off first chance you got, expecting me to stay behind, man up, and take the fall? Is that what your plan was, Frank?"

She'd insulted the hell out of him. "You know that's not true! How could I set you up if all you'd have to do is tell them that I was there too?"

"It'd be my word against yours," she said, gritting her teeth.

"Ballistics came back with two separate bullets from two separate guns. Of course they'd come looking for me!"

"That doesn't mean they'd find you, Frank," she said coldly. "That brother of yours give you money yet?" She jerked away from him.

Is that what this was about? Is this why she was here? "I don't have any money."

She looked like she didn't believe him.

He stood up. "If I had money, why the fuck would I still be in Paris, Texas?"

His argument fell on deaf ears. "I read about him, Jordan Gatewood. That fucker's got more money than the state of Texas." She walked over to him and stood close enough to kiss him. "Did you tell him who you were? If it's even true, I mean. Did you tell him?"

He thought about lying. But why? She already didn't trust him, and maybe she had good reason not to. The longer the two of them talked, the more he was starting to see things about himself that he didn't find too cool. "I told him who I was," he admitted. "And I told him that I wouldn't tell the press if he did what he needed for me to keep my mouth shut."

She seemed surprised that he'd told her that, but Colette still didn't look like she had any faith in him. "What did he say?"

This was the part he didn't want to talk about.

"He told you to go fuck yourself," she said dismally. "Didn't he?"

Frank dropped his gaze from her. "Pretty much."

"So that's it," she said, turning and crossing the room. "We've got nothing." Her voice cracked. "He could've given us enough to leave the country, Frank. Hell, he could've given us enough to fly to the moon, baby, but you punked out with him the same way you punked out on me."

Frank was getting sick and tired of people thinking he was a punk. "Not that it's any of your damn business, Colette, but I put my shit on the table for the man, and he chose to turn his nose up at it. I didn't go there and get in his face just to walk away with nothing."

She chuckled. "What the hell are you planning on doing, Frank? Go back to him and ask, pretty please give me some money, rich brother of mine. I swear I won't tell anybody. Pinky swear," she said, wiggling her little finger. "Why don't you let me ask him," she dared him. "Unlike you, Frank, I already know I've got nothing to lose. You're too much of a pussy to admit it to yourself. Let me ask big man for the money. Or rather, let me tell him to pay up or we tell them reporters the truth about who he is really is. I'll get it out of him. Watch me."

Colette was a liability. She was a trick with a great gift for blowjobs, but not much else. He had every intention of calling Jordan's bluff, or of at least making him think he would. Jordan had been paying Joel for years for his silence. Even if it did end up being Frank's word against Jordan's, Frank could make a hell of a lot of noise, enough to make Gatewood nervous. He had read that Jordan was in the middle of trying to take over another rival company. The last thing he needed right now was a scandal, and Frank could create enough of one to throw him off his game. But he was done with Colette. He'd decided that right here and now. Even if he did manage to get money from Gatewood, he didn't need to be dragging a meth head behind him, shooting off her damn mouth.

"I'll get the money, Colette," he said calmly.

"Yeah, right," she said, rolling her eyes.

"And I'll give you half, but when I do, we go our separate ways."

She stared at him. "You just telling me that to get me to leave?"

From the look on her face and the tone in her voice, Colette was pretty content with the thought of separating.

"We're too much trouble together, and we'd be far too easy to find. I'll get the money. You do whatever you want with yours, and we'll never have to lay eyes on each other again, but you've got to go back to Cotton, and you've got to be smart. If you lose your cool again the way you did with Reggie, then they will catch up with us, and we'll both go to prison."

She swallowed and shifted nervously from one foot to the other. "How long?" she asked, clearing her throat.

How the hell should he know? Frank had to give her something, though. If he gave her this to look forward to, to hope for, Colette could maintain, and he needed her to maintain.

"Two weeks?" he finally said.

She looked at him long and hard. Frank could almost hear the wheels spinning in her head. "Don't fuck with me, Frank," she threatened. "I swear, if you get that money and take off without giving me mine . . ."

"Two weeks, Colette," he said again, with more conviction this time. Of course he had no idea what would happen in two weeks. But it was something, and Colette needed something. Frank just needed more time. "Give me two weeks. If I don't have the money, then . . . I don't know, baby. You and me will just have to do what we have to do."

She laughed. "Oh, that's rich, Frank. And what is it that you and me are going to have to do? Go to prison for murder?"

He stared unemotionally at her. "That's one option."

It's Tempting to Pack Up Your Throne

Jordan arrived back at the office just in time for his two o'clock meeting with June and several others who'd come together to discuss the Anton buyout. He had made a fool of himself with Lonnie. But Jordan hadn't been thinking clearly. Even now she had this way about her that left him flapping around like a fish out of water, pushing him to limits beyond his natural boundaries. She brought out the worst in him. Lonnie, just her presence, brought out the animal in him. When things had been good between them, his feet didn't touch the ground. He was hungry for the woman. Jordan craved her beyond what was natural or moral. It was the reason behind why he'd lost it on her the way he did, two years ago. The line between loving Lonnie Adebayo and hating her had always been as thin as thread.

"Older investors are jumping the Anton ship like crazy," June explained to the group. "But there are just as many signing on as there are leaving. The new investors are younger, more aggressive players, all as anxious for this takeover to happen as we are."

"Anton is still refusing to file bankruptcy?" someone else asked.

"Robert Jorgensen is a stubborn, old bastard," June stated, in reference to the CEO. "He's a dinosaur when it comes to his business model, which is why it's failing, and has been for the last decade. He'll let the business crumble and fall apart into rubble before he'll take a Chapter 11. And that's good. Good for us. Stock prices at Anton right now are dirt cheap. Once the merger's complete"—June leaned back and looked like she had been born to make this merger happen—"that'll change overnight. A lot of people stand to make a fortune off this deal." She smiled and her gaze landed on Jordan. "And so do we. Isn't that right, Jordan?"

June had come into the business days after Jordan and his team had begun proceedings for buying out Anton.

"Mind if I sit in on a few meetings?" she'd asked him eagerly. "This is fascinating stuff, big brother. I could learn a lot."

In Jordan's mind, June was supposed to do just that, sit back, listen, watch, and learn. So, when the hell had she decided to take the lead on the whole goddamned thing? June had no idea who she was up against. She saw numbers. She saw investors and stock dividends. She saw an outdated business model. But Jordan saw something else entirely.

"Robert Jorgensen may be a dinosaur," he began calmly, "but he's no fool. And the worst thing you can do is to underestimate the man." His gaze fell on every pair of eyes in that room staring back at him and hanging on every word. "That old-ass business model you all are looking down your noses at netted Anton profits higher than any other U.S. oil company for longer than some of you have been alive."

June suddenly looked agitated and amused. "He's been losing money."

"He's made so much more than he's lost, June," Jordan shot back coolly. Jordan leaned forward, rested his elbows on the table, and laced his fingers together. "Do not make the mistake of taking Jorgensen for granted. The fact that he hasn't filed bankruptcy tells me that he must know something we don't."

"It only proves that he's an old fool," June retorted.

June thought she knew so damn much. Her tunnel vision was amazing, and the longer he worked with his sister, the more he realized how much she depended on her textbook knowledge of the business world, and how little she understood about the ugly makeup of corporate America.

"Of these new investors, who's bought up the most Anton stock in the last month?" he asked her. Of course she'd know. June was as efficient as she was intelligent.

She scrolled through pages on her laptop. "Probably a woman named Jennifer Mason."

Jordan smiled. "Jennifer Mason is Jorgensen's great-granddaughter," he informed them all. "She's a junior at Texas State, studying nursing, and I can almost guarantee that if you were to ask her about these stock options she's just spent so much money on, she wouldn't know anything about it."

June looked stunned and confused. Everyone else sitting around that table looked unimpressed because they were used to Jordan knowing these kinds of things and stealing the air out from under their sails.

"Jorgensen," June muttered, embarrassed.

"If he's buying stock in his own damn company like that, then what does that tell you?"

She glanced sheepishly at Jordan. "That he's not fighting too hard to keep this takeover from happening."

"You said it yourself, June. He's an old man. He's done. He's tired. And he's ready to let go of Anton."

Jordan leaned back, satisfied that he'd made his point, and that he'd shown his sister she was nowhere near ready for what the oil industry really had to offer.

After the meeting was over and everyone else left the room, June stayed behind. "You could've told me what Jorgensen was up to before we sat down at this little powwow and I made a fool of myself," she told him.

Jordan dismissed her annoyance. "You've got your numbers, June. You've put a lot of heart and soul behind them, and it's good stuff. I admire your due diligence and your faith in your expertise and, most of all, your ability to sell it."

She took her time responding. "But the devil's in the details."

"That's the only place he is," he said convincingly.

"I'm getting to you, though," she said introspectively. "Aren't I?"

He looked at her questioningly.

"I'm not stupid, Jordan. I know that the only reason you moved over and made room for me in this company is because I'm your little sister and you've always been taught to play nice with me, but you don't want me here," she challenged. "Except to sit back, and stare wide-eyed in fascination of you. You strong-arm me, but in such a way as not to hurt my feelings."

Now it was his turn to be amused. June was astute, and she'd pretty much nailed it. "The last thing I'd ever want to do is hurt your feelings."

"It's my company too," she finally stated. "And I have every right to be here that you do."

"I never said you didn't."

"So, maybe I haven't been around long enough to really see just how low all you corporate CEOs can really get, but I am learning, and I am taking notes," she said with conviction.

"You coming after my job, June?"

She thought about it before responding. "When's the last time you spoke to Mother?"

He looked caught off guard by the question. But Jordan reluctantly answered. "She doesn't speak to me."

"It's not a good feeling. Is it?" June said thoughtfully.

It was no secret that June and Olivia had never been close. Olivia doted over Jordan, and barely glossed over her daughter as she was growing up, because June was the rebel, the difficult one. June didn't buy into Olivia's program. When Olivia wanted her to be a debutante, June scoffed and made sure that she behaved so badly with the debutante committee that she embarrassed the hell out of Olivia. After June graduated high school, Olivia insisted that she go to an all-girls' private university in Massachusetts. June dropped the bomb on her over tea at the country club that Olivia belonged to that she was going to attend Berkeley in California.

"She talks to me a lot now," June admitted. "I mean, some days aren't so good. She either thinks I'm six, or she doesn't know me at all, but on those days when she does know me, it's not bad."

Olivia hadn't spoken to him since he'd had her put under a doctor's care and tucked safely away in that senior citizen community. He'd done it for her own good, to keep her safe from the police and public scrutiny, but Olivia didn't see it that way.

"You animal!" she'd screamed at him, as he walked out and left her in that room. "How dare you take me out of my own home! How dare you turn your back on me!"

Jordan waited until he thought she'd calmed down and went to visit her again. "Mother," he said as he sat across from her, trying to get her to listen to him, even just to look at him. "I love you. And I wouldn't have done this if I didn't think it was the best thing for you."

Olivia eventually cut her eyes at him. "Liar," she growled. "Just like him. Liars, both of you. Cheats and liars. You want to get rid of me."

"No, Mother," he tried to tell her. "But the police have been asking questions. I don't want them to take you from me. They think you shot Julian."

Olivia's expression hardened, her lips pinched tight. "I shot him. I shot the bastard for fucking that whore! And I'd do it again if I had the chance!"

Those were the last words she'd said to him.

His thoughts drifted back to the conversation he was having with June. Was she rubbing the fact that their mother was now her best friend in his face? It didn't matter. Jordan had done what he did to save Olivia, and if he had to make the choice again, he would make the same one.

"I'm happy for you, June," he said. "Happy that you and Mother are on better terms."

"She's the reason I came to work at Gatewood Industries, Jordan," June admitted. "'Don't let that bastard take what's yours, June,'" she said, repeating what Olivia must've told her. "Never in a million years did I ever expect to hear words like that coming out of her mouth about you, her golden boy."

June's words were subtly laced in venom, and even though he'd never give her the benefit of knowing it, they hurt.

"People change. But it's never been my intent to take anything away from you. My job is and has always been to preserve Gatewood Industries, to keep it, to grow it. But never to take it from you, baby sister."

June packed up her laptop and stood up to leave. "Then you won't mind one bit, if I decide to hang around a little while longer. I like it here and I belong here. Even you can't argue with that." June smiled at him, and left Jordan sitting alone in that conference room.

Nutty Nutmeg Phantasy

Desi Green was a New York City girl at heart. L.A. was nice, but it didn't fill her with the same kind of energy as Manhattan. She spent most of her time now between those two places, and it had been months since she'd last set foot in Texas. Finally, she'd come out of the fog she'd been living in most of her life, and looking back at everything that had happened to her in the last almost thirty years, it seemed like bad scenes from a bad movie.

Desi was strong because she'd had to be strong. Before she was barely old enough to vote, her freedom had been stolen from her and she spent the next twenty-five years of her life growing up in prison for killing a man she loved dearly. Mr. J had been everything to her and her mother, and Desi watched Olivia Gatewood shoot him, and watched him fall to his knees on her mother's living room floor. The next thing she knew, she was holding the gun that killed him, Olivia Gatewood vanished in a puff of smoke, and the police burst through the front door, put handcuffs on Desi, and her life was never the same.

"It's late, baby," Solomon said, coming out onto the balcony and wrapping his strong arms around Desi. "And it's chilly."

Desi laughed at the way he said the word "chilly." Solomon was a Texas boy, through and through. Desi melted in his arms as he wrapped the blanket he'd come out with around her too.

"Can't sleep?" he asked, nuzzling his face in the side of her neck.

She shook her head. "Got too much on my mind to sleep," she responded.

He felt so warm, and so good. Desi closed her eyes and let out a sigh. As anxious as she was about tomorrow, just his touch had a way of easing her fears and reminding her that she really was okay now and that the past was exactly where it belonged. Behind her.

She had a day filled with meetings tomorrow. Desi was finally getting a meeting with Macy's head of acquisitions to discuss the terms of carrying her product in their stores across the country. Until now, her Konvictions line had only been sold in small boutiques, and offered online from her company Web site, but distribution was getting to be too much for her to handle on her own. Konvictions was taking off, before she'd had a chance to really brace herself for it.

"Why the hell are you nervous, baby? You got this."

"Maybe I do, and maybe I don't," she retorted. "I won't take it for granted that I do until the ink's dry on the contract, Solomon. Weren't you the one who taught me that?"

He was an entertainment lawyer for some of the top artists in the music industry, and even represented some major sports figures. Solomon knew better than anyone not to get too comfortable too quickly.

"I did tell you that. Thanks for reminding me of how great a lawyer I am."

"You're welcome. So, that's why I'm up."

"Which is bad, because you're not going to be too sharp if you're falling asleep during the meeting."

"I won't sleep," she said, shaking her head emphatically. "Nope. I will not sleep until this is a done deal."

"And that's fine, because there are plenty of other things we can do right now besides sleep."

Desi laughed. "Oh, you got ideas," she teased.

"Plenty. But first . . ." Solomon opened the blanket, letting all that chilly air invade their cocooned bodies, and held a baby blue velvet box in front of her.

Tiffany's. He knew how much she loved Tiffany's. Desi laughed, took the box, and held it possessively to her chest. "How long have you had this?"

"Since yesterday."

"And you're just now giving it to me?"

"I was planning on giving it to you tomorrow," he said calmly. "Open it."

Even in the dark, it was impossible for that thing not to shine. Desi was hit by the light of the most brilliant diamond she'd ever laid eyes on. It was a ring. A perfectly exquisite ring, covered in diamonds circling the band.

"Marry me, Desi."

Desi stopped breathing. Before he'd said those words to her, Solomon had just given her a gift, a ring. *Marry me, Desi* changed everything just that quick.

She turned to him. Desi had every intention of saying something but the minute she looked into that handsome, chocolate face of his, she forgot what it was. And Solomon seemed intent on just letting her stand there, looking dumbfounded and speechless. He just smiled. Look at where she was now. Desi looked back out to the city, took a deep breath, and let it all soak in. She'd gotten good at that. Desi had moved past thinking that she didn't deserve the life she had now, because she had finally accepted that she not only deserved it, but she had earned it.

"Well?" he finally asked.

"What do you mean, well? You know what my answer is already, Solomon. You knew it before you even bought this ring."

She was long past feeling that detachment she'd come out of prison with. Because Solomon had been there, waiting patiently for her feelings to catch up with his. He waded through all her doubts and missteps with her, held out both hands, and helped her finally get past them. Any other man would've given up. His feelings would've been hurt, and he'd have shrugged her off and moved on to the next woman.

Desi sunk deeper into his arms, and sighed. "I will absolutely marry you, Solomon."

"And you'll never let me go?" he added.

She smiled. "Never."

"And you'll never do anything to make me wanna let you go?"

"I hope not."

"No, Desi. You've got to say it."

"I will never do anything to make you wanna let me go, baby," she purred.

"Then let's go make love, and seal this deal," he teased, kissing her neck, and turning both of them around to go back inside.

They didn't make it to the bedroom. Solomon backed Desi up to the sofa, spread his arms, and dropped the blanket on the floor behind him. Desi raised up on her toes and pressed her lips to his. Solomon slipped his hands underneath her nightgown, cupped her behind in both hands, and spun her around. He sat down, pulling her down on top of him. Desi's body melted on top of his.

Solomon stared so deep into her eyes that she wondered if he couldn't see her soul. "You're my wife, baby," he murmured.

Of all the things Desi had been in her life, guilty, not guilty, poor, rich, hopeless, nothing—being Solomon's wife was the only thing that mattered. He pushed his hips toward hers, took hold of her by the back of her neck, and pulled her face to his.

Desi drove her knees into the space on either side of him, and pumped slowly against him, driving him so deep inside her, until he touched places in her that no other man could ever possibly reach.

"I love you," she whispered between kisses. And more than that, Desi felt loved.

Solomon was still asleep when the phone rang. Desi had finally managed to doze off too, but just barely. "Hello?" she asked, without checking the number on the screen.

The other end of the phone was silent.

"Hello?" Desi asked again, irritated.

"Did I wake you?"

It was Lonnie. Desi hadn't spoken to Lonnie in nearly two years. The conversation had been brief, curt, and left Desi with more questions than answers. She carefully climbed out of bed and took the phone into the living room so as not to wake up Solomon.

"Where are you?" she asked.

Lonnie hesitated in answering. "Dallas."

"Dallas?" Desi asked, stunned. Whatever had happened to Lonnie happened in Dallas. So, why the hell was she back there?

"How are you, Desi?" she asked, as casually as if the two of them had last spoken a few weeks ago.

"How are you, Lonnie?" Wasn't that the million-dollar question? How was Lonnie? Or was it, *Where have you been, Lonnie?* Maybe it was, *What the hell happened to you, Lonnie?*

"I asked you first," Lonnie replied coolly.

"I'm fine. You?"

"That's what I hear, Des. I hear you're doing just fine."

Desi was thrown off by Lonnie's tone. But at least Lonnie was talking to her. When Lonnie first went missing, Desi believed that Lonnie had been killed and that Jordan had been the one to do it, but a few weeks later, Lonnie was resurrected.

"I'd like to see you," Desi said reluctantly. It was mostly the truth. But something about the sound of Lonnie's voice left Desi feeling uncertain about their friendship. "I'd like to see for myself how you're doing."

"I need to see you too, Des. Where are you?"

Desi paused. She wanted to see Lonnie, but not here. This New York trip was too important to add Lonnie into the mix. "I'll be back home this weekend."

Desi hadn't planned on flying back to Texas anytime soon, but if she were going to finally see Lonnie again, Texas seemed like the natural place to do it.

"Do you still have the house?" Lonnie asked. "We can meet there."

"That'll be fine, Lonnie. That'll be great, really."

Lonnie chuckled. "Yeah, Desi. Really great." Desi cringed at the sarcasm. "Call me back at this number when you get to town."

"Sure," Desi agreed. "I'll call you soon."

Lonnie hung up first without bothering to say good-bye. And Desi just stood there, dreading seeing her friend again.

All About the Watchtower

"*Your daddy* and I used to spend hours fishing in this very same spot." Edgar always sounded more like the old man he was when he sat slumped on top of that old plastic bucket perched at the edge of the Red River. He stared out across it, reminiscent of a time so long ago that it really was ancient history. "Sometimes, a man's got to slow down, and fishing will force him to do it."

Jordan didn't fish, so the analogy was wasted on him. He'd called Edgar's cell phone, but he didn't answer. Jordan called his house, and Edgar's wife answered, sounding like she was just waking up at three in the afternoon. She was the one who told Jordan where to find the old man.

Jordan came dressed to traipse around the muddy banks of a river—jeans, an old ranch button-down, boots. He closed the lid on Edgar's oversized tackle box and sat down on it next to him.

"If I didn't know you better, Edgar, I'd think you were purposefully trying to avoid me."

The years had added inches to Beckman's midsection, and in the sunlight, Jordan noticed deep brown markings beginning to mask the old man's face around his eyes and mouth. It seemed that Edgar's gene pool had managed to sneak through after all these years. From where Jordan was sitting, Beckman looked like a black man in white face.

Edgar huffed. "Of course I'm trying to avoid you. How the hell did you know where to find me?"

"Bridgette told me. She sounded a little out of sorts," Jordan jabbed. "Is she alright?" Of course he knew the answer to that question.

Edgar rolled his eyes in disgust. "Coke keeps you up all night," he said dismissively.

"When you going to rid of her, Edgar?" It was no secret that Edgar had a weakness for young women. He had lousy taste in choosing one worth having, though. Bridgette was a cokehead, the one before that, a thief, and the one before that, well . . .

"She's a damn good lay," he grunted.

"For who?"

"Is that why you came all the way out here to talk to me, son? You interested in fucking my wife?" He smirked.

Jordan laughed. "I wouldn't touch that bitch with a ten-foot pole, old man."

"Then what the hell do you want?"

"Tell me what you found out about Frank Ross and Cotton, Texas?"

"Nothing you couldn't have found out on your own, if you'd just put your own resources into it."

By resources, he meant time and money.

"I did, Edgar. I asked you to do it," Jordan said calmly.

"Since when have I become your go-to man, Jordan?" He looked at him sideways. "Since when am I supposed to jump every time you snap your fingers?"

"Since when is helping me a problem, Edgar? Maybe I've assumed too much. I've taken for granted that you've been a permanent fixture in my family, always so willing to step forward and to offer your services when needed. You feel I've taken advantage of that?"

The muscle in Edgar's jaw ticced as he clenched his teeth, but he didn't dare turn to look at Jordan. Edgar had always been there for the Gatewoods; going back to before Jordan was born, he had been Julian's best friend, his closest confidant. And he'd always been good at whatever task lay ahead of him. He'd been the best. Edgar was the only man he could trust, and the only one that Jordan knew for a fact didn't have it in him to ever let him down.

Edgar took a few noticeable deep breaths. "I'll be eighty pretty soon," he said wearily. This time he did turn to Jordan. "I am an old man, son, very old, and I'm tired."

"It's not like I asked you to personally ride out to Cotton and ask around about Frank Ross. You make a few phone calls, and it happens, Edgar. How is that taxing to you? I'd do it myself, but I don't have time, not to mention, I trust you, Edgar. And a man like me needs someone he can trust on his side."

Edgar stared back at him like he was speaking Chinese. Jordan waited for Edgar to say something. He wanted to understand where this reluctance was coming from.

"Two cops were killed in Cotton last year," Edgar began to slowly explain. "Some months later, Ross quit the force and moved to Paris."

Jordan perked up. "They think he killed cops?"

Edgar shook his head. "Nobody knows who killed those cops. They'd been keeping close watch over a drug dealer, Reggie somebody-or-other, but all of a sudden he ended up dead too. Ross had a partner, Colette Fisher. She's still a member of Cotton's finest," he said sarcastically.

"Is she a suspect?"

Edgar shrugged. "I have no idea. I just got a feeling about it. That's all."

"About what?" Jordan asked irritably.

"Maybe there's something there. Maybe there isn't. I really can't tell you, Jordan."

"Then why bring it up?"

"Because I said I'd look into it, and I did," he snapped. "I'm not a fuckin' golden retriever, son. I can't fetch you what you want and bring it to you exactly like you want it."

"You've made your fair share of miracles for me, Edgar," he said menacingly.

"Well, not this time! I got nothing! Nothing on Frank Ross, his partner, nothing! But I do have a suggestion." He had turned a scary shade of red.

"A suggestion?" Jordan said impatiently.

"Get rid of him, Jordan! You don't need the distraction, especially now! He's no one in particular, son, not worth your time, or mine! Frank Ross could go away and I doubt anyone would even notice! If you want him gone, then get rid of his ass and be done with it!"

That was his suggestion? To kill Frank Ross? Jordan just stared at him. "What the hell is really going on with you, Edgar?"

Edgar's eyes watered. "I told you I'm tired," he grunted. "And I don't have it in me anymore to chase after your messes, Jordan."

"Is it Bridgette?" Jordan probed.

"You know what it is," he muttered.

Jordan knew what it was.

"I'm tired of being held hostage by you, son, and I think I deserve better after all I've been through with you and your daddy."

"We've all got something, Edgar," Jordan said remorsefully. "Holding you hostage has never been my intention."

He rolled his eyes in frustration. "Say what you will, Jordan, but I know better and so do you." He glanced at Jordan.

Jordan was surprised by that statement. "Is that what you really think I'm doing? Holding you hostage?"

"What you know about me could put me in prison," he said, gritting his teeth. "It could get me the death penalty, and you use that! You use that against me, dangling it over my head like raw meat! I trusted you!" He pointed a thick finger at Jordan. "I trusted you because there was no one else!"

"I know you trusted me, Edgar," Jordan said carefully. "And I told you that your secret was safe with me. Have I done something to make you think it isn't?"

"Don't toy with me, boy!" Edgar's face flushed red again. "It's not what you say. It's what you *don't* say! It's what you imply!"

"What the hell have I implied? Tell me, man! You're talking in circles here! Have you been snorting that shit with Bridgette?" He reached out to Edgar, but the old man slapped his hand away.

"I did what I had to! I did the only thing I could! You know that! You said that yourself, Jordan! I did the only fuckin' thing I could!"

"You did, Edgar."

"I never expected you to judge me, Jordan! Not being who you are!"

The longer Edgar ranted, the more Jordan realized what was really going on here. Guilt was gnawing away at him. It had been eating at him for years, and Edgar was finally starting to buckle under the weight of it.

"I'm sorry if I ever made you feel that way, Edgar," Jordan said as sincerely as he could, and he meant it. Edgar had been like a father to him. In so many ways, he'd been more of a father to him than Julian ever had. "If it means anything to you, I'll back off." He raised his hands in surrender. "You don't need the pressure right now. I understand that."

Jordan stood up and started to walk away and leave that old man alone with his conscience.

"He's only your half brother, Jordan," Edgar called out. "Joel Tunson's bastard son . . ." His voice trailed off. "Make it easy on yourself, son. Make him go away and be done with it."

'Cause You Could Catch a Bad One

Jordan knew where she lived. Lonnie lived in a secure building, but she doubted that a door that required a code card to open and a nice person sitting at the front desk to welcome visitors and mail carriers would be enough to keep him from getting to her if he really wanted to. Time was running out for Lonnie. The only thing working in her favor now is that Jordan didn't feel the urgency of the situation, and he'd made it clear that he wasn't taking seriously the threat of using Frank Ross to expose him. She'd hoped for that. Lonnie had counted on it. Frank was never meant to be more than a ruse, a tactic of misdirection and a distraction to Jordan, and a way to buy her more time.

It was after one in the morning and Lonnie had spent the better part of the night Googling the hell out of Edgar Beckman. In her career as a journalist, Lonnie prided herself on her research skills. She had a knack for finding the obvious, but more importantly, she had a gift of being able to read between the lines of truth and speculation, and for being able to put together the puzzle pieces of circumstance.

She had a notepad filled with the vital statistics of Beckman: when and where he was born, a list of law firms he'd worked for through the years, including heading up his own practice twice, once at the beginning of his career, and again before he finally retired nearly a decade ago. He'd run for the position of mayor of Fort Worth in his fifties, which she suspected was the reason he even had a Wikipedia page. But there was almost nothing written about his upbringing or his immediate family. And like Phillip had said, Beckman was on his third wife now, thirty-year-old Bridgette Fontaine, a former cheerleader for the New Orleans Saints professional football team.

She'd noticed a pattern early on in her search of Beckman. And it was in his association with one of the wealthiest and most influential families in Texas, the Gatewoods. Lonnie stumbled upon photograph after photograph of Beckman shaking hands with or with an arm wrapped around some member of the Gatewood family. An old black-and-white photo of him with Julian Gatewood's arm wrapped around Beckman's shoulder or of the two of them in fishing gear, laughing together, was a clear indication that the two men had been close and more than just business partners.

Later, after Julian's death and at Desi's trial, images of Beckman sitting next to Olivia Gatewood and holding her hand, or escorting her and her children out of the courthouse surfaced, showing again how close he was to this family. More recent pictures of him and Jordan together at press conferences and sitting around meeting rooms together implied that he was as close as ever to the Gatewoods and that Jordan had filled the void in Beckman's life Julian had left behind, all except for the fishing part. She couldn't find any picture of Jordan wearing a fishing hat and casting a rod anywhere.

How do you topple a king? You find his weakness. She'd done that. Jordan's weakness was his name, Gatewood. But after you find his weakness, then what? You turn his most loyal subjects against him. There was no doubt in her mind that Jordan's biggest fan and cheerleader was Claire. Phillip wouldn't have taken the trouble of pointing out Edgar Beckman to her if Beckman wasn't important. He'd obviously had something to do with nullifying Julian Gatewood's original will in the probate courts. Which meant that he knew the truth. He knew that Jordan was Julian's stepson, and that Desi was Julian's biological daughter, at least, as he'd admitted it in his will.

If Beckman was Jordan's right-hand man then how could Lonnie get him to turn on his number one? The man thought enough of Jordan to see to it that he was magically made a Gatewood by blood, despite the glaring facts that disputed it. What else had he been willing to do for Jordan? And if he was buddy-buddy with Jordan, then he was dirty too.

Beckman's first wife, Annette Clark, died of breast cancer in 1985. They'd been married for thirty years, and had four children, three boys and a girl. Dominga Rojas was his second wife. Dominga was Chilean and was twenty-four when she married Beckman in 1987. They were married for seven years, until 1994. Bridgette Fontaine, his current wife, had been married to Beckman for three years. She was twenty-seven when she married Beckman.

Lonnie leaned back and sighed. The fact that the old dude liked them young wasn't a crime, but if he did have any dirt on him, she couldn't find it. "Come on, Edgar," she murmured to herself as she scrolled through pictures and articles, including wife number one's obituary and the grieving widower, Edgar, leaving the funeral surrounded by his children. "You're not that squeaky clean. I know you're not."

Any good and close friend of Julian Gatewood and now his son, Satan, had to have some dirty little gem hidden somewhere. Lonnie just had to look and then look some more if necessary. It wasn't long before she hit pay dirt.

"Persistence is a virtue," she said to herself. Lonnie had painstakingly done Internet searches on each of his wives, and come up with nothing on Annette Clark except for a photograph of her and Edgar and their family in a Christmas picture all standing in front of a tree. The grainy picture was published in the society section of a Dallas newspaper, and Annette looked like the disease had certainly gotten the best of her. She looked thin and weak, her hair thinning, and her dress cinched around an emaciated waist. She sat next to her husband, surrounded by their children, grandchildren, even staff that helped to run the house. Standing off to the side, and in the back row, stood a young, dark-haired woman, who bore a striking resemblance to Beckman's second wife, Dominga.

If I Were Giant Sized

"I got to be ready, Lonnie," Frank said to her over the phone. His paranoia had gotten the best of him and Frank had moved out of his house and into a motel outside of Dallas. He sat on the side of the bed, raking his hand over his head. "He might call my bluff, and if he does, I got to be ready."

Frank's life had been spiraling out of control for so much longer than he'd cared to admit. It was fucked the first time he took money from Reggie Rodriguez, lying to himself, and telling himself that it wasn't that much money, and that it wasn't that wrong to take it. A dirty cop is a thug—period.

"Jordan can smell weakness," she responded softly. "He can sense it if you're not sure of yourself, and if you can't sell this, he'll know it."

He picked his passport up off the table by the bed. A month ago, he was living in a fog, and under the roof of a lie that everything would somehow magically work its way out. Colette was a ticking bomb, and he was a fool. Was it any wonder that the two of them would end up in prison or dead?

Frank had been blowing up Jordan's cell phone number for most of the night. He was about to leave another message, when a knock came at the door. Call it instinct or intuition, Frank froze, his eyes fixed on the door to his motel room. All those years of being a cop had taught him to listen to his gut, no matter how ridiculous it might have seemed. No one knew that Frank was here. Not Lonnie and not even Colette. He placed the phone down on the bed, and reached for the gun inside the drawer of the nightstand.

Another steady knock.

Frank swallowed, eased up off the bed and over to the door, holding his gun at his side. "Who is it?"

His answer came in a spray of bullets. Frank dropped to the floor, and rolled over toward the bed. Frank hid at the foot of it, crouched low, and fired off several rounds. The door suddenly flew open, and three men, at least as big as Frank, dressed in black, burst through it, and tackled Frank like a defensive line. Punches landed in his face, side, and stomach. The crunch of his ribs stole his breath. Frank's gun was torn from his hands, and then everything around him went black.

The sunlight was blinding as Frank grimaced and squeezed his eyes shut. His head felt like it had been split wide open. Pain shot through his side, and air was at a premium. He had no idea where he was or how long he'd been here. It looked like a big, empty room. Frank felt the rumbling of what felt like a train passing by under his feet.

Frank hardly recognized Jordan when he opened his eyes. Gatewood sat across from him, wearing faded jeans and boots, a black pullover, and a ball cap pulled down low on his head.

"A good friend of mine told me that I should just end this." Jordan's voice sounded like he was talking through a tunnel. "I really don't have time for this, Frank," he said calmly.

Frank squeezed his eye shut as he cringed through the sharp pain stabbing his ribs. His head felt like it weighed a ton as he struggled to raise it and hold it up. What was he saying? That he wanted to kill Frank? Or was he just showing him that if he wanted him dead, that he'd have no problem making it happen?

Jordan must've read his mind because he answered Frank's question for him.

"I can snatch you out of your bed in the middle of the night, son," Jordan continued. "I have the resources to find you, no matter how deep you hide or how far you run, Frank."

Frank's arms dangled heavy at his sides, but he wasn't tied up. Frank was free to move, free to stand up, if he could, and probably free to walk out of this joint if he wanted to, but fear kept him in that seat.

"You're nothing to me, man," Jordan said. "Your threats are empty at best, and meaningless. I'm mildly annoyed by you."

If this isn't fuckin' rock bottom, then what is? Frank wondered, holding Jordan's glare, sipping small cups of air. Is this what his life had come to?

"You're a bottom feeder, man, and you need to take this lesson and make it mean something."

Frank finally gave himself permission to come apart. He'd watched Colette do it and he'd been trying to stay strong and in control for the both of them. But he couldn't do it anymore.

"I got nothing, man!" he gasped, swallowing through the pain.

Jordan shrugged. "Since when is that my problem?"

"Shit!" He stared dismally at Jordan. "There's nothing left!" Every grand idea he'd had to save his ass had gone up in smoke. Frank couldn't afford to sit back and wait for trouble to pass over his head like a bad storm. Colette was bursting at the seams and was on the very real verge of exposing the whole cop-killing case wide open, putting bull's-eyes on both their backs. She was crumbling, and so was he. This money was everything! It was the only thing! And without it, Frank and Colette might as well turn themselves in and confess.

"I can't help you," Jordan said, shaking his head, and starting to get up to leave.

"But you pay Joel?" Frank blurted out desperately. "You paying Woody and Malcolm too? But you can't pay me?"

He hated the sound of his own voice. Frank was finally a broken man, afraid for his life, and desperate enough to beg for help from this man.

Jordan stopped and looked at him. "What are you talking about?"

Frank grimaced. "Oh, now your ass has amnesia!" he growled. "I know about the money, man! I know what you giving that old man!"

Despite what he'd told Frank, Jordan had lied. It meant something to him. Keeping the secret that Joel Tunson was his real father had to have meant something to him if he thought enough about it to put money in the bank for him!

"You paying him to keep quiet! You paying all of them! So, why the fuck not me?" His voice cracked.

These might be the last words Frank ever said. He understood that he might not leave this room alive. But what the hell? He didn't have shit to lose.

"I wouldn't come to you like this if I didn't need it!" he said, raising his chin and gritting his teeth. "I could give a shit about you or your goddamned money, if I didn't have a good reason for coming after it!"

"And what reason would that be, Frank?"

Frank had no choice. He had to tell him. Jordan would kill him, or maybe Jordan would even turn him in, but without the money from Jordan, Frank was a dead man anyway.

"To save my ass," he said reluctantly. "I've done some things . . . I need it to save my ass," he said, dropping his gaze shamefully to the floor.

"You killed those police officers."

Hearing Gatewood say that shit out loud stripped Frank of any shred of dignity that he might've had left. He nodded.

So what if Jordan knew the truth? What did it matter? If Frank left this room alive and broke then it was over. Colette would be showing up in a week, looking for enough money to disappear with, and Frank would have nothing to give her. She wouldn't go back to Cotton and it would only be a matter of time before the sky fell on top of their heads.

"This money you're demanding from me is supposed to buy some distance between you and Cotton, Texas?"

Blood pooled in his mouth and Frank spat. "That's it," he said dismally. "Distance and a second chance."

Jordan started toward the door, and then stopped. "That's one hell of a mess you got yourself in," He sighed. "Go home, Frank," he said over his shoulder. "I'll be in touch."

The Wine That's Drinking Me

"*Claire! Oh, God! Claire! I can't believe what just—You need to call me! Please! I can't believe what he just did to me! Claire, please!*"

Claire immediately erased the first frantic message she got from Lonnie Adebayo on her phone. She'd just come from seeing her gynecologist to talk about increasing her chances of conception. Claire was high on the possibilities, and the last thing she needed in her life was Lonnie and her drama.

"*There's no reason why you can't get pregnant, Claire,*" her doctor told her. "*In fact, if you're going to do it, then the sooner you get started the better. You're in your mid-thirties now, and the pregnancy would be considered high risk but you've got all your moving parts.*" *Her doctor laughed.* "*So go make a baby.*"

Jordan finally wanted a child, and that's all Claire had ever wanted: him; a family. Claire was happy. For the first time in a very long time, she was happy, and she had something to look forward to. Lonnie Adebayo could go to hell!

Claire was beside herself with the anticipation of being a mother. On her way home from her doctor's visit, she stopped at a boutique specializing in baby clothes and furniture. The house was so big. Claire had already chosen the room for the nursery, the one next to the master bedroom. It had big, pretty windows that let in a lot of light. In her head, she'd already decided on a theme (owls) and the colors. A designer had been recommended to her, and Claire had already set up a meeting with her to discuss the possibilities.

"Isn't that adorable?" the saleslady asked, walking up behind Claire as she held up a snow-white bunting.

"It's lovely," Claire said, holding it up and admiring it. "Too warm for Dallas, though."

"Not always. Some of those ice storms can be frigid. Is this for you or—"

Pride swelled in Claire, and she blushed as she responded. "For me."

"Well, congratulations. Do you know what you're having yet?"

Claire found herself caught up in this fantasy and loving every minute of it. "Not yet. I'm hoping for a girl, though."

"When are you due?"

"Next winter," she lied.

"We have some beautiful little-girl dresses expected to come in in a few months. It's our winter line, and they are adorable."

Claire's phone vibrated urgently in her purse, but she ignored it and followed the saleswoman to the back of the store.

Jordan would think she was crazy if he came home and found out she'd bought all of these things. Claire spread a dozen neutral infant outfits across the bed and stood back, admiring them all. She'd waited too long for this. Claire had waited too long to finally be excited about the future of her marriage. Jordan had changed so much. He didn't ignore her or cringe now when she brought up talk of having a child. Instead, he actually listened, and he was—

Claire's phone vibrated on the nightstand. She glanced irritably at it and noticed the number belonging to Lonnie.

She would've turned the phone off if it wasn't for the fact that her husband was out of town on business and she didn't want to miss a call from Jordan. Claire made up her mind right then and there to have her number changed. She'd had that number for years, and of course she'd have to explain to Jordan why she needed a new one. She'd tell him that she was getting too many telemarketers calling her or too many wrong numbers. But she couldn't let Lonnie continue to get in touch with her.

She picked up the phone and saw that she had seven messages from Lonnie, and three texts. Claire deleted the text messages without reading any of them. Next, she decided to get rid of all those voice mails from Lonnie, deleting them before the messages could even begin to play. Claire's phone rang again, and it was Lonnie.

"What the fuck do you want?" she blurted out when she impulsively clicked over to finally answer it.

"I know that you got my messages, Claire," Lonnie shot back.

"You need to stop leaving them!" Claire snapped. "Leave me alone!"

"And your man needs to leave me alone!"

"What?" Claire asked. This bitch was crazy. Lonnie had lost her damn mind and she needed professional help.

"I saw him, Claire! Jordan knows—Jordan knows where I live! He came to my house!"

The sound of her world crashing down around her forced Claire to her knees. "No! That's a lie! No!"

Lonnie was crazy! Maybe she'd suffered brain damage! She was delusional. She was just wrong.

"I didn't want to tell you . . ." Lonnie's voice trailed off in a sob. "How'd he find me, Claire? How the hell did Jordan find out where I live?"

Crying. Claire heard the sound of a woman crying. She raised her fingers to her face and it was dry. Lonnie . . . Lonnie was crying. Claire was too numb to cry. Lonnie was lying. Of course she was a liar! All she ever wanted to do was to take from Claire the only thing she'd ever loved. Lonnie wanted Jordan, and she'd say or do anything to get him.

"You lying bitch!" Claire spat, using the bed as leverage to stand to her feet. "Jordan doesn't want you!" she screamed into the phone. "He never wanted you! Stay away from my husband! Stay the fuck away from him!"

"He found me! He came to me! God! Why would I want him after what he did to me, Claire? You saw me after Jordan finished with me! Jordan's a fuckin' pig! He's a beast! Open your eyes and wake up!"

Claire didn't realize she was shaking. She didn't realize that she was aimlessly wandering from room to room in the house, cursing and screaming into her handset. Lonnie had pushed her too far! And Claire was sick and tired of her games! Of her lies!

"He put his hands on me," Lonnie continued unabated as she sobbed into the phone, trying to match screams with Claire. "He touched me, Claire! Fuck! He put his filthy hands on me!" Lonnie's words evaporated into incomprehensible blobs of words.

He put his hands on her? Claire forced images from her mind of Jordan touching that woman. He touched her? No! No! He wouldn't touch her! Lonnie dirtied his hands, and Claire knew Jordan. He wouldn't dirty his hands with her again. Lonnie was trying to ruin their marriage. She was bitter and angry because in the end, it wasn't her that Jordan wanted. And he'd shown her how much he didn't want her.

"He should've killed you!" Claire spewed mercilessly. "I should've left you there!"

"He kissed me, Claire!"

Claire went silent, and she froze where she stood. Her mind wrestled with what Lonnie had just told her. She refused to believe it, but she couldn't help visualizing it.

"He grabbed me, pulled me into his arms, and kissed me," Lonnie repeated. "Oh, shit! I can still taste him on me! I can smell him! Tell him to stay away from me, Claire! I'm begging you! Please! I'm leaving town soon, but tell him to please—stay away from me!"

Lonnie hung up and Claire stood there, stunned, empty, and numb.

Lonnie had never considered herself an actress before now, but seeing as how her photography career was all but over, she sat there after hanging up the phone with Claire, considering the possibilities. Of course, not all of it was acting. Lonnie had started off faking the tears, but she'd surprised herself when real ones surfaced, bringing the very real panic she'd felt when Jordan had touched her. She cringed now, thinking of him putting his mouth on hers, but what made her cringe even more was how she felt afterward. Lonnie had spent private moments trying to explain her thoughts and feelings to herself, but there were no words, no reasoning that made sense. She was terrified of Jordan because of what he'd done to her. She loathed him, the sight of him, the sound of him, the smell of him. But for a moment, albeit brief, she had forgotten those things.

Lonnie was the spider and Claire was the pitiful fly caught in the web. Lonnie poured herself a glass of wine and raised it in a sympathetic toast to Claire.

Of course, Claire wouldn't mention that call to Jordan, and she wouldn't pass along Lonnie's message for him to leave her alone. If Claire mentioned any of what just happened to Jordan, he'd have more questions for her than he'd have for Lonnie. He'd wonder how Claire even knew Lonnie's name, because as far as he knew, the two women had never met. Jordan would become suspicious of his wife, and begin to focus on key events, like how Lonnie got out of that house that night. The only other person who had anything to do with that house was Claire. Maybe she could lie her way out of it, but knowing Jordan, he'd make up his mind about her before she had a chance to try.

Lonnie leaned back on the sofa, satisfied that things were finally starting to come together, one piece at a time, and slowly, but there was a method to her madness, and she could see it now. Maybe, if she was diligent and careful, she could actually pull this whole thing off.

Turn Me Upside Down

Jordan had just come home after being gone for two days on a business trip. Claire greeted him in the foyer with an unconvincing smile and looking like she hadn't slept in those two days. "Hey, baby," she said, almost too jovially. "How was your trip?"

He stared at her strangely. She sounded too forced, and had a look in her eyes that he couldn't quite read.

"It was fine," he said apprehensively. "Everything alright?"

She looked away quickly, and went into the living room. "Fine. I just missed you. That's all.

"I know you're starving. You're always so hungry after getting off that plane. Rosa's in the kitchen making your favorite: steak and eggs."

Claire flitted around the living room, touching everything, rearranging, and picking. It was a nervous busy. He hadn't seen her like that in a long time. Something had gone down while he was gone. She only got like this when she was upset about something, or someone—usually him. "What's going on, Claire?" he asked cautiously.

"Nothing, baby," she snapped, still wearing that plastic smile. "I've just got all this energy. I don't know what's wrong with me. I shouldn't have had that coffee at lunch."

Old habits die hard, even for a man who'd vowed to try and fix his crippled marriage. It was things like this that irritated him the most about her. Claire had a way of turning into an overwrought victim on a dime, and of pretending to be painfully fine, when it was obvious that she wasn't, making herself appear to be even more of the martyr. Jordan was tired. He'd spent the last day and a half flying halfway across the country to sit in a meeting discussing pipelines, and half a day putting a well-needed chink in Frank Ross's dumb ass. This was not what he expected to have to come home to.

"I'll be in the shower," he said abruptly, leaving Claire alone with her hurt feelings, or insecurities, or depression—hell, whatever.

Jordan let the hot water wash over him in the shower, cleansing his mind, body, and soul of all the debris kicking up in his life lately. His world was a muddled mess of petty annoyances, and he really wasn't in the mood to let Claire add hers to the mix.

The Anton takeover was getting hit with one delay after another. June was ready to forge full steam ahead into that shit like a freight train, without bothering to look where she was going, and she had half of his executive staff jumping onto her bandwagon like a bunch of silly kids at a parade. As annoyed as he was by the delays, injunctions, and stays, he rather appreciated them because they bought him time, time to read between the lines and to see what was really at stake here and just how much it was going to cost him, because deep down, he knew it was going to cost him more than just money. Jorgensen, the founder and CEO, had bought up so many shares of Anton stock, at dirt-cheap prices under his granddaughter's name, that the old man stood to make more selling it than keeping it. Jordan couldn't fault him for the strategy. Hell, he'd even made note of it, just in case the time came when he found himself in that position.

June was like a gnat buzzing around his ear. She had something to prove and she was stumbling all over herself trying to prove it. Yes, she was smart. Yes, that damn MBA had definitely been worth the money. And yes, she was more than capable of running things. But no—not while he was already busy running things. June was a whiz with numbers. She was a strong motivator of people, but June didn't have what it took to run a corporation the size of GII. She lacked the insight and vision that could only be gained by the experience of having people try to do whatever it took to snatch your shit right out from under you. Jordan wasn't where he was because he had a fancy degree. He sat perched on top of the food chain because he'd mastered the art of cutthroat, while still managing to stay in the good graces of the people that mattered.

Lonnie had turned out to be more of a distraction than the threat she tried to come off being when he first saw her again. Truthfully, when he first laid eyes on her again, Jordan thought he was looking at a ghost, and he was as scared of her as if she had been. But she'd done nothing more than amuse him at best. Lonnie had no fight left in her, not like she thought she did, and he almost felt sorry for her. If Frank Ross was the biggest threat she could bring to this table to get even with Jordan—then she was more of a pathetic mess than even she knew.

She'd been wrong about another thing too. Despite her appearance now, Lonnie was as gorgeous as she ever was. Embattled, and no longer perfect, but Jordan could admit thinking about her more than he should've. He had loved her, probably more than he'd ever thought it was possible to love a woman. Love like that didn't die so easily.

Regrets could eat a man alive if he let them. And most of the time, he tried not to let them, but where she was concerned, it was nearly impossible to let go. Too bad, he thought, disappointed. Too bad that the two of them were toxic together. Too bad that the past had carved a ravine between them so wide that it could never be crossed. Too bad she didn't just come to her senses, get on a plane, and fly back to wherever it was she'd come from.

"Jordan," Claire called into the bathroom. "Dinner's ready. Do you want me to have Rosa make you some fresh eggs?"

"No. I'll be down in a minute."

Jordan ate heartily as Claire moved lettuce around on her plate, and sipped on a glass of lemon water. The shower and the meal must've helped to refill his empathy glass because he was starting to remember what used to bring on these moods in Claire in the first place. Jordan's out-of-town trips weren't always business related, and he hadn't always been so intent on keeping those trips a secret from his wife. He finished the last of his steak, leaned back, wiped his mouth, and tossed the napkin on the table.

"How about you and me go dancing tonight," he said, smiling at her.

Claire looked surprised by the suggestion. "You're tired, Jordan. You just got back from your trip, and I know you must be exhausted."

Jordan noticed the hopeful gleam in her eyes. "We don't have to go out."

He stood up, and held out his hand for her to take. Claire reluctantly pushed herself away from the table, walked over to him, and took it. He led her out to the lanai, stopping along the way to pick up the stereo remote, and pressing the button to turn it on. Will Downing's voice fell like smoke from the ceilings, and erupted like lava from the floors. Jordan pulled her into his arms, held on to her so that she would know that she belonged in them, and that there wasn't room for another woman. The two of the slowly swayed from side to side, Jordan barefoot and still wearing his bathrobe, and Claire wearing a cashmere sweater and shorts. It was a perfect spring night. Crickets chirped from the yard, and the moon hung over the ranch like a giant disco ball.

Jordan had worked hard to damage this woman. The least he could do was to work just as hard putting her back together.

How did he know that she needed this? How did he know that the phone call from Lonnie had unraveled her like a ball of yarn, and that it had taken every ounce of strength she had to try and hold herself together? Lonnie was a liar. In the back of her mind, Claire had already known it, but Claire had buttons that were still so easy to push, and Lonnie knew how to push them. Jordan didn't want her. He wouldn't have done what he did to her if she'd meant anything to him. She was a piece of ass, and Jordan had had plenty more just like her, but he was different now.

He kissed the side of Claire's neck, and she purred. "Thank you for this," she murmured. "You have no idea how much I needed it."

"Then shame on me for not paying closer attention."

Diggin' a Ditch

It was a story as old as time itself. Old horny guy kills off sickly wife to marry young hottie. Lonnie's gut told her that it was no coincidence that Edgar Beckman married the cute housekeeper, Dominga Rojas, less than two years after his wife's death. Chances were pretty good too that he'd been kicking it with Dominga before the missus passed. So, Lonnie didn't find it much of a stretch that he could've very well wanted to speed up the process.

Annette Beckman was diagnosed with stage four breast cancer and passed away six months later. It was her second bout with the disease. Lonnie combed through the crumbs of information she could find about Annette until she pieced together a pretty unremarkable life of that decent woman. So, Lonnie decided to turn her attention to Dominga. She found very little on the beautiful, young Chilean before Annette's death. She did find a photograph of Edgar and Dominga

Beckman after their marriage at a fund-raiser. The striking brunette towered over Beckman, who wore her on his arm like a fine watch.

A lot was written about Edgar during his run for mayor of Fort Worth, but nothing about Dominga, except for one poor shot of her standing off to the side as her husband shook hands with the governor of Texas. Lonnie looked long and hard at the grim expression on the woman. Maybe it was because her man was so much older than she was, or maybe it had something to do with the fact that he was short and troll-like. Whatever the case, the beautiful Dominga did not look happy. It took another woman to instinctively know that expression. Dominga was married to a man she didn't love. When Beckman abruptly pulled out of the mayoral race, divorce papers were filed shortly thereafter, and Dominga vanished.

"So, where'd you go, girl?" Lonnie murmured.

Lonnie picked up her phone and dialed the number of a close friend of hers. "Hey Brad, it's Lonnie."

Brad Ackerman was a reporter friend of hers who wrote for the *San Diego Daily Sun* newspaper.

"Lonnie, baby!" he said excitedly. "How's it going? I heard you retired. Tell me it's not true."

"It's not true," she lied. "Hey, I'm in a bind, and was wondering if you could do me a favor."

"Sure, if I can."

"I'm doing a story on a missing Chilean woman, Dominga Rojas."

"Okay. How long's she been missing?"

"I'm not sure. Since ninety-five, maybe even longer, but definitely not before eighty-seven. She lived in Fort Worth for a number of years. I'm not sure when she got there, but I know for sure that she worked as a housekeeper or cook there for a while and then married an Edgar Beckman in 1987."

"What are you thinking? The husband killed her and hid the body," he said jokingly. Lonnie didn't laugh.

"Do you still have that South American contact?"

"I do. Do you want me to try and track down Dominga Rojas?"

"Could you? I could forward you an old photo of her. It's not real clear, but I don't know. It's better than nothing."

"Send it. I'll see what I can find. Am I working to a deadline?"

"ASAP?"

"What else is new? Okay, I'll get back to you as soon as I think I've got something."

"Cool. Thanks, Brad."

It was late, and Lonnie had hung up and was ready to call it a night when the phone rang. It was Frank. She hadn't heard from him in over a week.

"Frank. I tried calling. Did you get my messages?"

"I got 'em," he said, after a long pause.

"Well? Did you meet with Jordan?"

Again with the hesitation.

"Frank?"

"Yeah. Yeah, we hooked up."

Lonnie waited for him to elaborate, but obviously Frank wasn't in a very forthcoming-with-information kind of mood.

"Well?" she asked impatiently.

"He told me to sit tight. Told me I'd be hearing from him."

Lonnie sensed that something was terribly wrong. "What's going on, Frank? What happened?"

"What the fuck did you get me into?"

Lonnie realized that Frank must've finally met the real Jordan Gatewood. The really mean one.

"I mean, I didn't expect this to be easy, but damn, Lonnie."

"What happened?"

"What happened?" he repeated introspectively. "I'm done," he finally said. "Whatever you got against him, you need to pack it up and take it with you, Lonnie. You can't beat this. I'm telling you . . . you can't."

Lonnie almost felt sorry for him. "So, you're really going to let him run you off like that?"

"I got enough shit on my plate right now," he shot back. "I got my own battles to fight. I ain't got the time or energy to fight yours too."

"I didn't ask you to fight my battle for me, Frank," she said, feeling insulted. "I just thought that maybe you could make him uncomfortable for me, and get something out of it for yourself."

"Nah. You used to me get his attention so that you can do whatever else you've got planned without him looking. I may look dumb, but I know what's up."

Of course he was right. Frank Ross had only ever been a distraction for Lonnie, a way to get Jordan to look at something else and keep his focus off her.

"The thing is," he continued, "if I'm smart enough to see it, what makes you think he won't?"

Lonnie swallowed. He had a point. "I thought you said that he told you to sit tight. What'd he mean?"

He sighed. "Hell if I know, and hell if I give a damn. I'm just calling you as a courtesy, which is way more than you gave me."

Now she really was offended. "C'mon, Frank . . ."

"This phone is going in the trash. And don't even think about coming to the crib in Paris, because I won't be there."

What was he saying? "You sound like you're letting Jordan Gatewood run you out of the state of Texas!"

"Where'd you run to? I said I'm done, and I mean it. This is your fight. Stay here and fight if you want to, or be smart and leave that brotha alone. It's up to you."

He hung up without saying another word.

I Am the Captain of This Ship

This place smelled country. How many times had coming to this man's house flashed in his mind, and how many times had he pushed it away? Too many to count. Curiosity was relentless, sometimes, and it egged him on, but it was Frank Ross's declaration that had weakened Jordan's resolve and compelled him to finally make this drive and to look into Joel Tunson's eyes.

Jordan spotted him as soon as he got close to the house, standing over a plot of dirt, patiently watering it and wearing faded gray overalls. This was the man they said was his father, his biological father. As Joel Tunson heard the car pull up and park behind his, he turned around, and met Jordan's gaze with his own. Jordan had no idea how much time passed before either one of them finally moved, but there was no mistaking that each of them knew who the other was. And there was no doubt that they both knew this day would come. But there would be no happy reunions, or hugs, or apologies.

Jordan climbed out of his car. Joel crossed the yard and turned off the spigot on the side of the house. He was a tall man, at least as tall as Jordan, the color of mud with silver hair covering his head, and spiking from his face. Regrettably, Jordan couldn't miss the resemblance. Put him between Olivia and Julian, people would say how much he resembled his mother. But put him between Julian and Joel, they'd likely say something else.

The old man looked apprehensive and guarded. "I seen you in the paper, quite a bit," he volunteered.

Joel Tunson was missing teeth.

He waited for Jordan to respond, but Jordan had nothing to say about the fact that Tunson had seen him in the paper quite a bit.

"Do you wanna come inside? Mosquitos will be out shortly. They worst at dusk."

Houses like his lined streets along every small town in Texas, all of them tiny, and old, and, no doubt, offering refuge for old men just like this one. Jordan followed him up the steps to the porch, and then through the screen door held open for him by Tunson. He found it strange that he didn't feel anything for this man. Jordan wondered if the same held true for Joel. He wondered if the man felt anything for him.

"Thirsty?" Joel asked, leading Jordan through a small living room with worn furniture and creaking wood floors, into the kitchen with the linoleum peeling up in the corners. "I keep tea in the house. Got ice—if you thirsty."

"No," Jordan said, surveying the small room with the tiny gas stove, ancient refrigerator, and small window over the sink. "I'm fine."

Joel pulled a glass from the cabinet. "Suit yourself," he said dismissively, filling the glass with ice, and then pouring tea over it. He motioned for Jordan to have a seat at the small kitchen table. Joel sat across from him, and stared at Jordan like he couldn't believe that he was finally able to see him in person. "Look just like your momma," he said, nodding. "Olivia. How is Olivia?"

He hadn't come here to make small talk. This wasn't a social visit, and he had no intention on catching up on all the years that the two of them missed together.

"Tell me about the money, Joel," Jordan said unemotionally. The bluntness of his question seemed to catch the old man off guard. "Where have you been getting the money from?"

Tunson's eyes glazed over, and all of a sudden, he wasn't so thirsty anymore. He slid his glass off to the side. "That why you came here? 'Cause of money?"

"Yes," he said matter-of-factly, leaving no room for misinterpretation. Jordan had come here to ask a question, and he would leave as soon as he had the answer.

Joel turned introspective for a moment, taking his sweet time with the answer. "The money comes," he said simply. "That's all I know."

"Who sends it?"

He shrugged. "First I thought Gatewood was sending it. Sending it to keep me from saying anything about you being mine. After he died it kept coming. Didn't know what to think about that."

Jordan wasn't his.

Joel looked wounded. "I can see you don't like hearing that any more than Olivia did."

Jordan wouldn't be baited. He came here for a reason. Just one. "When does it come? And how much?"

Joel's expression hardened. "Well, if you ain't the one sending it, then I guess that ain't none of your damn business. Is it?"

This time, it was Jordan who was caught off guard. But his defenses were high, and he wasn't about to lose sight of what he'd come here for. He wasn't going to let this old fool drag him into some kind of personal confrontation, because he didn't give a damn enough about Joel Tunson to even want to argue with him.

"It's going to stop," he threatened. "You've gotten your last dime of Gatewood money." It was a dig, and Jordan could see the sting in the old man's eyes.

Joel stood up slowly, disappeared into the living room, and came back a few minutes later with a faded yellow pillowcase, stood over Jordan, and dumped stacks of money in front of him. "Take your goddamned money! I never wanted it! That motha fucka took my wife, and he took my son! What the hell would I want his money for?"

There had to have been hundreds of thousands of dollars on that table.

"Whoever's putting it in my bank can go to hell!" Joel growled. "Be it you! Or Olivia! Or who the hell keeps sending it!" He stalked around to the other side of the table, and glared at Jordan, nostrils flaring. "You don't have to like it, but I'm the one who made you!" His chest heaved. "I'm the one who carried you in the house when I brought you and your momma home from the hospital because she was too tired to carry you! I'm the one who rocked you to sleep, and who played with you out there in that yard!" He pointed. Joel's eyes glazed over with tears. "She begged me to let you both go! Said, if I loved you, I'd want better for you than I could give! Said that Gatewood could give you all the things a boy could want! Said she'd hate me for the rest of her days if I didn't let her go!" Joel's voice cracked. "I'm the one"—he pointed his finger hard in his chest—"who loved you, Theodore! Even more than she did!"

Joel tossed the empty pillow case on top of the pile of money, and stormed out of the kitchen. "Getcho goddamned money and get the hell outta my house!"

Jordan sat frozen, even as the sound of the screen door echoed through that shack of a house. He had come here to ask one question. That's all. He'd expected to leave with one answer. Jordan stood up, stared at all that money, slipped on his Ray-Bans and left. Joel was back to watering his plot of dirt. He didn't turn around when he heard the screen door slam as Jordan left the house. He didn't turn around when he heard the sound of Jordan closing his car door, or starting up his engine. Jordan didn't even see him turn around in his rearview mirror as he drove slowly down the street, leading away from that old house—the house he'd lived in after he was born.

What a Wild-Eyed Beast You Be

"Frank, man, what the hell is going on?" Lawrence, his old partner before he was paired up with Colette, called him. "Is it true?"

Frank suddenly had that sick feeling in his stomach. It was late. Phone calls this time of night were never good. Frank swung his feet over to the side of the bed. "What're you talking about?" This was it. Frank had been sitting on pins and needles pretending that he wasn't waiting for this moment, but it was never far enough away from his thoughts. Shit, if it hadn't already hit the fan, it was about to.

"They arrested Colette, Frank. For murder. Says she shot some drug dealer. Is it true?"

Frank groaned without realizing it, squeezed his eyes shut, and swallowed the bile boiling up in the back of his throat. They had her. That meant that they had him, too.

"What the hell's up, Frank? You know anything about this?"

Frank opened his eyes. He hadn't heard from Lawrence in months, maybe even a year, and now all of a sudden, the dude had his cell phone number. Frank straightened his back. He took a deep breath to help clear his mind. Lawrence didn't call him because he was a concerned friend. He called Frank because they were trying to get him to confess.

Desperation engulfed him and the instinct to save himself took over reason. He had to think fast. Frank had never been much of an actor, but if he was smart, he'd act his ass off now so good he'd deserve an Oscar. "They arrested Colette for murder?" he said, doing his best "Damn, how could that happen?" impression. "Nah, man. That can't be—Nah! Not Colette. Somebody must've made a mistake, Lawrence. You know Colette. She's a good cop, a damn good cop. Nah!"

Lawrence waited too long to respond, which confirmed what Frank suspected all along. The man was sitting in an interrogation room, maybe with another cop, maybe with Colette sitting right there across the table from him. He'd cast a hook out into the pond and had hoped Frank would nibble. Frank didn't take the bait.

"They got a witness, Frank. A witness that saw Colette arguing with this cat named Reggie. He had his younger brother in the backseat of the car, crouched down so that Colette couldn't see him. Said the kid was sixteen."

"The kid's lying!" Frank shot back. "I worked with her for years, man. I know her. I know her better than I know myself. Colette wouldn't do that, not unless he had it coming. Not unless he pulled a gun on her or she felt threatened." Frank's mind was reeling. The words were popping into his head faster than he could say them, and he couldn't help but to marvel at just how good of a liar he really was.

Again, Lawrence took too long to say anything. Frank held this mental picture of him sending hand signals to another cop in the room, or scribbling down notes. Maybe he had his hand over the mouthpiece of the receiver while someone else gave him direction. In any case, Frank knew that one wrong word from him would be the end of his freedom. His palms were sweating. Frank concentrated on taking long, slow, even breaths.

"She's saying something else, Frank," Lawrence finally chimed in. "Saying that you and her had something to do with killing Ed and Jake." His voice trailed off, and he paused. "She's said that y'all shot them—"

The sound of the world crashing down around him was deafening. Frank raked his hand across his head. Sweat broke out on his face. "What? Are you—is this some kind of a joke, Lawrence, man?" Frank laughed nervously. "You know that shit's not funny, man. I don't know what kind of game y'all playing, but it ain't cool," he said evenly.

"That's what I heard, man," he said dismally. "I heard she said that she's not going down for this by herself."

"No." He shook his head. Lawrence was baiting him. It was the oldest cop trick in the book. He was dangling some shit in front of him to get him to slip up and say the wrong thing.

"Colette's in a bad spot. This ain't looking good. Not looking good at all."

"No, man! No! She didn't kill nobody! Neither of us are killers! You know I wouldn't do no shit like that, and you know that Colette wouldn't either!"

"They got her, Frank. They got the kid who said he saw her do it. They got ballistic that matched the kind of gun that killed that dude to the same kind she bought for her personal use, a few years back."

"How do you know all this?" Frank challenged. If Lawrence wanted to play games, then Frank was going to play it too, and call his ass out on his bluff. "How you know so much, Lawrence? You sound like you're working the case!"

Lawrence didn't respond right away. "Did you kill those cops, Frank?"

Frank shook his head as if Lawrence could see him.

"Frank?"

"I can't believe that you'd think I'd be capable of doing something like that," he said quietly. "How long have you known me, Lawrence? How long were we partners? I came to the hospital when your last kid was born, man. You took me out to get drunk after my divorce was final."

"Did you kill those cops, Frank?" he asked again, more gravely this time.

Frank had pieced it all together in his head. Colette was arrested for killing Reggie and she fell apart.

"I wouldn't shoot another cop," Frank said quietly. "And fuck you for asking." He hung up the phone, and then looked at the door, knowing that at any moment, they were coming for him.

"He'll run," Colette said, sitting across from Lawrence. Her eyes were swollen from crying, and bloodshot for being up all night. She was tweaking for another fix. The drugs had done this to her, turned her into what she was now. Colette could admit that.

The detective standing over Lawrence shrugged. "He won't get far."

Colette craved a cigarette, but she knew they wouldn't give her one. "I saw that kid," she volunteered. "I saw him, and I could've shot him too." Her gaze dropped. "But, I couldn't shoot a kid . . ." Her voice trailed off. "It wouldn't have been right."

"You had no problem shooting your fellow officers, though," he said matter-of-factly.

She smirked. "They weren't boy scouts." She glanced at him. "They wanted in on a bad deal," she volunteered. Her mind warned her to shut the hell up, but Colette and her mind hadn't gotten along together in years. She was caught, and she was going to prison. But she wasn't going by her damn self.

"The two of you could've just let them in on whatever it was you had with Rodriguez," the detective said. "You didn't have to kill them."

She thought about it, and tried to recall the details of that day. "Jake pulled his gun first," she said introspectively.

"So you say," he challenged her.

"Frank saw him. We only pulled our weapons because they did."

"Well, they're not here to corroborate your version of the story."

"Frank can."

"But will he?"

She wasn't going to do this by herself. Even if he did run, he didn't have the money to go far enough away. That stupid-ass scheme of his to get that rich man to get him money had fallen apart. Unless, of course, he'd lied. Maybe he did have the money, and maybe he never had any intention of sharing it with her.

"You get him here," she said. "If I go to prison, then he's going with me. If I get the death penalty, then Frank's gotta have it too. It's only fair."

Your Glory Was Lost That Night

Jordan hadn't visited his mother in months, but he'd followed the money trail back to her. The last time he visited, she didn't know who he was. Jordan introduced himself to his mother as if he were a stranger and they sat and talked for an hour about the Stylistics concert she and her best friend, Margaret, had begged Olivia's father, the doctor, to go to. The time after that, she remembered him, but she ignored him.

The disdain on her face this time when she spotted him crossing the green lawn headed in her direction was a sure sign that she knew who he was today. Olivia lay stretched out on a chaise, wearing a wide-brimmed hat, a pretty orange and yellow sundress that covered her legs down to the ankles, and a white shawl draped over her shoulders. Even at seventy-three, she was a lovely woman. Looking at her now, and knowing what he knew, Jordan could see how a man like Julian would go to any lengths to have her. What had attracted her to a nobody like

Joel Tunson was anybody's guess. But nothing about her looked like it had ever belonged with him.

"Hello, Mother," he said, leaning down and attempting to kiss her cheek.

Olivia shrugged away from him.

Jordan accepted her rejection of him, but she wasn't about to get rid of him that easy, not today. He pulled up a lawn chair and sat down next to her. She flipped through her magazine, pretending that he wasn't there. Jordan found himself looking at his mother with a new set of eyes today. To say that his getting to finally meet Joel Tunson face-to-face hadn't affected him would've been a lie. In the days since that visit, Jordan found himself starting to put certain things in perspective and to accept them.

Once upon a time Jordan had worshipped this woman. She had been his queen and everything about her was perfect. She was beautiful, loving, kind, and considerate; graceful, delicate, and gentle. When Julian's affair had come to light, right after his death, Jordan loathed the man for daring to misuse his mother like that, to humiliate her the way he had done with Ida Green. And when Desi Green's book came out, implicating Olivia as the person who'd actually pulled the trigger and shot Julian that night in Ida's living room, Jordan packed her up as quickly as he could, and tucked her away here, put her under a doctor's care, and dared the police to try and take her away from him. He couldn't wrap his head around the idea that she had actually been the one to shoot Julian. But that was then.

"How are you feeling?" he asked, strictly out of courtesy.

Of course, she didn't respond. She would talk to him, though. Before he left this place, Olivia would finally open up and tell him what he already suspected was true—that perfection was just an illusion.

"Joel Tunson asked about you," he said coolly.

She stopped turning pages.

"Asked how you were."

She had taught him to protect those things that mattered most to him, to cherish family and to always show them loyalty, especially when the rest of the world was watching. He wondered where she'd learned those things from—who'd taught them to her—when she took her infant son and her beautiful self away from one man because she preferred another.

"He doesn't want your money, Mother," he continued.

Olivia abruptly cleared her throat, closed the magazine, and slipped her sunglasses onto her face.

"Why'd you send it to him?"

"Because I know he needed it," she suddenly said. "He needs it now; he's always needed it."

He had no love for the man. Jordan didn't know Joel Tunson from the man on the moon, but even he couldn't turn a blind eye to the kind of humiliation and pain he must've felt when another man came banging on his door, demanding that he hand over his wife. And how he must've suffered when his woman, his wife, begged him to let her go, and "Oh by the way, I'm taking my baby with me."

"Whether he needs it or not, he never wanted it."

"That's fine," she said curtly. "I'll stop sending it."

"Why'd you really send him money?"

She pursed her lips together and turned her face away from him, trying to make him disappear.

"Answer me, Mother."

"I don't have to, Jordan."

"Turn around and look at me," he demanded in a tone he would've never dreamed he'd ever take with his mother.

She did look at him. She looked at him like he'd lost his damn mind.

"You paid him thinking that it was going to keep him from what? You thought it would help to keep him quiet? You thought that giving him that money would keep that secret locked away in that little shack he lives in? Were you protecting me? Or you?"

"How dare you!" she said, clenching her teeth. "How dare you talk to me like that, Jordan! I am your mother!"

"Yes, you are! You are my mother who took me away from my poor-ass daddy. You are my mother who shot my rich stepdaddy! You are my mother who won't talk to me because I'm trying to keep you from going to prison."

"If you don't like your station in life, then you're free to take a walk," she said bitingly.

Whoa! Jordan reeled back in his seat a little at the sight of this lovely, old woman finally baring her claws like the feline she was.

"Had I stayed with him, where do you think we'd be? Joel is a nice man, Jordan. He's always been a nice man, but make no mistake—he's never had shit and I didn't want that for me or for you!"

"But more for you?" The thought flicked on in his mind like a light switch.

Of course the gracious Olivia Gatewood was offended. "Careful how you speak to me, Jordan," she said with warning. "My power of attorney put you where you are now. It wouldn't take much for me to have it revoked. I could just as easily hand over the helm of Gatewood Industries to your sister."

Jordan found himself mildly amused by the threat. "And all this time I thought I got my prowess from my dad—Julian—when I really got it from you."

"I'll warn you one last time, son—be careful."

He leaned closer to her. "He let us go because you begged him to," he said solemnly. "He said that you told him you'd hate him forever if he didn't."

Olivia stared down at the magazine lying in her lap. "I did what was best for us, Jordan. You can accept it or you don't have to. I don't really care anymore."

"You got what you wanted. So did Julian. You got each other."

"Yes." She nodded. "We did."

And both of them were miserable because of it, but looking at her, Jordan figured he didn't need to remind her of that. Olivia already knew it.

"Like I said, son, if you aren't happy with your position in this family, you're free to take your behind back to Joel Tunson's shack and learn to fix cars and mow grass," she said sarcastically. "Really get to know the man who made you."

Jordan shook his head and laughed. He stood up to leave. "No, Mother." He pulled back her hat and kissed her head. "He's not the man who made me, and Julian wasn't that man, either. But you are."

She looked up at him. "Don't ever come here and talk like this to me again, Jordan," she warned. "Or you will find yourself sleeping in Joel Tunson's spare room."

He leaned down and kissed her cheek. "Thank you, Olivia," he whispered, "for all that you have done for me."

He walked away. If threatening him made her forget how shitty she'd treated Tunson, and how shitty Gatewood had treated her, then so be it. The bottom line was Olivia Gatewood was a motha fucka, but he should've known that when he found out that she set up an eighteen-year-old girl for murder.

Black Bird from a Dark Heaven

"*Edgar Beckman has sat on and or chaired the board of directors of Gatewood Industries since Julian Gatewood went public with the company back in sixty-eight,*" Phillip said over the phone.

The man never stayed in one place too long. After leaving Lonnie in Dallas, he flew to Beijing.

"*He's not just a family friend, Lonnie. He's more than that. Beckman is an advisor, confidant, and yes, I would go as far as to say that Jordan Gatewood doesn't make a single business decision without probably running it past Beckman first.*"

Lonnie had been studying this copy of Julian's will since Phillip had given it to her. "*This will doesn't really prove that Desi Green is Julian's biological child, or that Jordan isn't. Is it worth the paper it's printed on without anything else to support it?*"

"*You have Jordan's birth certificate,*" *he responded.*

"I have a copy of a document that could be his birth certificate," she said, disappointed. "Revealing it would cause some drama, sure, but the Gatewoods would eventually just make it disappear."

"It's as worthless as you believe it is."

Lonnie thought before answering. "It's just . . . it's not enough, Phillip. So what if I have it published in the local paper that Jordan's not a Gatewood? It's sensationalism at its best, and even though it would raise questions, the bottom line is, who cares? The man's a mastermind when it comes to running this business, and he's made too many rich people richer. If Gatewood Industries loses its golden boy, then it loses money, and if it loses money, then so do the rich bastards who back it. Who really cares who his daddy is?"

"His mother."

"She only cares because it puts a dent in an otherwise stellar, bright-and-shiny reputation. And more and more, Jordan could give a damn. So, like I said, who cares?"

"One person might," he said, and then paused. "Desi Green? Maybe she would care if she found out that Julian was her biological father, and not Jordan's."

Would Desi care? She was busy traipsing all over the country, pushing shoes and purses and living like a celebrity. Did she care anymore about what the Gatewoods had taken from her?

"Other than Olivia Gatewood, the only other living person who would possibly know the truth is Edgar Beckman. He was Julian's personal attorney," he explained. "By all indications, he worked for Julian long before Gatewood Industries became what it is today. The two even went fishing together, according to you."

Phillip was reaching. "So?" Lonnie asked irritably.

"You said it yourself, Lonnie, that day at lunch? It was obvious that when Beckman saw you, he knew you. Now, how could he possibly know who you *are, unless Jordan had shared that with him, and why on earth would Jordan mention you to a man who was merely a member of the board, unless the two of them were as close friends as Edgar was with Julian? He went so far as to forge that man's will to hide his declaration of Desi being his child. He's practically Jordan's shadow. How far do you think he'd go for Gatewood Industries' superstar?"*

"It's a stretch, Phillip," she said, doubtfully.

"It is. But you're good at stretching."

Lonnie's last conversation with Phillip had left her more frustrated than anything. In all her years of experience working as a journalist, she counted on facts to make her case for a good story, but in most cases, the best investigative reporters began the chase for those earth-shattering stories based on nothing more than curiosity or speculation. Sometimes, it was like a dog chasing its tail and Lonnie wasted a lot of time and energy only to end up with nothing, no story at all, but every once in a while, she hit pay dirt.

Beckman lived on an estate just outside of Fort Worth. She didn't know how much Jordan had told him about her, but the look on his face that day in the restaurant was a good indication that he knew more than she wanted him or anybody else to know. She was here now, to formally introduce herself, and to share with him all the fascinating things she'd found out about him too.

A buxom, young blonde answered the door. "Edgar Beckman, please?" Lonnie asked politely.

The woman didn't smile, say hello, or so much as fart, before she turned and started to walk away, leaving Lonnie with the impression that she was supposed to follow her inside. She led a trail through the massive living room, into the kitchen, and then finally out to the back of the house to the pool.

"Edgar?" she said in her Southern twang. "You have a visitor."

She brushed past Lonnie and disappeared back inside the house.

Beckman stopped in the middle of putting, pulled down his sunglasses, and stared stunned at Lonnie.

The silence between the two of them was eerie. He took reluctant steps in her direction. Lonnie felt obligated to at least meet the stout, old man in the middle.

"What are you doing here?" he finally asked.

She wore three-inch heels and stood eye to eye with the man.

There was something about him, something she couldn't quite put her finger on, but there was something familiar about his face—his features?

"I came to formally introduce myself," she said confidently.

So maybe he knew that Jordan had kicked her ass, but he also needed to know that Lonnie wasn't the victim.

"Lonnie," she said. "Lonnie Adebayo."

He looked unimpressed.

"What do you want?" he asked abruptly, reaching down to pick up his drink that sat on the patio table.

Some pieces of the puzzle were still missing, and Lonnie had to be careful of what she said, and how she said it. Beckman liked to fish; so did she. Only Lonnie had come here to fish for him to fill in the blanks for her. He was a lawyer, an old one, but lawyers were master wordsmiths. They talked too much, and said too little. The fact that he was old meant that he had mastered the art of talking shit.

Lonnie reached into her purse, and pulled out the copy of the will that Phillip had given her, and handed it to him.

He took it reluctantly, unfolded it, glanced at it, folded it back, and held it out to her.

"That supposed to mean something to me?"

He was good. Cool. Unruffled. Damn. If she ever needed a lawyer, she'd definitely want one like him.

"You and Julian Gatewood were close."

He stood there. "Leave my house."

"You and Jordan just as close?"

"Get the hell out," he demanded again.

"Not until I tell you a story, Edgar," she continued. "About a beautiful Chilean woman named Dominga Rojas." Lonnie expertly rolled her "r."

All that lawyer cool blew away in the wind, and dangerous color suddenly flushed across that old man's face, and that's when Lonnie realized what it was about him that she found so familiar. Edgar Beckman was a black man, or at least, he had black in him, and he was "passing."

Lonnie felt the smirk creep across her lips. Without even trying, he'd just given up another secret, one that was almost better than the first.

Beckman found the chair beside the table and sat down, casting a forlorn gaze across the lawn. He looked tired, all of a sudden, like a man who'd been carrying something for far too long and wanted nothing more than to lay it down.

Lonnie sat down too, and began to relay a story to him that she was sure would be incredibly close to the one he already knew.

"She came to this country to live with her aunt," she began calmly. "Dominga's mother wanted her to learn English, and to go to American schools in the hopes that she would have a bright future, because she was such a bright girl."

Brad had gone that extra mile for Lonnie. She knew he had a contact in South America, but she had no idea that that contact had been Chilean himself, and he took it upon himself to find Dominga's mother and to actually sit and talk to the woman about her daughter. He ended up getting some real personal shit from a heartbroken woman, desperate to know the truth about her youngest child.

Edgar sat like a statue.

"Her aunt was a housekeeper, and she agreed to take Dominga in, as long as she pulled her own weight and helped to make money to support herself," Lonnie continued, carefully scrutinizing the man's face and his body language.

"She worked for you, Edgar, and after your wife, Annette, passed away, you married Dominga."

He finished what was left in his glass.

"She was so young and so beautiful. But then, you divorced her and poof! Dominga Rojas vanishes like a quarter in a magic trick."

Edgar swallowed.

"Her mother hasn't seen or heard from her in years, Edgar." Lonnie relished saying that to him. She saw his body go rigid, even though he tried to hide it. She noticed how he turned his head away from her. "What did you do to Dominga?"

He cleared his throat, turned back to looking out at the lawn, and swallowed again. "You need to leave my house," he said hoarsely.

"It's not like Dominga not to call her mother," Lonnie continued. "But her family was poor. They didn't have much, so no one looked for Dominga Rojas-Beckman for long." Lonnie reached into her purse again, and pulled out a copy of an article she'd found on the Internet. "I wonder if this is her?"

The headline read, WOMAN'S BODY WASHES UP ON GALVESTON'S EAST BEACH.

"The article said that the woman was about five-five with dark hair, and was undoubtedly Latina. But she had no face, and her hands and feet were missing." Lonnie held it in front of his face, but Edgar swatted it away. "Do you think she might've slipped and fallen in, Edgar?" she asked condescendingly.

This time, he did turn to her, and Edgar's eyes bulged out of his head until she thought he'd explode.

"She left me!" he growled. "Found herself some young, rich stallion, took everything I gave her, and ran off with him!"

Lonnie leaned back. "But why hasn't she phoned her mother? Dominga adored her mother. Her mother doesn't believe that her daughter would go this long without speaking to her unless something was terribly wrong," Lonnie continued softly, almost sympathetically. She watched the stout and defiant Edgar Beckman begin to slowly dissolve right before her eyes. She was on to something. Lonnie didn't know the details but her gut warned her that poor Dominga's mother would spend the rest of her life waiting for her daughter's call.

"What did you do to her, Edgar? Where's Dominga?" Of course, she didn't expect him to confess. The questions were rhetorical, and they were asked to make him remember the dark thoughts that he undoubtedly worked hard to keep hidden, even from himself. But still, Lonnie had come here to plant a seed. "Does Jordan know?" she asked softly. A vein running along Edgar's temple suddenly swelled and pulsed. "You trust Jordan the way you trusted his father, Julian? Did you trust him with your secrets? Would you trust him with your life?"

He opened his mouth and Lonnie waited for him to cuss her out or threaten her or something, but Edgar said something even more shocking.

"I'm too old for this." His voice cracked. He suddenly shrank in his seat, lowered his head to his hand, and began to rub his eyes.

If Lonnie didn't know better, she'd think that he was crying. And that was it. She had somehow made an impact, and at least for now, that's all she needed to do to Edgar Beckman. He would do the rest to himself.

"Maybe we'll talk some more later, Edgar," she said softly, as she stood up to leave. "Was that your wife who answered the door? She's lovely," she lied. "Don't bother getting up. I'll see myself out."

Lonnie let herself back into the house, and saw the missus standing in the kitchen, nibbling on cheese, and looking out at where her husband and Lonnie were talking.

Lonnie stopped. "Just so you know," she offered, "he takes his vows very seriously. Till death do you part." Lonnie picked up a piece of cheese and popped it into her mouth. "I'm just saying."

I Am Screaming

Desi hadn't been in this house in months. It was her house, the first house she bought with the money she inherited, but it never did feel like home. Texas didn't feel like home anymore either. She found it strange that you could spend your whole life in a place and never find a connection to it, but she'd managed to do it. This place was dusty and hollow. It had furniture in every room, but there was no spirit in this house, because she'd never bothered to put hers into it.

Desi took her bags upstairs to the bedroom, peeled out of her clothes, and took a shower. When she finished, she dried off, wrapped a towel around her, and climbed into her bed. She'd come back to Dallas because Lonnie was here. But that was the only reason. Lonnie had disappeared over two years ago. One minute she and Desi were as thick as thieves, and the next, Lonnie was gone. For weeks after Lonnie's disappearance, Desi thought the worst, that Jordan had killed her and gotten away with it.

It was months before Lonnie finally did call. In that time, though, nobody was even looking for her. The police said they could find no evidence of "foul play," which meant that they weren't going to touch Jordan Gatewood with a ten-foot pole. But when Lonnie did call Desi, she didn't sound like the Lonnie Desi had known. Lonnie had been pensive and withdrawn. Something had happened to her, something horrible, but she wouldn't say what it was. Desi knew, though, that whatever it was, Jordan had been the one to do it.

"Hey," she said into the phone. "I'm back in town. Yeah, I got in this morning. At the house. Okay. I'll see you soon."

Desi had made up her mind to move on with her life and to turn her back on the Gatewoods forever. She had been given the opportunity of a lifetime when she got out of prison. Desi had inherited more money than she knew what to do with, and a second chance. Lonnie had helped her. She'd come to Desi's rescue when no one wanted anything to do with her, and stood by Desi's side, exposing the truth behind her conviction.

The sheriff from Blink, Texas, came into the house that night after Mr. J, Julian Gatewood, had been shot, and saw Desi holding the gun in her hand, but Olivia Gatewood had put it there, after she shot her husband. Her fate was decided in that moment, and there was nothing Desi or her mother could do after that but to sit back and let it happen. Gatewood money paid for her conviction, and they got it. And Desi spent the next twenty-five years of her life in prison for something she never did. But Lonnie was there for her. Lonnie helped Desi to expose the setup behind her conviction, and all the king's men—from the sheriff, to the judge, to the court forewoman—all had to answer, in one way or another, for the role they'd played in seeing to it that Desi was sent to prison. Desi's conviction would likely never be overturned, but at least her truth was out there, and it had hit the *New York Times* bestseller list, so it was out there pretty damn good.

She dressed, and went downstairs to make herself a cup of tea. Desi was starving, but of course, there was no food in the house except for a can of chicken noodle soup and a package of stale crackers. She had no intention of staying in town any longer than she had to, so she doubted that she'd buy any groceries. Half an hour later, her doorbell rang, and Desi got up to answer it. It was the first time the two of them had ever met face-to-face. Until now, they'd only ever spoken on the phone to each other.

"Wow," Desi said, feeling overwhelmed. "You look so much like him."

June smiled and carefully studied Desi. "Thank you. That's the nicest thing anybody's ever said to me." June reached for Desi and the two hugged. "Welcome home, Desi."

All Wise Men Today Grieve

Dominga let him love her when he needed to most. When Annette lay dying, and smelling like death and medicinal and old, Dominga let him kiss her. She let him touch her and hold her. She let Edgar make love to her. Dominga was his sweet, raven-haired beauty—young, warm, so full of life and light.

"You need to smile more," she whispered to him, her accent thick and melodious, her tongue like velvet. The lines of her were perfect and flowed like rhythms. Her beautiful, golden brown skin was smoother than silk. Dominga's full, plump lips made his mouth water and his cock sit up at attention.

"It's hard to smile sometimes," he responded, lovingly stroking her hair. He lost himself in the dark pools of her eyes. "But you—you make me smile, lovely Dominga."

She wrapped her luscious lips around the head of his cock, and Edgar gave himself fully to her. He was hers in a way that he had never belonged to Annette. He was weak with Dominga, like clay in her hands that she could mold into any shape she wanted him to be, and he loved it. He loved her for it.

"*I love tasting you,*" *she told him.*

He loved tasting her too. Edgar pulled her up from the end of the bed, turned her over on her back, spread her legs, and lowered his face, burying it between the heavenly space between her caramel thighs. There was no sweeter taste, no aroma more sensual than her. Dominga was his fantasy. She was the kind of woman a man dreamed of loving and of loving him.

"*I love you,*" *he said, looking up at her, his face covered in her juices.*

She bit her bottom lip, and then smiled, batting thick, dark lashes at him. "*I can tell.*"

He became impatient for Annette to die, but he knew that she would. Eventually, she did, and Edgar and his children buried the woman he'd spent so many years of his life with. But he had a new future waiting for him in Dominga. And as soon as he could, to the protests of his children, he married her. She became his, and Edgar's obsession began to take over, and swallowed them both. Dominga began to resent him for it, and he resented her for possessing him like a demon. He began to watch her, to track her every move. She was a passionate, beautiful woman, and young—so damn young. Too young.

Dominga waited until he was away on business to misbehave and take a lover, a black man, Isaac. Isaac was a tall, dark, handsome Cuban and every chance she got, Dominga disappeared with Isaac, but she had no idea that Edgar was watching.

"*Edgar!* Por favor *no!* Vamos, *Edgar.* Por favor, voy a estar con ustedes! *Please no! Let's go, Edgar. Please, I'll be with you!*"

Edgar pulled the trigger. Isaac's body folded and dropped to the floor.

"*Edgar?*" *Dominga was shaking. Her lips were trembling, and he stared at them, wondering if she'd used them to make love to Isaac, the way she'd made love with him.*

He and Jordan Gatewood weren't so differnet. Both of them had loved women who had betrayed and mocked them, women who had toyed with

*their devotion and crushed them. Lonnie Adebayo was to Jordan what Dom-
inga had been to Edgar, and just like Jordan, Edgar destroyed that woman
with his bare hands. Unlike Lonnie, however, Dominga had no guardian
angels watching over her. The thought of shooting her the way he'd shot her
lover never occurred to Edgar. He did use that gun, though, beating her with
it until there was no trace of her beautiful face.*

*Edgar moved mechanically. Edgar thought methodically, as he systemati-
cally removed her hands and feet, using a hacksaw he'd had in the trunk of his
car. She couldn't be identified, he reasoned. Without hands and feet, and face.
When he finished, Edgar put the hands and feet in plastic bags, went to the
bathroom and washed his face and hands. Dominga was dead. He stared at
his reflection in the mirror, thinking that thought over and over again, waiting for it to sink in, but it couldn't. Something inside him blocked it. Dominga
was gone.*

*He left Isaac in that dirty, tiny house of his. Edgar didn't care about Isaac
or if they found him or could identify him. Let them. Dominga was his wife.
Dominga was gone. Dominga was his—*

*He carried her to the car, wrapped in a blanket from the bed. It smelled of
sex. Her sex. Edgar was careful not to get her blood in his SUV. There was so
much blood. But he was careful. He drove to Corpus because it was close. He
opened the plastic bag and dropped the hands and feet into the water and
Edgar stood there and watched them sink. And moments later, he watched her
sink too. Dominga was gone.*

*He filed divorce papers a few weeks later. Nobody questioned the fact that
beautiful, young Dominga left him. After all, Edgar was too old for her. Poor
Edgar, with his broken heart, and silly notions that beautiful Dominga loved
him for anything other than his money.*

Guilt doesn't adhere to the rules of time. Most things fade with time: regret, eyesight, memories. But guilt feeds on time, and as it feeds, it grows, and when it runs out of time, it begins to gnaw on the guilty. Dominga was the only woman he'd ever loved. Dominga was the last woman he'd made love to. She was the only one he could ever make himself truly want.

"Edgar?" Bridgette had come down the stairs and found him sitting in the library. "Baby, it's late," she said, sweetly rubbing his shoulders. Bridgette was a toy at best, an amusement that he lavished with gifts and money, but she meant nothing to him. "You should come to bed."

He platonically patted her hand. "I'll be up shortly, sweetheart," he promised.

She sighed, and quietly left him sitting there alone, in the dark.

Lonnie Adebayo was a smart woman. Jordan had failed to mention how smart. Edgar had suspected that she was cunning, but he had underestimated her too. She had been savvy enough to do what he would've done in her position. She'd studied her enemy, Jordan, and she'd made the connection between him and Edgar. He had no idea how she'd done it, but she'd done it and that was all that mattered. And then she'd done something else extraordinary. She'd set Jordan aside, and turned her attention to Edgar.

From their meeting, he could tell that most of what she said to him was her just pissing in the wind. She didn't know the details, but she had a theory and put it to the test. She had her finger on the big picture and it was the big picture that mattered. So what would she do with what she knew about Edgar, or what she suspected she knew? Would she go to the press and resurrect Dominga? And if she did, would they believe her enough to even be curious? Edgar was an old man. Did he really care anymore?

He picked up the slip of paper she'd casually left him with her number on it, and dialed it.

"Hello?" she answered.

Edgar had played these types of games for longer than she'd been alive, so he knew the rules. He knew them well.

"What do you want from me?" he reluctantly asked.

It was a simple question. That's all it needed to be.

"Proof."

"Of what?"

"Desi Green's lineage."

"Why?" he asked curtly.

"Do you really care?"

Edgar thought about it. "No."

Like the Cat That Collared Me

"We've got you on the camera in the parking lot of the supermarket where you and Colette met up, leaving your car and climbing into hers the evening that Ed Brewer and Jake Boston were shot, Frank, corroborating Colette's version of what happened."

They'd caught Frank coming out of San Antonio, driving down Highway 35 headed toward Laredo. He'd taken what was left in his bank account and filled up his gas tank, hoping to make it across the border before they caught up with him.

"She said that you and she were taking money from Reggie Rodriguez, in exchange for letting his people deal without being arrested."

Chuck Baldwin was the detective questioning Frank. Frank remembered when Baldwin first came on the force. He was young and scared—now look at him, all large and in charge and shit.

"Ed and Jake wanted a piece of the action? Is that true?"

Frank had the right to remain silent. So, he did.

"According to Colette, the two of you weren't getting all that much from Reggie. Maybe Ed and Jake thought you were cleaning up more than you were?"

Reggie gave them a grand a week, which was change considering how much he was bringing in, but Chuck didn't need to know that.

"Maybe it's just me, but if the two of you weren't getting much from Reggie, then why bother to shoot Ed and Jake at all?"

Because Jake was a hothead, who pulled his gun first. And Colette was a methhead who pulled her gun next. Ed was looking out for Jake, and Frank was looking out for Colette. One thing led to another, and all of a sudden, the whole world turned upside down. Chuck didn't need to know all of that either.

"I'll be honest, Frank," he said with a sigh. "This isn't looking too good for you, man. Colette's adamant about her side of the story, and the only reason she's telling it at all is because she knows she's going down for Reggie, and she figures that she might as well take you with her. Now, if I were you, I'd speak up now. Say something to help yourself out here, Frank. Don't let her take you down with that sinking ship without a fight, man. It ain't worth it."

Chuck Baldwin was a good man, a good cop. He had Frank almost convinced right now that he really did care about what happened to him. If Frank hadn't seen this ploy so many times before in the past, he might've fallen for it, but he knew better than to say shit. If they wanted to prove he shot those men then they'd have to do it in court. Frank made up his mind to do all his talking through his public defender.

A few days later, Frank and Colette appeared together in the courtroom, awaiting their bail hearings. She looked at him as the two were brought into the courtroom together. They locked on to each other, and

Colette's eyes filled with tears. She mouthed "I'm sorry" to him. Frank turned away.

His hands and ankles were cuffed. Frank was a fuckin' criminal. A year ago, they were giving him a plaque and pats on the back. *"It's been good working with you, Frank. Man, you are going to be missed around here. If you ever change your mind and want to come back, just give us a call. We'll keep your locker warm."*

Colette was led up to stand in front of the judge first. Some vague-looking public defender appeared like a rabbit out of a hat next to her. The district attorney rattled off the charges, making Colette sound like a regular mass murderer. Then her defense lawyer mumbled some kind of half-assed plea for leniency and bail, which the judge revoked. Colette broke down crying, and two police officers scooped her up, and dragged her out of the room.

It was Frank's turn, and with each step, his stomach turned. It was almost over. Frank had been living in denial for so long that now he was starting to feel a sense of relief that this whole thing was coming to an end. It reminded him of having a bad tooth that needed to come out. His knees threatened to give out from under him as the realization was finally setting in that he was going to prison for killing those men. And when it was all said and done, Frank stood to lose his life.

He fixed his eyes on the gavel sitting in front of that judge. Frank barely even noticed his lawyer sidling up next to him. He heard the shuffling of papers, and the nauseating sound of that judge's voice as he read off the charges in front of everyone in that courtroom. He was numb and detached from this whole scene, because he already knew how it was going to end.

"Your Honor, my client is charged with this crime based only on the heresay of another defendant," he heard his lawyer say, loud and clear. This one didn't mutter under his breath. Frank looked at him. This one looked like he was wearing a million dollars.

"A defendant who was also arrested for taking the life of another victim in a crime of which, according to the CTPD (Cotton, Texas Police Department), my client had no involvement whatsoever. Until recently, Mr. Ross was a decorated officer with said police department, with exemplary annual performance reviews and a spotless record."

"He's accused of killing two other exemplary police officers, Your Honor," the prosecuting attorney retorted.

"Ah, yes," Frank's attorney said pompously, holding up a document in his hand. "A Mr. Edward Brewer, placed on disciplinary suspension twice for citizen complaints of unnecessary roughness, and Jake Boston, who transferred to the Cotton Police Department from the El Paso Police Department, where he was also placed on a leave of absence pending investigation for domestic violence against his then girlfriend."

"Your honor, the victims are not on trial here," the DA argued.

"Neither is my client."

"Not yet," the DA's representative snapped.

"That's enough," the judge commanded. He took his time considering Frank, and then made the decision. "Bail set at one million." He raised his gavel and struck it down on the bench.

Frank's heart sank into his stomach. "A million fuckin' dollars?" he murmured.

"The angels are on your side today, Ross." his expensive-looking lawyer said matter-of-factly, packing up his briefcase. "You'll be out within the hour." He glanced at Frank, and then followed him as he was led out by the uniformed officers.

Like the Devil in the Church

"*But you canceled* the last board meeting, Jordan," June said, taking two steps to every one of his to try and keep up with him as he walked back toward his office. "We're all anxious to get this over with, and by the numbers, if we're going to do this, then we have to do it now, before someone else comes in and snatches Anton right out from under our noses."

His patience with her was running thin. "This isn't up for debate, June," he snapped. "Reschedule the meeting for next week, after I've had a chance to take a look at some things." She followed him into his office and closed the door behind them.

"June." He spun around and glared at her.

She put her hand on her hip. "Jordan."

Jordan glanced at his watch. He didn't have time for this shit now. He'd agreed to meet with Edgar for lunch. "We'll talk about this later. I have a meeting."

"Just tell me what it is that's keeping you from wanting to move on this now? Anton is in a prime spot for us to come in and sweep it out from under Jorgensen's feet. It's done, and it's going at a bargain price," she said, sounding like a used-car salesman on late-night television.

"I have my reasons," he said simply.

"Why can't you share them with me? Why can't you share them with the board? Maybe if you did then they'd be willing to take a step back and do it your way, but because you don't, and with everything I've shown them . . ."

"Numbers!" he said, suddenly snapping. June and her damn numbers were starting to get to him in the worst way. "This business isn't just about numbers, June! How many times do I have to tell you that? And how many more times do I have to tell you to respect me and my position and to stop selling that shit to my board members?"

"Your board members, Jordan? How about our board members? This is my company too, and I have every right to be here as you."

"But you haven't been here, baby sister," he retorted. "You've been in Atlanta, with your husband and your kids, running your little non-profit," he said condescendingly. "I've been here, June!" He drove his finger down on top of his desk. "For damn near thirty years, I have been here, carrying this damn company on my back to where it is now! These people have seen what I can do! They have trusted what I can do until you came along and started to undermine that!"

"I'm not undermining anything, Jordan! I'm just—"

"Forgetting your goddamned place, June. That's what you're doing." Jordan was hitting some serious nerves in his sister, and he could see from the look in her eyes that he'd crossed a line. He quickly composed himself. "There is an order to things, June. You've got to know that. You're a smart woman, and I know you understand what I'm saying. I've headed up this company since before you graduated high school, and it's taken me a very long time, but I think I've figured out what I'm doing. A corporation this size needs good, strong, and unshakable leadership. We both can't go around pounding our chests and acting like each one of us, in our own right, is in charge. We do that and we'll rip this company apart from the inside out, June."

"You know that's not what I'm trying to do," she said defensively, folding her arms across her chest. "But I'm also not trying to let the opportunity to grow GII into one of the largest and most profitable oil companies in the world pass us by, either." She paused. "You've been preoccupied, Jordan. I can see it. We all can. I don't know what's going on with you, but something is, and I'm just worried that you might not be your usual, clear-thinking self. That's all."

Now, she'd offended him. "There's nothing going on with me that I would ever allow to get in the way of me running this company."

"Are you and Claire alright?" she asked, concerned. "I've spoken to her a few times, even tried to get her to go out for a drink or lunch. Seems she's good at avoiding people."

"Claire's fine," he said dismissively.

"Are you fine, big brother?" She was pushing, and he didn't appreciate it. "I know you, Jordan. I've studied you my whole life." June smiled. "I know when something's bothering you, and something is."

June thought she knew him. She knew an idea that was Jordan. He was her big brother, the one who looked out for her, took care of her, and threatened to beat up any boy that she brought home because she believed she was in love. But she didn't know that Jordan was only her half brother. That her father was the namesake for this company, and his was a broken-down old man living in some no-name town who had handed over Jordan and his mother to another man out of shame and guilt. June had no idea that Julian never gave a shit about him. That Jordan was the part of the package he had no choice but to take when he made up his mind that he wanted Olivia Tunson. No. June didn't know any of these things. And she didn't need to know them.

She didn't have any idea that he'd nearly killed a woman with his own hands and that that woman was out for revenge now, or that death and killing were nothing new to him. She didn't know that he had brothers, and probably cousins and nieces and nephews, completely unrelated to her. June had no idea what kind of man Jordan really was. If she did, she'd have skipped her happy ass out of his office and staked a claim to her father's corporation.

"Claire and I are trying to have a baby," he said, thinking that the word *baby* to a woman would be like kryptonite to Superman, and that it would get her off of him.

June's expression softened and a slow smile creased her cheeks. "A baby? *You* want a baby? I thought you hated kids, or is it just mine you hate?"

"I don't hate your kids, June. They just need ass whoopings. That's all." He was teasing, but not really.

"I told you, I don't believe in spankings."

"You told me that."

"So, what brought this on?" she asked, looking at him suspiciously.

"A man can't want to have a kid with his wife?"

"Sure, but you were always quick to bring up the fact that you had one, even though she's grown now and barely knows you, and that you weren't interested in having any more."

June had a gift for doling out digs. Jordan had a daughter living in California with her mother. He sent money, and sometimes gifts. Every once in a while, she called him, or he called her. That was the extent and the nature of their relationship.

"Well, I want one now," he said.

June nodded introspectively. "Good. You need one."

He frowned. "What the hell is that supposed to mean?"

"Kids help to keep it real, Jordan," she explained. "They put things in perspective and keep it there, especially when we get too full of ourselves and forget what's really important."

Again, he was offended. "You need to be careful," he warned.

She laughed. "Or what? I'm not twelve anymore, Jordan. All I'm saying is that I think you'd be a great father. Probably even better than you know."

June turned and started to leave.

"Don't forget to reschedule that meeting," he reminded her, relieved that this whole scene was over. But he still didn't trust June as far as he could throw her.

"Consider it canceled," she said over her shoulder, as she disappeared into the hallway.

Jordan left soon after she did, stopping at his assistant's desk. "Please follow up and make sure that each member of the board knows that the ten o'clock tomorrow morning is canceled."

"Yes, sir."

Please Fill My Glass Deep for Me

As composed and polished as Jordan appeared to be, Edgar knew that this boy was a sloppy mess, a direct result of the sloppy mess that Julian had been. Both men were suckers when it came to women, and both men left behind debris dirty enough to ruin them.

"You look miserable," Jordan said, sitting down at the table across from Edgar.

The lovely brunette who had brought Edgar his drink before Jordan arrived appeared like magic at the table again. "May I get you something to drink, Mr. Gatewood?"

"It's a little early for me, Marci. I'll just have an iced tea."

Edgar's head spun around like it was on a swivel as he watched her walk away. His usually lifeless cock pinched against his zipper.

"She's even younger than Bridgette, Edgar," Jordan reminded him.

Edgar smiled. "Is she?"

He'd been a dirty old man too long to change now.

"How's Bridgette?" Jordan asked.

"Worn out," Edgar answered roughly.

The best Jordan could do with that answer was to raise a curious brow, but it was the truth. Edgar had learned not to fall in love with a woman. He'd taught himself that after Dominga. Women were like new cars to him now, or a new pair of shoes. In the beginning, they were beautiful, but after a while, they lost their luster.

"How's your woman problem going?" Edgar casually asked, referring to Lonnie.

Jordan expressed a smug assuredness as he thought before answering. "Not as much of a problem as I thought it'd be."

"Meaning?"

"Meaning Lonnie came back here with more bark than bite. The shit she was planning had no teeth, Edgar. Her intention was to sic Frank Ross on me in the hopes of making me sweat, but his ass is useless and she is not the woman I thought she was."

Jordan sounded and looked almost sorrowful.

"I expected more," he muttered.

"You sound disappointed."

"No, I'm relieved. The last thing I need right now is drama, pending the buyout of Anton. I've got enough to worry about with that, and the fact that Claire and I have decided to have a child, finally," he admitted sheepishly.

"Claire's wanted children since the two of you were married." Edgar smiled. "You on the other hand did not."

Jordan was thoughtful for a moment. "I'm not close to my daughter. The older I get, the more I regret that. And I need an heir. I need a legacy that goes beyond just me."

Jordan's foolish, pompous ass had bought into the lie that was him and owned it hook, line, and sinker. He truly believed that he was all his mother had promised him that he was. Edgar had no choice but to take some of the blame for the man that Jordan Tunson, now Gatewood, had become. After all, he'd orchestrated it himself, drawing the notes with his own hands because Julian was too love-struck and pussy-whipped by that country mouse in Blink, Texas, to see straight. But Lonnie Adebayo had Jordan by the balls and he didn't even know it, because he was too busy playing king of the hill at Gatewood Industries, and at the house with his lovely, delusional wife.

"Is that right?" Edgar asked, finding it hard not to sound condescending.

Jordan looked curious. "Are you drunk already, old man?"

Edgar raised his glass and smiled. "Not yet, son. But I'm working on it."

"Don't you think it's a little early?"

Edgar flagged the lovely Marci back over to the table.

She smiled at him and it warmed him all the way down to his toes. "Another one?" she asked, resting her hand on his shoulder.

Edgar fell in love just like that. "Please," he said, smiling back at her. When she left, he looked at Jordan. "If she asks me for my credit card, please remind me to give it to her."

Jordan laughed. "I don't think you're her type, Edgar." He motioned his head across the room at a much more handsome, younger man sitting at the bar. "He's a running back for Dallas, and the two of them have been locked on to each other since I sat down." And then he laughed. "Stick with Bridgette. At least you already know that she loves you for your money."

If Edgar had had any qualms before about the conversation he had wanted to have with Jordan, he didn't have them anymore. Jordan's careless and sloppy ass had no business doling out advice about women.

"Do you know why I told you about Dominga, Jordan?"

At the mention of her name, Jordan suddenly sat up, looked around the room in case someone heard Edgar say her name out loud, and leaned closer to Edgar. "Let's talk about this somewhere else," he suggested covertly.

Edgar found it amusing. "Let's not."

Jordan stared cautiously at him.

"It was a lesson on being thorough," Edgar continued coolly. "Maybe it's the lawyer in me, or maybe it's the reason I turned out to be a damn good lawyer, but there is no greater asset, in my experience, than being thorough. Nothing as pertinent as crossing all your *T*'s and dotting every last *I* with finality. With Dominga I did those things."

Jordan looked mortified. How dare he.

"You failed to cross your *T*'s and dot your *I*'s where Miss Adebayo was concerned," he said, deadpan. "Which is why I'm here."

"You're here to hit on that young hostess and to drink too much, Edgar."

"I'm here to tell you a story, Jordan. The same one I told her." He took a deep breath before starting. "Julian Gatewood loved nothing more than dipping his dick into the sea that was Ida Green. It was a fascination I never understood because Ida Green was absolutely the most unremarkable, commonly sweet woman I have ever met." She was a woman Edgar had made a conscious effort to forget, much in the way he'd tried to forget Dominga.

The expression on Jordan's face told Edgar that the boy had no idea that Edgar had known Ida. Edgar found himself suddenly relishing the fact that he was about to tell Jordan something that would surely make him fall off out of that chair he sat in.

"I sat at her table and on many occasions ate food she prepared, and laughed and had a good time with my best friend, Julian, and for all intents and purposes, his family. It seemed that the only time he was ever really happy was when he was with Ida, and Julian was just a man, like any man, free of the stresses and obligations of being one of the richest men in the state of Texas."

"You know Desi," Jordan stated resentfully.

"I have always known her, son. I was there when she was born in the hospital, pacing the floors right alongside her daddy."

There were no words to explain the expression that crossed Jordan's face. But Edgar could imagine the bomb exploding inside him.

"Lonnie Adebayo found out all she needed to about my Dominga, Jordan," he said unemotionally. "And I'm too damned old to spend even a night in prison."

"You've spoken to Lonnie?" Jordan asked, stunned. Edgar sat silent. "What did you tell her, Edgar?

"What do you think?"

"You told Lonnie that Julian was Desi's father?" he asked, clenching his teeth. "Is it true?"

"Every bit the truth, son. Just like it's true that he's not your father. I'm the only reason the world doesn't know either of those truths. Julian would've hated me if he knew what I'd done, but I did it for his own good and the good of Gatewood Industries and its name. I did it because he was a stupid fool, just like you."

Jordan reminded Edgar of a bullet loaded into a gun. He looked about ready to shoot out of his chair, aimed right at Edgar.

"You've underestimated that woman. She wanted you looking the other way so that she could do what she really came here to do, which is to set you up."

"How?" he asked angrily.

"I have no idea how. But if I was a betting man, I'd put every dime I had on her," Edgar burst out laughing.

If I Had No Greed Too Big

"*Keep your mouth* shut," Frank's new lawyer told him. Alex Richards was his name, a slippery white dude with oil-slick black hair, dark eyes, and a nose that reminded Frank of a hawk. "Stick close to home, and make sure you have your phone on at all times in case I need to contact you."

Frank was no fool. This cat cost money, big money that Frank sure as hell didn't have. "Who hired you?" he asked, as the man pulled his car up in front of a run-down motel off Cotton's main drag.

"They'll be watching you," he continued coolly. "I wouldn't put it past them to put a wire tap on your phone. Your ex-partner is still in their custody, and they'll no doubt use her to try to get to you. If she calls, and she will, just know that they're listening, so hang up, and then call me. Understood?"

Frank nodded.

The man handed Frank a room key with the number 322 on the tag. "I'll be in touch." That was his signal to get out of that man's Lexus.

He stood there and watched the smoke gray car pull out of the parking lot and turn the corner. Frank didn't know if he should jump up and down for joy or run off into the woods somewhere and hope to God nobody, especially that dude, ever found him.

After he showered, Frank finally had a chance to look at his cell phone. He had at least twenty calls on that damn thing, some from Colette before he was arrested, but most were from Lonnie. Maybe she was the one who got him this high-priced lawyer. The last week had been a whirlwind for Frank, and he really didn't feel like talking to anybody, but if she'd done this for him, then he at least owed her a thank-you.

"Are you alright?" she asked, as soon as she answered the phone.

He rubbed the burn from his eyes, and sighed. "I take it you saw what went down on the news?"

"No. It's not being broadcast at the state level, but I did see it on the Internet. Where are you?"

"At a motel in town."

"Cotton?"

"Yeah. I'm out on bail but I can't leave the city."

"So, you did manage to get bailed out?"

If she hired that lawyer, then she had to have been the one to bail him out too.

"I don't know how you did it, Lonnie, but I appreciate it."

"It wasn't a problem, Frank."

"And that lawyer— That dude's scary, girl. Where'd you find him?"

"A friend of mine owed me a favor," she explained. "He's one of the best."

"No doubt. So, what next?"

Lonnie hesitated like she was thinking about something. "Did you really kill those cops, Frank?"

Just that quick, Frank's brain jumped back into ex-cop mode, and he put on a suit of armor. "Would you have bailed me out if you believed that I did?"

Lonnie sighed. "No. No, I guess not."

"Sorry I couldn't come through for you, Lonnie," he said, disappointed. She'd stepped up her game to get him a chance at getting off with this thing, and he had fallen short on her quest to put some heat on Gatewood. "I should've trusted you from the beginning. Maybe if I had . . ."

"No worries, Frank. It is what it is. You hang in there. I'll be in touch."

Frank didn't remember falling asleep. The sun had gone down when he finally did wake up, still wearing that towel he'd wrapped around his waist after he got out of the shower. He was starving, and because he knew that he didn't have anything in that place to eat, Frank put on his clothes, and headed out to find something. Fortunately, that motel was right off the highway, so there were a lot of places to eat within a few blocks of the place. Frank found a diner on the corner.

"I'll have the steak with mashed potatoes, gravy, and the vegetables."

"To drink?"

"A beer."

A few minutes into his meal, Frank got company: Lawrence Brooks and Quincy Simpson, both esteemed members of the Cotton Police Department.

Larry squeezed in right next to Frank. He'd been the one on the phone, trying to get Frank to confess before he was arrested.

"Fuck the formalities, brotha. How the hell did your broke ass manage to get that kind of money to get bailed out?" Larry asked unapologetically.

Quincy just sat there, drilling holes into him with those big-ass bulging eyes of his.

"That lawyer didn't come cheap either," he chimed in. "What kind of friends you got?"

Had they been following him? Maybe the two of them had been staked outside his motel room. How else would either of them have known he was here?

Frank took his lawyer's advice and said nothing. He carved off a huge slice of steak and shoved it into his mouth.

"You really going to let Colette take the rap for this herself?" Larry asked menacingly. "Colette don't have the connections you do, man. That fancy dude you got might just be able to convince a jury that you ain't guilty, but you saw what she was working with. You gonna let her go down like that?"

"You and Colette were more than partners," Quincy added. "That's what I heard. Heard she was your girl, your real girl."

Frank flagged the waitress. "Another beer, please."

She asked the other two if they wanted anything, but both declined.

"Ed and Jake were no saints, Frank," Larry continued. "You and Colette weren't the only ones they were trying to shake down. Neither was Reggie."

Frank swallowed what was left of his beer and stared at Larry. Like, what did his dumb ass expect for Frank to say? *Really man? Aw, then that's good, so yeah. Yeah, we shot 'em. We blew holes in both their asses!*

This wasn't a game. Frank was fighting for his life, and he'd take whatever help he could get to get him off. Colette had dug her own damn grave. Drug addiction had left her off-balance and impulsive. If she hadn't shot Reggie, maybe neither one of them would be in this damn situation right now. And maybe, Frank could've gotten his hands on a way out of Texas, and even the country, if he'd played his cards right. Larry had asked him if he was really willing to let Colette take the fall for this herself, and the answer was simple. Now that he was free, at least temporarily, and had one of the best lawyers that money could buy, even if it wasn't his money, Frank had a chance. So yes. She could take this one on the chin her damn self.

Frank had suddenly found himself a little bit of hope. More than he'd had in weeks. It still wasn't too late. Yeah, Gatewood had shown his ass a few weeks ago with Frank. He'd kicked Frank's ass and showed him just how far he was willing to go if Frank didn't back down, but what about now?

Maybe Gatewood had no idea what was happening to Frank now. But even if he did, especially if he did, would he really want the truth coming out now, when Frank was looking at murder charges? Would he really want his name, his reputation tied to this shit? Frank seriously doubted that Jordan Gatewood would want anything to do with Frank's ass now, but maybe that was the motivation the man needed.

It's the Best That I've Had Lately

"*Why do you* have this thing about waking me up in the middle of the night?"

Phillip had awakened her like Prince Charming, with a kiss. He was such an ugly, sexy man and the fact that his voice was about twelve octaves deeper when the sun set didn't hurt his case either. He stood up, undressed, and crawled into bed next to her, spooning behind her. Phillip's erection swelled the longer he stayed pressed up against her.

"You should let me make love to you," he whispered in her ear.

Lonnie cringed. "And you should stop asking me to let you make love to me. You know I don't want to."

"Are you afraid I'll hurt you? Are you afraid that you won't enjoy it? Because I can make certain you do."

Lonnie didn't know what she was afraid of. She couldn't even bring it upon herself to get off on her own anymore because even the fantasy of sex was unappealing to her now.

"Close your eyes," he told her.

Lonnie looked over her shoulder at him. "Why?" She suddenly felt panicked. "What are you going to do?"

He softly kissed her lips. "Just close them. Trust me and close them."

He was Phillip Durham, the man who had come for her whenever she needed him to. He was always there for her, and Phillip had never lied to Lonnie.

"I won't hurt you, Lonnie. I never would and you know this."

The warmth of his breath washing over the side of her face was soothing. Phillip's heart beat slow and deep against her back. It was comforting and made her feel secure and safe. He pulled her so close to him that their two bodies nearly felt like one. Lonnie wanted to fall back to sleep. With one hand, Phillip lightly began to stroke her belly with his thumb. The rhythmic pattern of his breathing began to lull her into a calm and peaceful place, the kind of place Lonnie couldn't get to without taking an Ambien. His touch was relaxed and careful.

"You are so beautiful to me," he whispered. "Do you understand that? Do you understand how lovely you are to me?"

Lonnie felt herself smiling. Phillip raised his hand from her stomach and brushed his fingers against the side of her neck. He nuzzled his nose against her, inhaled, and released a low, lustful moan. "Lovely," he whispered again.

Lonnie didn't realize that his hips were grinding against her, or that her body had begun to open up to accept his advances. She gradually thrust her pelvis against his. Phillip's thumb grazed against one of her nipples that had aroused to become erect. She gasped at how sensitive it was. Lonnie almost opened her eyes.

"It's alright," he said, breathlessly, over and over again, like a chant.

He had slipped his fingers between her panties and her skin.

Lonnie's body reacted instinctively at first, but the kisses he planted on her neck relaxed her even more. With one long, slender finger, Phillip tenderly began to stroke the lips of her pussy. Soon, he began to part them, and dip his finger slightly between them, grazing it gently across her clit.

Lonnie gasped and began to spread her thighs even more to accommodate him. She felt the wetness in her build at the excitement of being touched. She wanted this so much. Lonnie wanted to savor every second of his stroke, she thrust her hips against his palm, hungry for him to push deeper inside her. She hadn't felt like this in so long—sexy, desirable, feminine.

No one knew how to make her cum the way Jordan did. No one's dick felt as good inside her as his. Lonnie's knees were drawn toward her chest, her thighs wide open, as she held him by the back of his neck, watching every delicious stroke of him as he drove deep inside her, and pulled himself out to the tip, until the head of his beautiful cock kissed the moist opening of her pussy.

He had her. Lonnie's eyes locked on to Jordan's and she knew that despite her best efforts to resist him, and to make him believe that she could take him or leave him—he had her.

Lonnie abruptly grabbed hold of Phillip's hand, pulled it from inside her underwear, crawled out of bed, and disappeared inside the bathroom, where she slammed the door shut behind her.

"I—I'm sorry, Lonnie . . ." Phillip's voice trailed off. "I thought you were enjoying it," he finished dismally.

She was enjoying it, but for all the wrong reasons. Lonnie suddenly had tears in her eyes. "It's not you, Phillip," she said through the door. It's me." She stifled a sob. "I'm just one fucked-up bitch. That's all."

Phillip was scrambling eggs the next morning. He poured Lonnie a cup of coffee when she sat down at the kitchen island. She could scratch her own eyes out for how she'd acted with him the night before, but Phillip was a master at letting things ride. He kissed her cheek, put eggs on her plate, and asked her where the salt and pepper were as he scoured through the cabinets. If she'd have apologized to him for what happened, it would've offended him. And he didn't seem to need an apology.

"So, this Edgar character killed his wife," he casually mentioned over what he considered breakfast.

White people could make breakfast of coffee and eggs. Lonnie was sorely missing some bacon, sausage, toast, grits.

She nodded. "He didn't come out and say it, but I implied it, and he didn't really deny it."

"Do you have proof?"

She shook her head. "In cases like this, proof is overrated. Beckman's own conscience convicted him right in front of my eyes, and he never had to admit a thing, even though I had nothing and he maybe knew that I had nothing, but I had enough, and that's all I needed, because he caved," she said in one continuous breath.

"You're good at that." He smirked.

"Bullshitting people?"

"Yes."

"I know, right. But that's because I can usually read people, and I read old Edgar like the Bible. It was almost as if he couldn't wait for someone to find out. Like he was relieved that he didn't have to know what he did and have to keep it to himself."

"So now what?"

"Well," she said as she scooped more eggs into her mouth. "He gave me a name of Julian Gatewood's old secretary. Harriett Grainger. Apparently, Harriett was real protective and loyal to Julian before he died." Lonnie took a sip of coffee. "Beckman said he couldn't guarantee anything, but that it was rumored that Harriett left Gatewood Industries after Julian died, and took a bunch of things with her. He said that she especially didn't trust Beckman, so he suspected that she kept a close watch over everything he did."

"Why?"

"Because she was like a mother hen to Julian. Watched over him like a hawk, to the point of being obsessive. And she was nosy."

"Is she still alive?"

"She died fifteen years ago. But she had a daughter, living in the house she inherited from Harriett. Gloria Dawson. I don't know. I just think that there's got to be some kind of proof that Desi is Gatewood's biological child."

"And what if there isn't?"

She shrugged. "I don't know," Lonnie said dismally.

"And what if there is?" he asked, sounding hopeful.

"Then we have the final answer to our last question of how do you bring down a king."

He smiled. "And the answer is?"

"You dethrone him."

"Well, I have to give you a high five." He held up his palm. "You've masterfully turned his subjects against him."

Lonnie slapped his palm. "Only Edgar. There's still Claire."

"His wife."

"She'd drink his dirty bath water if it meant keeping him."

He frowned. "What?"

"It's an American analogy," she explained. "It means that she'll do anything for Jordan, and she'll turn a blind eye to every bad thing he does."

"Sounds like she's going to be harder to break than Beckman."

"Claire's a delicate woman," Lonnie explained introspectively. "She fights tooth and nail to stay balanced but she's really standing on the edge of a cliff. She just needs one big push to send her over."

The Bullets in Our Firefight

"Lonnie?" Desi couldn't believe that it was really her. She stretched out her arms. "Oh, God! Lonnie!"

Talking to Lonnie over the phone didn't make her real. Not as real as she was now as Desi embraced her. Lonnie was heavier; her hair much, much longer. Lonnie was rigid and cold. She was wounded.

Desi pulled back from hugging her, carefully pushed her hair aside, and stared at the scar crossing her eye and disappearing into her hair line. All this time, she hadn't been able to shake the feeling that something terrible had happened to her friend, but even when she did finally get that call she'd been hoping for all those months, Desi could tell that there was something different about Lonnie, just from the sound in her voice.

The two of them stood in Desi's living room. "What happened?" Desi asked shakily. Lonnie had never said over the phone why she'd disappeared all of a sudden. She'd never told Desi what had happened to her, but now she couldn't deny it. "Tell me what happened, Lonnie." Desi had tears in her eyes.

Lonnie stood at attention like some defiant soldier. "Guess, Desi. And I'll bet you get it right the first time."

Desi brought her hands to her face and shook her head. "I knew it. I knew it."

Jordan.

"Why? What— He found out that we were friends," she said. "He found out that you knew me?"

That's exactly what happened. She knew it even if Lonnie never did admit it herself. The way Lonnie stood there, so guarded and defensive, staring down her nose at Desi like she blamed her for what he'd done to her. And maybe she should've. Maybe what happened to her, whatever that meant, had been because of Desi.

"I'm so sorry, girl," Desi said tearfully. She reached for Lonnie again, but Lonnie withdrew, and Desi understood why. "I'm sorry."

Lonnie walked past Desi, and sat down on the chair farthest across the room. Desi hesitated, but decided to sit on the sofa. The tension between them was unnatural and powerful. This woman had been as close to Desi as a sister, maybe even closer, and now it felt like they were more distant than strangers. It was almost as if they were enemies.

"Congratulations," Lonnie said, breaking the awkward extended silence between them. "On the success of the book. I read it, Des. It was a powerful story," she said earnestly. "I mean that."

"I couldn't have done it without you, Lonnie, without your help."

Lonnie showed no emotion. "I think you redeemed yourself to a lot of people. And I think that it was good for you to finally tell your side of the story."

Desi didn't know what to say. She wasn't sure how to take Lonnie.

Her words said one thing, but her actions, her body language, and the expression on her face said something else entirely.

"And kudos again for your new fashion line." Lonnie forced a smile. "I checked it out online. Nice. I ordered some shoes."

Desi smiled. "You could've asked. I'd have given you some shoes."

"Again, I think you've got a winner on your hands with Konvictions. And you deserve it. Success. You deserve all of your success."

"How are you, Lonnie?" Desi asked, to change the subject. She felt uncomfortable as hell listening to Lonnie go on and on with accolades over Desi's accomplishments when it was painfully obvious that she really didn't mean any of it. "Are you still working?"

"No," she said curtly. "Not as a photographer. I do some freelance writing, but that's about it."

"Well, what brings you back to Dallas?" Desi asked guardedly. She suspected that she knew what the answer might be, but Desi hoped she was wrong.

Lonnie looked at Desi almost as if she knew that she didn't need to answer that question.

Desi looked away.

"I knew that night that he was above the law, Des. Jordan can do just about any damn thing he pleases and some high-powered team of lawyers will come to his rescue, just like they came to Olivia's when she shot Julian, and it would've been my beaten and bloody ass they'd have arrested for trespassing against his fist."

She was right. Those people had too much money and influence to be held accountable to the law like everybody else. "It's a shame," Desi muttered. "But it's the truth."

"I thought about waving a copy of that birth certificate in front of the audience on the nightly news, but even that wouldn't do any good.

It's a piece of paper. Ultimately, Jordan would make a joke out of it, and a fool out of me," Lonnie said matter-of-factly.

She was right about that too. The Gatewoods were used to weathering scandal. They did it better than most people did, and they always managed to come out the other side of it better than when they went into it.

"I need your help, Desi," Lonnie finally stated.

"Of course, Lonnie," Desi said wholeheartedly. "You know that all you have to do is ask. Whatever you need, girl. I'm here."

Lonnie reached into her purse, pulled out a slip of paper, and handed it to Desi. "She lives in Tyler, and I'd like for you to pay her a visit, Desi. She has something for you. Something she won't give to anybody else but you."

"What's this about? Who is this?" she asked, studying the note Lonnie gave her.

"It's about you finally getting what's yours, and me finally seeing Jordan get his."

"What is she supposed to give me?" Desi asked.

"Proof, Desi. Proof that Julian was your real father."

Desi leaned back on the sofa and sighed. Not this again. For years, speculation that she was Julian's daughter filled Desi's fantasies, but there had never been any proof that he was, and even if he was, what difference did it make now?

"If Jordan knew, he'd lose his fuckin' mind," Lonnie said menacingly, a glint of life flashing in her eyes for the first time since the woman walked into Desi's house. "It would be the nail in the coffin for him, Desi. He's not Julian's son, and he knows that now, but to find out that you are Julian's blood relative . . . Do you know what that could mean?"

Desi didn't bother to answer. Jordan wasn't an issue anymore and she'd been living her life just fine not hearing his name, but lately it seemed that everybody was trying to push him back to the forefront of Desi's life. Desi was his Achilles heel, still, and apparently the worst way to get to him, even after all this time, was by using Desi. Lonnie knew it, and so did his sister, June.

"You could lay claim to everything Gatewood, Desi, from the corporation to the name. Hell, you could change your name to Gatewood if you wanted to. What do you think that would do to him? What do you think it would do to him if you filed a petition for your rightful percentage of that business? And you could, Desi. There are lawyers out there, good ones, who would sell their own mommas to take on a case like this. Even the publicity alone would be enough to—"

Desi tossed the piece of paper on the coffee table, stood up, and paced across the room.

"What's wrong?" Lonnie asked, confused.

"Do you hear yourself, Lonnie?" Desi asked, exasperated. "Do you hear what you're saying?"

Lonnie looked offended. "I know exactly what I'm saying. The question is, do you hear what I'm saying? Do you see the possibilities here, Desi?"

"Oh, I see them. But you know what else I see? I see you trying to drive a butcher knife in Jordan's chest and then keeping him alive long enough for him to see that there's a butcher knife sticking out of his chest."

"What the hell does that mean?"

Desi felt so sorry for Lonnie. It had been two years since the two of them were last together in this house, plotting and planning ways to get back at the Gatewoods and everybody else who'd done Desi wrong, and in those two years, Lonnie was still stuck in this space in time, held there like she was the one locked up.

"I don't know what he did to you, but I'm sure that if I use my imagination, I could figure it out," Desi finally said, feeling so over-wrought for Lonnie. "But damn, Lonnie! How long do you plan on running around in this maze?"

"Maze?" Lonnie stood up, looking pissed.

"You're like a rat in a maze chasing the trail to Gatewood cheese," Desi argued. "Why can't you leave it alone?"

Now she was just livid. "How fuckin' dare you say that to me!" Lonnie stalked toward Desi like she was going to hit her, and Desi couldn't help herself. She hadn't spent twenty-five years locked up without learning how to fight. Instinct kicked in and she balled her fingers into fists.

Lonnie stopped short and pulled her hair back. "Look again at what he did to me, Desi!" This time, the tears did come. "He raped me! Over and over and over!" she said, pounding one fist into her palm. "Jordan beat me to within an inch of my life! He left me, thinking that I was dead, Desi! He intended for me to be dead! And you think that I should just let that shit go? Did I let it go when you got out and his people had stolen twenty-five years of your life? Are my two years any less important?"

Desi felt small and broken. "I-I didn't mean it like that, Lonnie."

"I helped you, Desi. I helped you to get your money and your name." Her voice cracked. "And you owe me. The least you can do is to help me make his ass regret he ever put his filthy hands on me!"

Desi felt tears begin to well up in her own eyes. "Yes, I owe you," she said tearfully. "I owe you my life, Lonnie, and if you ask me for it right here and now I'll hand it over to you without a second thought."

Lonnie grimaced. "I don't want your damn life," she said bitterly. "I want you to do what I told you to do. Call that woman, Desi. Go see what it is she's holding, and bring it back to me. Get the proof that you need to finally show this man who you really are, and more than that, who he isn't!"

Desi felt so sorry for Lonnie and angry with her at the same time. "I don't need to show him anything. I know who I am, Lonnie! And I don't have shit to prove to Jordan . . . or to you!"

"But I need this," she argued. "I give a whole hell of a damn what he thinks, Des!" She shook her head in dismay. "He still scares the shit out of you," she said, disgusted. "My God, Desi, you strut around the world selling shoes and talking with your head up like you're somebody special, like you've overcome and risen to the mountaintop, but"—she looked Desi up and down and frowned—"You're really just that pitiful little martyr fresh out of prison and scared to take a piss without asking for permission."

Desi stared back at Lonnie like she'd lost her damn mind. But Desi recognized this tactic for what it was, because she'd seen it too many times when she was locked up. Desperate women saying desperate things to get other desperate women worked up and fighting. The difference was that Desi wasn't desperate.

"I'm so sorry for what he did to you," Desi said, as sincerely as she could. "And I'm sorry for my part in what happened, Lonnie."

Lonnie huffed and rolled her eyes.

"But Jordan's not my problem anymore."

"No, Desi!" Lonnie shot back. "He's my problem! And if you cared so much about me that would be enough to make him yours! Hell! I did it for you!"

"I never asked you to!"

"And you never told me not to either! And because you didn't, this is what he did to me!" she said, pointing at her face.

"You're right, Lonnie!" Desi shouted. "You're so right! I owe you! I will always owe you, and I'm willing to pay up and make it right in any other way but this! He's dangerous, girl! You got away with your life, Lonnie! If you keep pushing this, you know it's not going to end well."

Lonnie wiped away her tears and angrily pushed past Desi on her way to the front door.

Desi followed her. "Don't leave! Lonnie, girl . . . c'mon! We need to talk about this!"

Lonnie turned once more before leaving. "I'm all talked out, Desi," she said quietly. "I'm through with your pathetic ass!"

We're Strange Allies

Frank had moved out of that motel and rented an apartment. It wasn't much, but Frank had gotten a job doing janitorial work at an insurance company. He didn't make much, but he made enough to afford a studio apartment. In a town as small as Cotton, he might as well have been Billy the Kid. His notorious ass couldn't go anywhere without being recognized, so he did the best he could to try and keep as low a profile as possible. He still had heat on him, watching him go from home to work. But other than that, Frank's life had been pretty uneventful the last month.

He spent most of his time alone, watching television in his place. He shopped at a local convenience store around the corner from him. But the time he spent alone, he spent figuring out how to get Gatewood to stand up and pay attention this time. And the fact that he had cops watching him every hour of the day and night actually played in his favor. The last time he had approached Gatewood, Jordan had sent three muscle heads to rough Frank up, and to drag him unconscious out on his back. Frank had his own built-in security force sitting outside his place in an unmarked car.

Frank had called Jordan's private number and left a message. "In case you haven't heard, shit's hit the fan in my neck of the woods. If you didn't want it getting out before, I know you sure as hell don't want it out now. Call me back."

Frank had placed that call during his fifteen-minute break one night while he was working. They might have had his place wired for sound, so he didn't risk making the call from there. Thirty minutes later, Frank's disposable cell phone rang.

"What the hell are you doing calling me?" Jordan blasted him over the phone.

Frank propped his mop up against the wall in the bathroom. "I called to let you know that I ain't going away, man!" Frank growled. "That shit you pulled before ain't working this time. Them three motha fuckas can't touch me, Jordan, man, and you need to wake up and see and hear what I'm selling!"

"Have you lost your goddamned mind?"

"Shut the fuck up and listen!" he said, trying to keep his voice down just in case anyone happened to have been working late. He hadn't seen anyone, but he wanted to be safe, rather than sorry. "I told you what I needed!"

"Yeah, you told me, motha fucka."

"Shit's hit the fan, Jordan. My ass is facing murder charges, and the last thing you want is for me to open my damn mouth and link you to a fuckin' murderer. I'm not asking again, man."

"Well, why don't you tell me what you want then, Frank?" Jordan asked too damn cordially.

"Half a million," he shot back. "And I want you to fire up one of those damn jets you got and fly my ass out of the damn country!"

"Anything else?"

This asshole was playing games. "I'm serious, Jordan. I will tell the world that we're brothers. I'll tell them that Joel Tunson is your daddy and mine, and point those damn reporters to that old man's house and let him tell it his damn self! Don't fuck with me, man. I'm serious. All of a sudden, you won't be shit. The board of directors will snatch that company out from under your ass and leave you swimming in a sea of drama of my ass on trial for murder."

Jordan Gatewood had known what it was like to be neck deep involved in a murder trial. He'd managed to survive the scandal with the murder of his father by Julian's girlfriend's daughter, but that was a long time ago. Frank wasn't high on Jordan's priority list of family members, but the fact that his name and Frank's name were tied together by Tunson would be more than enough to soil this pretty life of his.

"How about this, Frank," Jordan offered. "I'll give you everything you've just asked for, if you give me back my damn bail money and the bill I'm footing for that expensive attorney of yours."

The bottom dropped out from underneath Frank. Jordan's bail money? His lawyer. No! No! Why would he . . . "Fuck you, man! You didn't pay for shit!"

"Then who did?"

Frank swallowed, but that lump in the back of his throat swelled to the size of a cue ball. "Lonnie said . . ."

"Whatever Lonnie said to you was a lie, Ross. I'm the reason you're not sitting in jail right now, man. I'm the reason you probably won't ever go to prison for what you did as long as you sit your ass down and do what you're told."

Lonnie had told him that she'd paid his bail—that she'd called in a favor for that lawyer.

"She played the fuck out of you, Frank. That's all she's been doing since she found out who you are."

This wasn't making any sense. Frank fell back against the wall and tried to put the pieces of what was happening together in his head to make them fit. "Why the hell would you . . . Why would you put up my bail, Jordan? Or hire me an attorney? What the fuck?"

Jordan was quiet for a long time. Frank had almost thought the man had hung up on him.

"Now you see what you're working with?" Jordan asked calmly. "Lonnie's a liar."

"Why would you do this? Why would you help me?"

Again, Jordan took his time answering. "I don't know," he said, barely audible to Frank. "I met Joel a few weeks back," he admitted. "I'd never even seen the man."

Frank couldn't believe it. This motha fucka was helping Frank because he had had a Kodak moment with his biological?

"I could give a shit about you, Frank," Jordan said, sounding like the man Frank expected him to be. "But we're blood. Not brothers, just blood. I saw you were in trouble."

Frank couldn't believe it. "That's it? You acknowledge that we're related because you talked to that old man, and all of a sudden you decide to step in and help me?"

"I can stop."

Frank paused. This was not what he expected. This was not the conversation he ever thought he'd have with this man. And all of a sudden, Frank was a ball of confusion standing in that men's room, scratching his head.

"Alex is one of the best, Frank. He's got a whole team working on this, and if you listen to him, and do what he says, your chances of walking away from this situation are damn good. But make no mistake, you will owe me. One way or another. You will repay this debt, and it won't be cheap."

So much for brotherly love or whatever.

Super Cool, Super Mean

"*How did you get this number?*"

"*It doesn't matter how I got it. I got it. And we need to talk.*"

"*Talk,*" she huffed. "*What makes you think I have anything to say to you?*"

"*I have plenty to say to you, Lonnie. Meet me at the Jolt Bar in the Joule Hotel on Main Street tomorrow at six.*"

"*And if I don't?*"

He paused, and sighed. "Six. Please."

Jordan had been out of town the last few days on business in Colorado. He'd told Claire that he wouldn't be home until Saturday afternoon, but that wasn't true. He'd come back Thursday night and checked into a room at the Joule. He needed time and he needed to be completely alone so that he could think and put together these pieces of a puzzle started by Lonnie Adebayo that were gradually coming together.

June had been right. Jordan had been preoccupied lately by too many strange nuances going on in his life all at once that were gnawing away at him, bit by bit, biting him like mosquitos, until he found that he wasn't fully engaged in any one thing. Lately, he'd been scattered all over the place, his mind pulled in what felt like a hundred different directions all at once. The Anton deal needed his undivided attention, but Jordan hadn't been able to give it. More and more, he was beginning to understand what was happening.

Frank Ross had been a pawn for Lonnie—that piece in a chess game that you didn't mind sacrificing if it meant getting that all-important checkmate. She'd waved him in front of Jordan's face like a red flag, knowing that—at least momentarily—Jordan would be sucked into the potential drama that could come from Ross revealing the truth that he and Jordan were brothers and had the same father.

It was weak. In the beginning, Jordan hadn't realized just how weak, but as time went on, he knew that it would be Ross's word against his and a copy of a document that someone could've easily bought off the Internet for a few bucks. He could make the Frank Rosses of the world vanish, taking their accusations with them, just by snapping his fingers. Lonnie knew this.

His intention to take over Anton Oil and Gas was public knowledge, and Jordan had been foolish long enough to not take into account that Lonnie would be paying attention to what was going on with Gatewood Industries and his role in it. The Anton deal was at the center of all of this. And while he was focusing all of his attention on Ross, she was searching long and hard for a way to get to him, through the Anton–Gatewood Industries merger. Lonnie had found it—courtesy of Edgar Beckman.

"I'm sorry, Jordan." June had called him while he was in the air. "But we

couldn't put it off any longer. Three other companies, including Exelon, the British oil company, put in bids to buy Anton. We had no choice. We had to act fast, and so the board voted unanimously to move forward. Needless to say, we won. We won the bid, Jordan. Anton is ours."

With news of the merger, the value of GII stock tripled overnight. Those who invested in Anton days before the merger bought Anton stock for pennies on the dollar. One of those investors rolled over him like a herd of cattle. It was Desi Green, which meant that she was a Gatewood stockholder and she'd just made millions off of this deal.

Lonnie walked in looking like she'd stepped out of his dreams, wearing tight jeans, high heels, and a red blouse that draped low in the front and outlined the curve of her hips. He still hadn't gotten used to the longer hair on her, but he understood why she wore it that way.

The waiter appeared at the table at nearly the exact moment as Lonnie. "I'll have a Riesling, chilled," Lonnie told him as she sat down across from Jordan.

"You rang?" she asked sarcastically.

"Thank you for coming," he said cordially. Jordan had no fight left in him. She'd played him like a guitar and made a fool out of him, out of his whole goddamned corporation, and there was nothing left for him to do but to congratulate the winner.

Jordan raised his hands and began to clap. Lonnie stared at him, confused, but what else could he do? "That was one well-played game, Lonnie," he commended her. "Had me looking left while you were making your move on the right."

Lonnie remained expressionless.

"I have to say," he continued. "I haven't had my ass handed to me like that in many, many years. I didn't think it could happen. Not to me. Not like that."

Lonnie didn't say a word, and she didn't need to. Jordan remembered now what it was he'd always seen in her. As beautiful as she was, that wasn't the reason he'd fallen in love with this woman. Lonnie was brilliant and capable and cunning. She was a problem solver, a bullshitter, a liar. She was him in a dress, and the narcissist in him loved her for it.

"How'd you get her to do it?" Jordan asked. "How'd you talk Desi into buying in to Anton?"

She hesitated for a moment and then smiled. "I reminded her that she owed me a favor."

"And told her that she could make a fortune?"

She shrugged. "A win-win for both of us."

He paused and studied her carefully. "Are we even now?"

One corner of her lips turned up into a smile. "As even as we'll probably ever be, Jordan. My life changed that night you tried to kill me, and I'll never get back to who I was before then, but maybe I can build a new me, a better one."

Jordan shook his head. "God! I can't believe what I did to you." He shamefully dropped his gaze, but recovered and stared deep into those dramatic eyes of hers. "It's a shame," he admitted.

"He was so much more than that."

He cleared his throat. "I loved you, Lonnie. Hell, I—think I still do."

"I don't want to hear that," she said, shaking her head.

"But I have to say it because despite that night, and what happened—I have never felt any other way." He needed to say this. He needed for her to hear it even if she couldn't bring herself to believe it.

She stared blankly at him, almost as if she were waiting for the punch line.

"So, what's next? And don't tell me that Frank Ross is going to go forward to the media with the truth about who my father is, because that's not going to happen. He's knows now that it wasn't you who bailed him out of jail, Lonnie." Jordan laughed. "But, nice move on making him think it was." Jordan stopped laughing. "I own him now. He owes me."

She shrugged. "No big deal. Frank served his purpose," she said indifferently. "You can keep him."

He nodded. "Like a pet." He locked gazes with her knowing that she was thinking the same thing. "You going to be leaving town now?"

Lonnie hesitated before responding. "You going to let me?"

Jordan shrugged. "All's fair in love and war, baby." He raised his hands in defeat. "I concede. It's the least I can do."

"Then my work here is done," she said and sighed, "and I'll be on a plane first thing in the morning."

His gaze lingered long enough to make her uncomfortable.

"I will miss you," he said sincerely.

Lonnie managed to smile. "I almost believe you will."

The two of them finished their drinks, and left the hotel together. Jordan held the door open for her and then followed her outside. Lonnie stopped abruptly, and turned toward him, standing inches away from him. The light breeze in the air carried the scent of her perfume toward him.

"I'm going to take my toys and go, Jordan," she said, as she reached up and touched his lapel. The gesture seemed strange to him, but nothing about their relationship had ever been normal. "War is hell," she said, looking up at him. "I would tell you to take care of yourself, but it would just be words."

"Not for me," Jordan said, giving in to the urge to lean toward her and kiss her forehead.

Lonnie surprised him, put her hand around the back of his neck, and pulled his lips to hers. "Now, we're even," she whispered, sweeping her tongue into his mouth, and kissing him the way she used to. Moments later, she broke the seal of her kiss, smiled at him, and glanced one last time over his shoulder, setting off a strange alarm inside him. Jordan turned and saw his wife, sitting parked across the street, watching with horror the scene that had just unfolded. By the time he turned around, Lonnie was pulling away from the curb in her car.

Feeling It Deep Tonight and I'd Rather Die

"I know you don't believe me, Claire. Be outside the Joule at six thirty and you'll see that I'm telling the truth."

The only sound Claire could hear was the sound of her own breathing. She sped away before Jordan could reach her because there was nothing he could say anymore, nothing else he could do to make her believe that he gave a damn about her.

"Claire!"

There would be no babies! There would be no more of her believing his lies! No more hoping that somehow he had changed! No more of her pretending that the two of them would recover from this mess called a marriage!

"Claire!" Jordan burst into the bedroom. "Claire—?"

She had packed some of her things by the time he'd gotten there. Claire had to get out of this house and as far away from him as she could.

"Claire! Baby—"

He touched her! Claire jerked away from him. "Put your hands on me again, Jordan and I'll—"

Claire didn't recognize the sound of her own voice. But that was because she wasn't the same woman. A moment, that one moment when she saw him kissing that woman, everything about Claire changed into a complete and total stranger. Inside she was different! Just different, hollow and different, angry and different.

"Claire! She set this whole thing up!" he argued. "She directed that scene like a movie! Claire!" He grabbed her again, and Claire spun around and hit him hard across the face.

Jordan stood there. A moment flashed in her mind that he would do to her what he did to Lonnie in that house, but he just stood there. She hit him again, and again, and again.

"Enough!" he said, grabbing her by the wrists.

"I know what you did!" Claire exploded. The words burst through her mouth like water through a dam and she realized how relieved she felt to finally say them. "I know what you did to her." She was crying now. Claire jerked away from his grasp, and backed away from him as if she were truly seeing him without the mask he'd always worn with her. The truth flooded her gut and burned her lungs. It scratched at the back of her throat, and Lord, she had to say it! She had to tell him everything.

"I went to the house that night, Jordan!"

Claire's mind flashed back to how fragile she had been that night. She'd tried to take her own life over him. She'd loved him so much that she'd have rather died than live without him, and he just left her there! He left her alone in that hospital, discarded and dismissed like she was a nuisance to him.

"I saw her lying there on the floor!" Claire said, turning her nose up in disgust. It was as if she could smell the funk of what had happened in that room all over again. "Bloody and beaten and almost dead!" Tears streamed down her cheeks. Claire's hands shook, her whole body shook as she wrestled against completely falling apart long enough to get away from him and to get out of that house.

The look on his face was classic.

"I got Lonnie out of that house and I took her to the hospital and I begged her not to call the police." She sobbed and struggled to catch her breath. "I'm the reason she's alive, and I'm the reason that you didn't go to jail, Jordan! Don't call the police! Don't call the police! I begged her!"

He looked at Claire like he didn't recognize her. But Jordan had no choice but to believe her. She'd given him every ounce of her, every inch of her body and soul and still, he wanted that bitch! He could have her!

Jordan shook his head vehemently. "No, Claire! No, sweetheart!"

"No? Yes, Jordan! Yes, I've been here this whole time, knowing in the back of my mind what you're capable of, and still loving you! Still wanting to be with you and to have your baby! Yes, I have! But you? You want her? You choose her over me?"

"No!"

"I saw you with her with my own eyes! I saw you kiss her!"

"She kissed me!"

"And you let her!" Jordan was garbage. He was like any other man, led around like a dog on a leash by his dick. Claire had wasted herself on him, loving him, and needing him. "I am so sick of you," she said, gritting her teeth. "I've bought into the hype, Jordan—that you're so much more than you really are." She said this with disgust.

"You need to calm down, Claire," he warned. "I know you're angry, but what you saw out there wasn't the truth! I'm with you! I love you! I want to be with you!"

"I don't want you!" Those words coming from her mouth sounded like they'd come from someone else, because from the moment she'd met him, Claire could never fathom saying something like that to the man she loved so deeply.

Claire pushed past him, grabbed her suitcase off the bed and her keys off the nightstand, and hurried downstairs.

Jordan stumbled over to the side of the bed and sat down before his knees gave way out from underneath him. It was Claire? That's how Lonnie made it out of that house that night? But he'd left Claire in . . .

"The hospital," he muttered dismally. She'd known all this time. "Fuck!"

And Lonnie had known. This whole time, she'd been biding her time, waiting anxiously to make this last move, and he'd played right into her hands.

He had no idea how long he'd sat there. Jordan tortured himself going through a play-by-play of everything that had happened since Lonnie came back into his life. She had systematically, and maybe even unwittingly, unraveled every chord until all that was left of him was a raw and open wound. Jordan found himself in unfamiliar territory, outsmarted, and off balance. All of a sudden, he was the underdog, the victim, and fodder.

He didn't even remember picking up the phone or dialing the number. Jordan had no kind of plan in mind when he called, but he knew that it was the place to start.

Frank Ross answered the phone. "Hello?"

"Call Lonnie," Jordan instructed him. "Tell her you're back in town just for a night, but that you want to see her."

Frank was quiet for a few moments. "Where?"

"That motel you were staying at, outside of town." Jordan's mind moved like methodical components of a machine. "She knows that I paid your bail, so don't act like you still believe that it was her."

"She's going to ask me what I want."

"Make it up, Frank. Make it good. And make sure she believes you."

Frank sighed. "What time?"

Jordan glanced at his watch. "An hour. I'll call you back in a few minutes with the room number. Tell her to meet you there."

Jordan hung up.

Sugar Wishes Don't Change What Is Real

"You bought Anton stock?" Lonnie squealed over the phone to Desi. "Is that true?"

Desi paused. "Yeah, Lonnie. I bought it."

"When? Why didn't you tell me? How much?"

"A few days ago, and I didn't tell you because . . . I don't know. And I bought a lot."

Lonnie was beginning to get the feeling that Desi buying that stock had nothing to do with her. "Why'd you buy it, Desi?" she asked cautiously. "I thought you wanted to be done with Gatewood."

"It came highly recommended, Lonnie. And after speaking to my accountant, I thought it was a sound business move."

A sound business move? That didn't sound like the Desi she knew. "Who recommended it?" When Desi didn't answer, that really raised Lonnie's suspicions. "Desi? Did you see Gloria Dawson?" Desi could at least tell her that since Lonnie was the one who'd provided her with the lead in the first place.

"Not yet."

It figured. All of a sudden Desi had her own agenda that she was working toward, which somehow included buying up stock in an oil company, making money off Jordan.

"We need to get together and talk, Des," Lonnie said sternly. She didn't like the vibe she was getting from the woman all of a sudden. "When can I come over?"

"Lonnie, I'm about to get on a plane. We'll talk again when I land. Okay?"

Desi hung up before Lonnie could even say good-bye.

Frank's dumb ass was taking a huge risk leaving Cotton while he was out on bail for murder. He'd called her, all shaken up over finding out that Jordan had footed the bill for his bail and lawyer.

"What the hell does it mean, Lonnie?" he'd asked desperately over the phone. "Why would he bail me out? What's he want? What's he up to?"

He'd begged her to meet him at that motel he'd stayed in before when he was in town. Lonnie agreed but only if he drove his ass back to Cotton first thing in the morning. Jordan had told her that he owned Frank. Even she didn't know what he'd meant by that, but she owed Frank some solace, even if it was just a shoulder to cry on. She'd think of something to try and ease his concern, though. The fact was, Gatewood money could afford some of the best lawyering in the country, and if Jordan had bought Frank a lawyer, then chances were good that Frank would walk, guilty or not.

Lonnie pulled into the parking lot but didn't see Frank's car parked anywhere out front. Technically, the man had jumped bail, so of course, if he had a brain cell in his head, he'd have either gotten rid of his car or parked it somewhere else. Maybe he'd been really smart and caught a bus into town. The fact that he'd even come back here in the first place was odd, but Frank was operating on adrenaline and instinct and, no doubt, fear. All those things together could drive people to make dumb decisions.

Lonnie walked up the stairs and all the way down the corridor to the last room, number 224, and knocked. The door swung open—it was Jordan's face she saw on the other side of it. It happened so fast that Lonnie didn't have a chance to react. One minute she was standing in an open doorway, and the next, her body was flung onto the bed, the door slammed behind her, and Jordan's hand was pressed down on her neck, holding her in place on that bed.

Not again! she thought, pounding his arms and face with her fists. Lonnie tried to kick at him, and raised her knees between their bodies to get him off of her. She tried to scream, but Jordan put too much pressure on her throat.

"Stop it!" he commanded, slapping her hands away.

Lonnie felt his other hand sliding up her thigh. Jordan fumbled with the buckle of her belt, jerking it from around her waist once he got it loose. Her purse! Where was her purse! Lonnie had a gun. She stretched out her arm and felt for it across the bed. All of a sudden, Jordan flipped her over and, still holding her by the neck, managed to force her jeans down past her hips.

She grabbed the other side of the bed and tried to pull away from him, but his grip tightened, and Lonnie couldn't breathe. He grabbed her panties and ripped them off of her.

Hell no! No! She couldn't let him do this! Not this time!

Jordan forced her again onto her back. "Look at me!" he growled, pulling her to the edge of the bed. "You look me in the face, Lonnie! You see me! It's me!"

Jordan was inside her. Lonnie opened her mouth to scream, but he'd cut the sound off with his hand. Angry, hot tears flushed from her eyes and burned trails down the sides of her face. Not again!

He lowered himself on top of her and as he did, his hold on her began to lessen. Jordan bore holes into her as he stared back at her. He opened his mouth and pressed it to hers. Jordan didn't blink. He didn't close his eyes. And in between his kisses, he whispered.

"Look at me, Lonnie." He stroked her pussy with a slow, even rhythm. Jordan let go of her neck and as he drove deeper and deeper inside her, Lonnie let her legs relax, allowing them to part and open wide to accommodate him.

Jordan's kisses were intoxicating. She couldn't believe . . . Lonnie couldn't believe how good he felt inside her. The bedding began to get soaked with her juices, flowing hot from between her legs.

"Remember how good we are," he whispered, not taking his eyes off of her. "Remember this, baby?" Jordan's eyes clouded over with tears. "Remember us?"

She did remember. Lonnie dug her nails into his back and thrust her hips up to meet his. What the hell was wrong with her? What was it about him? No other man had ever hurt her the way he had, and no other man could make her cum the way he could. The room filled with sounds of her moans. She needed this! She had needed him inside her like this, and she hated herself for it.

Lonnie's tongue mated with his. The familiar flavor of Jordan made her drunk with him, and before long, she quivered, shook, and cried out as she came all over him. "Jordan!" she gasped. Clarity came back to her almost immediately. He had no right being inside her!

"Get off!" she cried out, slapping against him, and pushing him away. "Get your hands off me!"

He pressed his weight down on top of her, thrusting and stroking, unaffected by her attack on him, holding her in place until finally, he came too. Lonnie was repulsed all of a sudden. She hated him. That hadn't changed and it never would.

"If you're going to kill me you'd better get that shit right this time!" she threatened. "Make sure I'm dead, Jordan!" she said, breathless. "Make sure you don't miss!"

Jordan caught his own breath, stood up, and adjusted his pants. Lonnie kicked at him, but he moved before she could make contact.

He laughed. "That's my girl," he said. "A regular Smokin' Joe Frazier."

She scoped the room and saw her purse lying on the floor near the door. He saw it too. Jordan walked over and picked it up, searched through it and found the gun. He looked back at her, the smile gone from his face and put it in the pocket of his sportscoat. He watched as Lonnie stood up and pulled up her jeans. *Jesus! I don't want to cry! Stop it, Lonnie!* she commanded herself, but she broke down. Jordan waited until she was finished and finally able to compose herself.

"Like it or not, Lonnie," he finally said, "you're in my soul, girl. And I am so very, very inside yours."

She looked at him. "Fuck you, Jordan! You disgust me! You make me sick to my stomach!"

He shook his head. "I will not apologize for this, baby." He leaned forward and rested his elbows on his thighs. "Because it's the most satisfied I've been in years." Jordan stood up, buttoned his shirt, slipped into his sport coat, and headed for the door. He stopped and turned to her. "Don't let what I did define you or ruin you, Lonnie," he said remorsefully. "Be better than that. You are better than that." Jordan turned and left her sitting in the room alone.

There weren't enough sorrys in the world for him to make amends for what he'd done to her. But even she had to admit that he was right. Lonnie had been holding on too long to that ugly part of her past and it was time to finally let it go.

As she was making her way down the stairs, Lonnie spotted Jordan getting ready to get into his car. He'd just unlocked the door when Claire suddenly appeared in the parking lot with a gun.

"Go home, Claire," he told her, glaring nervously over his shoulder at Lonnie.

"To what, Jordan?" Claire asked.

Jordan took a step toward his wife, but Claire pointed the gun at him, stopping him dead in his tracks.

"I never meant to hurt you, Claire. Lonnie's leaving, baby, and we'll never see each other again!"

Claire's face flushed red. "I can smell her on you from here!"

"It's you I want, Claire! It's you I need, and we can fix this! Claire, put the gun down, baby. I want to fix this! I want to make it right again between us!" He took a step toward her.

For a moment, it looked as if Claire believed him. Claire wanted to believe him and she started to lower her gun.

For the first time, she noticed Lonnie, and a look of resolve crossed Claire's face. "You love her the way I love you," she said pitifully to Jordan. "Too much."

"I love you, Claire," he told her.

Claire pointed that gun to where she knew it would do the most damage; a place where death would be inevitable.

The gun went off. Jordan looked back at Lonnie. Lonnie would never forget the look in her eyes.

Never be bullied into silence.
Never allow yourself to be made a victim.
Accept no one's definition of your life;
define yourself.
—Harvey Fierstein

Yolanda "Lonnie" Adebayo
September 20, 1964–May 28, 2012

What If God Shuffled By?

"*Momma left me* this house when she died, but I only moved back into it after my husband passed."

Gloria Dawson was in her sixties. When Desi called and told her who she was, it was as if she'd been waiting on her.

Gloria lived in a small bungalow in the middle of town. Desi followed her through the kitchen and into a back room, filled with boxes from floor to ceiling.

"She loved Mr. Gatewood," Gloria gushed about her mother. "She met him before he built his company and used to come by the library all the time to do his research. Momma worked there at the time."

Gloria found the box she was looking for, and pulled it down on top of the small table in the room. "When he started his company, he asked her if she wouldn't mind being his secretary because he trusted her," she said, smiling. "Being that she was a librarian by trade, Momma had a way about filing everything that most people were clueless about. She said that if he didn't trust those people he worked with, then she couldn't trust them either."

"Let me get that for you," Desi volunteered, reaching for the box.

The two women went back into the kitchen, where Gloria opened the box and began thumbing through file folders until she came to one in particular.

"She made me promise never to give this to anybody else but you or your mother." Gloria held it out for Desi. "Mr. Gatewood made her promise to keep it safe, keep it hidden, no matter what happened."

Desi lay the file flat on the table and carefully opened it. The first thing she saw was a lock of hair tied with a purple ribbon.

"I believe it was your mother's," Gloria said. "But that's just a guess."

Desi saw an old black-and-white photograph of Ida sitting in a hospital bed, smiling, and holding a baby.

"That's you," Gloria said with a smile.

Desi leafed through the deed to the house, some kind of land deed, and a copy of Julian's will.

"He had two." Gloria held up two fingers. "One was filed with the probate courts, but was pulled back, and another one was filed in its place. I don't remember which one that is."

Desi stopped when she saw a picture of Ida in that hospital room holding Desi, with Mr. J standing beside the two of them. Gloria had nothing to say about that one.

The last document in the folder was Desi's birth certificate, listing Ida as her mother and Julian Gatewood as her father.

"You won't find that on file with the county. There's another one out there, I believe. But Momma said that was the real one."

Desi looked at her. "I can keep these things?"

"Of course, dear. After all, they belong to you."